Hell Hounds of High School

Patricia Marie Budd

iUniverse, Inc.
Bloomington

iUniverse books may be ordered through booksellers or by contacting:

iUniverse
1663 Liberty Drive
Bloomington, IN 47403
www.iuniverse.com
1-800-Authors (1-800-288-4677)

Because of the dynamic nature of the Internet, any web addresses or links contained in this book may have changed since publication and may no longer be valid. The views expressed in this work are solely those of the author and do not necessarily reflect the views of the publisher, and the publisher hereby disclaims any responsibility for them.

Any people depicted in stock imagery provided by Thinkstock are models, and such images are being used for illustrative purposes only.

Certain stock imagery © Thinkstock.

ISBN: 978-1-4502-4266-0 (sc)
ISBN: 978-1-4502-4265-3 (hc)
ISBN: 978-1-4502-4267-7 (ebook)

Printed in the United States of America

Library of Congress Control Number: 2011902323

iUniverse rev. date: 04/15/2011

"Patricia Budd's teaching career has no doubt brought her close to some of the characters you'll find in the Hellhounds of the High School. These characters nearly jump off the page with their fiery independence and shout at you, 'I've got something to tell you!'"

Alberta Author, Mar'ce Merrell

"A cynic in the classical sense of the term, Mrs. Bird conveys the teacher's angst as she tries to reconcile a populace lagging in dedication to youth education and her own desire to make a difference. *Hell Hounds of High School* uses a language that both students and adults can enjoy, raises issues that parents can learn from and poses problems that anyone working in the education industry can appreciate."

George Franko, teacher

In honour of Phil McKay,
the man who taught me what it means to be a teacher!

Acknowledgements

This book is dedicated to all my students past, present, and future. I love you!

Thank you Fort McMurray, Alberta, Canada! You are an amazing city, my home and a fabulously fun place to live! Since having moved here I have been inspired to write like never before.

Many thanks (ironically and honestly spoken) to the infamous 30-2 class—*you know who you are!* And to the notorious 10-2 class—Yes, *I mean you!* Don't worry, 20-2s (especially the first bunch who locked me out of my classroom by piling all the desks in front of the door), I haven't forgotten you—and *I never will!* No, you're not sweat hogs like *Welcome Back Cotter* but you've certainly given me a good run! ☺

This book was a delight to write, and a wonderful opportunity for me to laugh at myself along with all my students and everyone else out there who has ever hated a teacher (or a teacher who has ever hated a student).

Although I admit to having caricaturized myself in some ways, this book is entirely fictional. All the characters are a product of my warped imagination—even Mrs. Bird.

Special thanks go to:

- My artist, Tara Nakano, you are f—in' awesome, girl!
- Chris Scott (as always) for the endless labour you put into content editing. It's Bushwakkers pub for life, girl!
- Michelle Gavigan for helping with the sales of my first novel. You're the best! I love you.
- Jill? Jane?—Joanne Williams for inspiring "Remembering the Good Ones."
- Scott Simpson and Chris Blasius for the expression "sh—tered."
- Shayla McGlaughlin for the expression "pony ride."

- Gerry Murphy for reading and responding to the counselor's scenes.
- George McGuigan for reading and responding to the principal's scenes.
- Lisa Poder and Robert Yaro for reading and responding to the second draft.
- Michael Taylor for organizing two years of student teacher paintball (and for shooting me in the a—, an event that ends up in my book, but in the way I would have preferred it to have happened.)
- Everyone I've ever worked with—no, you are not in my book—but I do love you and thank you for your continued support.
- Shane Cranner, Chase Nagorsiki, and Kelsey Bulbuc for filming my gorilla and robot routines.
- Corene Kozey, Marichal Binns, Shonna Barnes, and Lorna Dicks—women, you are my backbone of support. Thank you!
- Simon Budd for putting up with a full-time English teacher, full-time writer, full-time saleswoman, and (God knows I try) full-time wife. God blessed me the day I met you.
- And, especially, my mother, Edith Gavigan. You were right, Mom. There is something good in every student.

☺ ☺ ☺ ☺ ☺

The Bitch and the Ass

Together, the bitch and the ass make the perfect metaphor for the teacher/ student relationship. The bitch growls, snarls, and exposes sharp teeth whilst constantly harping at the stubborn ass to make it move. Nipping at the ass's hooves, the bitch desperately attempts to make the animal go to work. All the while, the ass stubbornly stands still, refusing to pull its load.

The bitch and the ass

☺ ☺ ☺ ☺ ☺

Prelude: Early January

Astounded is hardly the word for it! Seated at the dining room table, Priscilla Bird (Mrs. Bird to her students) reads and rereads the paper before her five times. "William," a mystified Priscilla calls out to her husband.

"Yes, dear," William replies from the kitchen. Priscilla has designated the kitchen as William's domain since he is far more adept at cooking than she is. The fact is, Priscilla is far too busy marking to do any cooking, thus her silent expectation is that her husband fill that void in her life. It is a lucky thing for Priscilla that he complies as her previous diet of fast food had been injurious to her health. Since marrying William and being introduced to a healthy diet, she seldom ever gets sick anymore.

"Come listen to this," Priscilla encourages from her perch in the dining room.

William casually strolls into the small room, which is currently cluttered with a vast array of Priscilla's work. A briefcase is lying on its side next to Priscilla's chair, its contents spilled out onto the floor. The chair next to her holds a pile of essays as does the chair opposite. On the table, essays are spread all over in a cluttered mess. Standing behind his wife's chair, William places his hand on her shoulder and gives it a slight squeeze as he glances over to see what she is working on. "What is it?" he asks.

"A student essay." Her response is terse. Priscilla is leaning back in her chair with arms wrapped tightly under her breasts, looking down her nose at the paper.

"A good one?" he asks.

Looking up to see the half-quizzical expression on William's face, Priscilla, too, feels the need to half smirk. "Expecting more teenage nonsense?"

William shrugs. "That's what you usually share with me."

"Sorry to disappoint you, dear, but this paper is good—very good." Her reply is a bit too curt.

"You don't sound too enthused," he says as he gives her shoulder another squeeze. There is too much tension there, as always. "Usually a good paper brings out the chipper in you."

She shakes her head, and loose strands of hair caress his wrist. "It's too good, William," she says. "Too good to be true. Listen." Lifting the paper off the table, she begins reading:

> *Jimmy Buffett's song "The A—hole Song" is one of the great existentialist quandaries of the twentieth century. In "The A—hole Song," Buffett questions what exactly has produced the a—hole persona of the driver who "nearly cut [him] off the road" (Buffett line 2). He wants to know whether this man was "born an a—hole" (Buffett line 6) or if he "worked at it [his] whole life" (Buffett line 7). In this one line, Jimmy Buffet is asking whether God created the a—hole or if the man, through choice and action, turned himself into one.*

"Wow, that kid's smart," William replies. "He must be one of your best."

"No, he isn't." With tears glistening, Priscilla smiles softly. "He's my worst."

"Holy cow!" he exclaims. "How did you get that out of him?"

"I don't know." Shaking the paper at her husband, Priscilla announces, "This boy is the amalgam of every bad student I have ever had." Pausing momentarily to consider, "In fact, he is the culmination of—"

"In other words," William reasons, "he has reached the highest point of stupidity—"

Before William can finish, Priscilla points out the less-common use of the word culmination. "Or, rather, has sunk to the lowest point to which a student can possibly descend."

"Is it okay for him to use that song? I mean it does have swearwords in it."

"Oh, aren't you little Mr. Mischievous. Trying to help me knock him down a peg or two, are you?"

"Why not?" William inquires.

"Well, to begin with," Priscilla says with a sigh (she now has her thumb in her mouth and is tapping her nail against her teeth), "the boy does not swear." Her head reverts to shaking. "Jimmy Buffet swears." Pointing to the paper with emphasis, she continues, "And everything Greg says about the song is accurate."

"Is that the kid's name?" William smirks. "Not *the* Greg?"

Leaning her head back, looking up over her glasses, Pricilla reiterates, "*The* Greg."

William bends down to kiss her. "The one Wood calls Mc*You-know-what* McGregor?"

"Yup." She tilts her head for another kiss. William complies. "Look at the title page." She hands the page to her husband.

title page

He's reading silently, Priscilla surmises, *as he doesn't want to risk saying out loud anything this kid might have written*. She chuckles at her thought and taunts her husband, "Afraid to read it out loud?" William grunts a response and hands her back the title page. "You know," she says with an impish smile, "for a not-so-very-pious man, you certainly have strange views on swearing."

Noting the rise in William's brow, Priscilla advocates, pointing directly to the boy's name, "I'd call him Mc*You-know-what* too—" William's expression turns into a scowl. "But I don't." She places her hand on her heart as if making a vow, "When I give my word, William, I keep it. I call him Gregory McMiscreant McGregor."

Pleased, William laughs. "*Miscreant* is a much better word. More suiting an English teacher, don't you think?"

Priscilla responds with an affirmative grunt. Retrieving the title page, she takes a moment to reexamine the boy's name. "The *A* word seems better suited to McGregor."

"You can think what ever you want, my dear, just as long as you refrain from using the words."

For her part, Priscilla complies with a half-muttered, "Yes, dear." She is too busy staring at the essay as if faced with an impossible conundrum to worry about foul language. Pondering, she mutters, "I can't believe this is the same kid." Jumping up from her chair, Priscilla backs into William. "Move, please." Priscilla Bird, in teacher mode, shows no heed to her treatment of others. Heading towards William's den, she calls over her shoulder, "I need to use your computer."

"Why?" William demands.

"I need to get on the Net. All I have to do is type the word *plagiarism* into the search engine and all kinds of sites pop up that will help me determine if this boy has plagiarized."

"How?" William's voice has softened some for this inquiry.

Priscilla, unfortunately, ignores William as she races down the hall to his office. It is spacious, their having converted the second largest bedroom for this purpose. His desk spans two walls; his computer sits advantageously in the corner. Sitting down in William's high-back chair, Priscilla instantly converts it from the lean-back position to the upright position. There is no relaxing when this woman works.

Following his wife into his office, William inquires, "So how can the Net help you determine if this kid plagiarized?"

"Easy." Priscilla is all smiles. She is certain she has finally got her hands on the evidence she needs to get this boy out of her class and out of her hair forever. "All I have to do is type in one line from his essay and the whole text or its web link will appear."

"Sweet," William replies. "Do you really think he cheated?"

"I have to consider the possibility." Priscilla, swiveling the chair around, presents her husband with a grave countenance. "This boy has not written a thing for me all semester, and, suddenly," she says, waving the paper for emphasis, "he hands in this. For all he's bothered to show me, the boy could be illiterate." Looking at the work, a dark cloud covers her eyes. "He means this as a statement—a statement I can put up with from the average kid—if it's his own. But if he stole it, well, William," she looks her husband in the eye to emphasize the severity of the crime, "that is intellectual theft, and I will slam him down hard for it."

Priscilla taps a key to wake up the iMac. Using Google as her search engine, she types in the word *plagiarism*. When she gains access to an online plagiarism catcher, she immediately begins her sleuth work.

Mrs. Bird as sleuth

After two hours, Priscilla finally admits defeat. "William," she calls.

Her husband, having abandoned Priscilla and her search one hour and fifty-seven minutes ago, reenters his office.

Swiveling the high-back chair to face her husband, and staring up at him with disbelief, Priscilla exclaims, "He didn't cheat."

"Are you sure?" he inquires.

"Well," Priscilla grimaces, now chewing on her thumbnail. "I can't prove he copied anything from the Net." William slaps the back of her head. "Ow!" Priscilla ejaculates, "what did you do that for?"

"Stop chewing your fingers." Priscilla has asked him to hit her every time he catches her biting her nails, a nasty habit she has had since her own high school days.

"Sorry, it's just ... this kid has me so wound up."

"I can tell," William adds. "Your nail biting has gotten really bad since you started teaching him." Pausing for a moment to study his wife, he says, "You shouldn't let one kid get to you so much."

"I know," she sighs, "but it's so da— da— *darn* hard." She accents her difficulty in avoiding the curse by tapping her fist on William's desk.

"You can't fix every kid's problems," he reminds her yet again.

"I know that, but, when I started teaching him ..." Her hands open and start shaking in the air as she tries to grasp at the concept that is alluding her. "And I heard all the rumours about what a bad a-jackal he was ..." This time she pounds her fists on her thighs. "I swore I would drag him by his ears into a pass." Sighing now, she closes her eyes and places her fist on her forehead. "And now all I want to do now is get him the Hades out of my class." William smiles. "Don't laugh at me."

"I'm not laughing," he says as his cheek muscles twitch to subdue the impending outburst. Once he appears to be under control, he begins, "So, what's next?"

"Well ..." Priscilla pauses a moment to ponder her options. "He may not have copied off the Net, but he could just as easily have hired someone to write for him."

"Who?" William asks.

"That, I don't know. My first guess would be one of my thirty-dash-one students. I taught them the concept of existentialism."

"Well, there you go," William says in an encouraging manner.

"Uh huh," Priscilla grunts as she shakes her head. "None of my current academic kids are smart enough to have written this essay. No, wait," she adds judiciously, "Richard is smart enough, but he's too dry and pedantic ... and this essay," she gives the paper a little shake, "has its own unique style." With a slight tilt of the head, she considers, "Scott—now he's witty enough, but he lacks the higher-level thinking skills required of such prose." She slaps the side of her face in wonder. "Nope, it wasn't one of my current kids, and it doesn't make me think of any of my past kids either." Now with her thumb rubbing her temple and two fingers rubbing her forehead, Priscilla's sigh is both audible and lengthy. "If he cheated, William, there is absolutely no way I can prove it."

"What are you going to do then?"

"The only thing I can do. Accept it as his work. Grade it as his work and congratulate him on it.

In the Beginning

When Mrs. Bird was twelve, and known as Miss Priscilla Fledgling, a friend took her upstairs in her parents' old Victorian home and had her listen to Cheech and Chong's "Sister Mary Elephant." The first thing this impressionable young bird thought of as she listened to the rising clamor through the scratch of the old Victrola was, *I have been in that class!* She also took the time to ponder just how stupid that old teacher was. What this chickadee never considered, or would have ever conceived possible at that time in her life, was that she would someday *be* Sister Mary Elephant! Yet, here she is today screeching out "Class? Class? Shudd-uuuuuup!" Then, after a pause, a quiet, "Thank you."

Twelve-year-olds listening to Cheech and Chong

If, at twelve, the future Mrs. Bird couldn't conceive of herself as a teacher, imagine the repulsive reaction to this fate that Priscilla as a teenager might produce. You see this young bird was not very popular in high school. In fact (as politically incorrect as this is about to sound), the only other student lower on the totem pole than our little Tweety Bird was the boy in the wheel chair. Priscilla always knew when Rick was home sick. When Rick was at school, the other kids would get their jollies by offering to push him down the wheelchair access ramp. Of course then they'd let go to see how long it would take him to get the brakes on. You see, this ramp, like most wheelchair ramps in long hallways, was built on two levels, which means a wall awaited poor Rick halfway into his descent. Rick was destined to smash into this wall over and over until his reflexes improved—and they got pretty darn good over time. As well as being confined to a wheel chair, Rick was almost blind. One day, a group of cool kids thought it would be neat to throw ink in his face, pretend it was water, and see if he could tell the difference. Oh yes, the teenage beast can be truly brutal.

So, imagine the days when Rick was not at school and young Priscilla had to traverse the jungles of teenage warfare unarmed and alone. She suffered brutal onslaughts of sexual abuse. With long legs and a short upper body, she was awkward. Having a flat chest and short hair made her look boyish. Kids liked to call her "the school board." Priscilla used to help Rick by wheeling him around the school and getting his bag open and closed for him, but the rest of the students made both their lives so miserable. "So, Priscilla, are you Rick's girlfriend?" or "How do you two f—?" The two made a silent agreement to avoid each other and, therefore, the abuse. Now pose the question to this teenage girl, "So, Priscilla, do you think you will end up as a high school English teacher?" Just try to imagine the look on her face!

Teenage Miss Fledgling with shocked expression

There is more to that expression than just Priscilla's repulsion of the teenage beast. Priscilla was none too bright in her youth. Actually, that's not fair. She was bright enough and could hold her own in a debate. She was quite active in all the various seventies demonstrations and fought passionately against the injustices of the world, but that was outside the teenage jungle called the high school. Inside those walls, Priscilla became a meek, frail dove that flittered about avoiding all human contact. Her sense of self was so low, the terror level in her heart so great, that she paid little to no attention to the lectures in class. English class was the worst—okay math was, but she had her math teacher wrapped around her little finger.

You see, her math teacher had no control over the students, and, feeling sorry for Priscilla, he would often send her to the library to get her out of harm's way. Although Priscilla wasn't smart enough to do the math work on her own, her math teacher felt obliged to pass her anyway. No, she had math figured out: make sure she always got Mr. Belleson, keep getting sent to the library, and keep getting pity marks. English wasn't so easy. Her English teachers always seemed to have a handle on classroom management so Priscilla had to listen and learn, but she couldn't. Her mind was always on survival. Still, she did her best. She even stole her sister's boyfriend's poem once to earn a grade of 100 percent and bring her average up to passing. Throughout her high school career, her English average was a very shaky 55 percent.

So how did this particular young woman manage to become an English teacher? Simple. She partied a few years, went east to study mime, got sick of poverty, and got accepted into university as a mature student. Why English? While she was a mime, she wrote and produced a play in Toronto, and the English department thought that meant something. They wanted creative writers in the English classroom. Priscilla, cocky now having had a play produced in Toronto, actually believed she could do this. Well, let me tell you, university was some fun. Priscilla learned the meaning of work there! And she really did learn how to write—spelling, grammar, and the whole nine yards. Pardon the cliché, but, when her university professor told her they were going to cut her from the program if she didn't do something about her spelling and grammar *right now*, Priscilla turned on the problem-solving mode of her brain and worked it out. Since her professor was a woman, Priscilla wasn't inclined to sleep with her for marks, so her solution was to hang out with the brightest students in her class. She successfully purchased their friendship with spirits and beer, and got them to proofread all her work in exchange. And it worked. Transformation complete. Today, our little Priscilla is an English teacher.

Mrs. Bird Today

☺ ☺ ☺ ☺ ☺

Mrs. Bird Today

How does one describe someone as vastly complex and absurd as Mrs. Bird? She is an enigma in Pandora's box. Upon first introduction, people believe they have divined her character. According to Mr. Wood, the social studies teacher, "Bird is the most outrageous and eccentric person I have ever known." Miss Payne, the math teacher, says, "She's far too set in her ways." While the principal, Mr. Willow, thinks she is too outspoken for her own good since she often blurts out exactly what's on her mind. "Bird," he often reminds her, "you really need to think about the consequences before you start spouting out the words." First-year teachers love her because she is always there to help them out and, more importantly, always gets them sh—faced that first Friday of every school year. "Poor dears," she is often heard lamenting in the staff room, "they can barely afford the rent, let alone life's elixir." William, her husband, worries she might be a binge alcoholic since she goes out every Friday after school with the staff to booze it up and grumble. No one really knows what to expect from this old bird, except perhaps the unexpected.

An old bird is exactly what she is, has become, and forever will be (by choice if truth be known). Puffed up and fatted for Christmas dinner, she struts about her classroom like a mother hen (albeit a mother she never shall be). Her appearance at school is at odds with her personality. She wears various combinations of peach sweaters, cream blouses, and grey and navy blue skirts, bottomed off with terminally comfortable footwear. Her day begins with her hair tightly knotted in a bun that is always disheveled by day's end.

At home, her appearance changes. The first thing to go is the bun. As soon as she enters the door, she rips out all the pins and pulls away the elastic so her salt-and-pepper hair falls around her shoulders. No longer encased in sweater, blouse, and skirt (they are scattered behind her in a trail from foyer to bedroom), she throws on a yellow-and-maroon sweat suit with H.E.L.L. plastered across the seat of the pants. H.E.L.L. stands for Father Hubert Edward Lucius Laurence High School, and 1999 (which is 1666 upside down) was the one year they got away with printing the initials on the annual school sweat suit. This educational institution was named after the priest who had ensured the existence of a Catholic School System in this northern boomtown (also affectionately referred to as hell by its citizens—but never in front of the aforementioned name). A scandal hit the Catholic community that year, the year of 1999. "How dare they!" the high and moral mighty cried, "How dare they accent the buttocks of young women with the *acronym* of the Holy Father!" Memory of this always makes Bird snort. *Irreverent Father is more like it,* she always says (to herself of course!).

After dismantling her teacher look, Bird lets out all the burps and farts she has held in all day (to the chagrin of her loving husband), makes her apologies, then flops herself down on the couch to watch reruns of *Welcome Back Cotter* on the Deja-Vu channel, envying the man for having such well-behaved students.

Mrs. Bird sitting on couch watching TV

☺ ☺ ☺ ☺ ☺

Mr. Bird

Mr. Bird working out

William A. Bird, Priscilla's loving, supportive husband, may be shorter than his wife, but he suffers no insecurity. William has a strong inner core that matches his muscular girth. He is the only one who can actually control Priscilla. Whenever her voice gets too loud at home, he shushes her, telling her she is stuck in teacher mode. His most common expression when dealing with her is, "I'm not one of your students, you know."

On the rare occasion when they cook supper together, Priscilla has a tendency to take control. "William, peel those carrots." "Chop that onion." "Not that way, dear. Cut the root off first." "Cut the celery smaller." With their tightly packed kitchen only adding to the tension, the two inevitably begin to argue. Just to let her know he is *not* an ensign on some ship, William stands at attention, salutes, and responds, "Aye, aye, Captain," using an accent reminiscent of *Star Trek*'s Scotty. To which Priscilla always responds, eyes open tight and lips pursed, "I wasn't *that* demanding."

William loves to box. Their entire basement (with the exception of the laundry room) is dedicated to his workout equipment. A punching bag hangs from the ceiling next to which is a peanut bag. As well as a skipping rope and weights, his room contains a NordicT track skier, a treadmill, and a Bowflex Home Gym. Priscilla uses this room once every month or two but William is down there every second day.

William's hair is thin; well, his head is nearly bald. Choosing to follow Bruce Willis's example (if you're going bald you might as well just go bald), he shaves his head every morning. It has become a relaxation ritual for him. Considering he is married to a workaholic, obsessive, perfectionist high school English teacher, relaxation rituals are a necessity in this man's life.

Is William perfect? Does Priscilla wear rose-colored glasses when she looks at him? Who cares? Before she met William, her life was a lonely existence as she jumped from failed relationship to failed relationship. She met William when she was thirty-eight, and they married when she was forty. Priscilla is now forty-eight, and William is fifty. Both were childless when they met, and childless they remain—but they have each other, and that is enough ... for William at any rate.

Gregory McGregor

Gregory McGregor

With a fresh, innocent face surrounded by thick, curly locks of dark, reddish brown that accent the deep blue eyes of the Irish, Gregory McGregor—*Greg*, if you please!—is capable of winning over just about any woman he wants. He is a beauty and a charmer who truly understands human politics. Life for Greg is a series of games that boil down to one essential rule: manipulate or be manipulated. Just shy of five foot ten, Greg maintains the illusion of height by dating girls no taller than five six. His current squeeze, Susie Cardinal, is five foot five and a half. Although he never admits it, Greg feels a true connection with Susie. It really is more than just sex with her. Unable to understand what is going on inside him emotionally, he keeps her at arm's length while simultaneously finding it impossible to date anyone else.

Living in hell at home, having to abdicate to the absolute control exerted by his father's drunken and drug-enhanced bouts of rage, Greg works at maintaining control in every other aspect of his life including friends, girlfriends, and, most importantly, the classroom. You see, the classroom is a public venue, and gaining and maintaining control there ensures a reputation throughout the student body. As there is no higher claim to fame in the average teenager's life than notoriety for escapades committed in the classroom, Greg is notorious for causing daily disruptions. Greg is always presenting these numerous outrages via the vehicle of innocent inquiries. Take, for example, an incident that occurred in his grade ten English class:

"So, Miss," infuriating polite he asks ever so innocently, "How many times did Romeo and Juliet f— before they died?"

Miss Payne, unfortunately teaching English in her first year even though her major is math, kicks him out and sends him to the office.

Greg loves going to the office. It gives him further opportunity to test his manipulative skills. Here he argues the justification of his query on an intellectual level. "Romeo and Juliet's sex life," he claims, "is a very important part of the play." Adding even greater insight, he adds, "In fact, Shakespeare goes to great lengths to show that it is their sex drive that gets them into so much trouble."

Although Mr. Willow smiles, he chastises Greg, "Was it really necessary to use the *F* word?"

Greg is willing to accede the point; he's had his fun for the day, and he is certain Willow has fallen for his logic. "No, sir, you're right. The word *sex* would have worked just as well, but, really," he insists, "Miss Payne is so uptight that it wouldn't matter what word I used."

In her subsequent meeting with Mr. Willow and Greg, Miss Payne insists that the question was not necessary at all and that Greg was just using it as an opportunity to disrupt the lesson.

Greg counters this by suggesting that Miss Payne is stifling her students' quest for knowledge.

In the end, Greg wins. He has been called to the office three times during English, and all he has to do to atone for his escapade is apologize to Miss Payne, in private of course.

Mr. McGregor

Mr. McGregor

Greg and his father are drug dealers. Mr. McGregor not only grows his own dope, he also buys it from a dealer in Edmonton. Greg provides the teenage clientele. They live in a small, two-bedroom condo with a skeleton

21

for a cat, a basement for a litter box, and all the original flooring, carpeting, and furniture (dating back to the eighties!). There are punch holes in the doors, smoke stains on the ceilings and walls, and cigarette burns on various carpets and furnishings. It may smell, but it's home.

Mr. McGregor is an older version of Greg. He bleaches his longish hair blond to hide the onset of grey. His hair, however is no longer thick and luscious, and two bowling lanes recede up each side of his head. What little is left of his hair is pulled back into a ponytail. He seldom shaves more than twice a week so his face is grizzled. Crow's-feet etch his temples, and furrows dig deep into his brow. He has a wry grin, just like his son, and, like Greg, his pupils are constantly dilated.

Greg does partake of some of the drugs in which they deal; however, he does not follow Mr. McGregor into his latest adventure in the wonderland of drugs: crack. Mr. McGregor grew up in the fast lane and has never slowed his engine down. His body is ragged as a result. No longer the muscular man of his youth, he is stringy and gaunt.

A typical father/son conversation in the McGregor home goes as follows:

"Eddie's coming up tomorrow," Mr. McGregor mutters through a mouth full of cereal.

Flicking a cigarette ash off his plate, Greg mutters, "Cool." He picks up his toast and munches down on it.

Mr. McGregor puts down his spoon and replaces it with his cigarette; the ashtray next to his plate is overflowing. After drawing heartily on his Players, he exhales the smoke with the following proclamation, "He's bringing up two kilos. Party Thursday night."

Greg shakes his head. "Friday."

Mr. McGregor shakes *his* head. "I work Friday."

Greg shrugs his shoulders. "I can get more kids out on Friday." He takes another bite of his toast. Looking at it he adds, "I can always run the deal."

Mr. McGregor's eyes squint as he peers at his son, and his mouth tightens into a scrunch. After a short pause, he adds, "I'll call in sick."

Greg, still looking at his toast, addresses it, "Whatever." After a slight pause, he adds, "You inviting the boys?" Finally he takes a bite.

Mr. McGregor puts down his cigarette. "Of course."

Still talking to his toast, Greg asks, "Not worried they'll rat?" He takes another bite.

A long pause ensues. Mr. McGregor picks up his smoke, inhales slowly, then blows smoke into his son's face. "Nope." Greg coughs slightly. This is a typical routine so Greg no longer waves the smoke away in a convulsive fit whilst swearing. Mr. McGregor smiles. "As long as we set 'em up, none'll nark."

Greg leans back, his shoulders braced against the top of the back of the chair, and his tailbone stretched to the front of the seat. His knees are open, his ankles are touching, and his left hand is draped over his thigh. The fingers of his right hand slowly tap the table. Smiling, he is the picture of relaxed innocence. "If you're sure."

"I'm sure," Mr. McGregor says dryly. Grumbling he adds, "You stick to the teenage clientele. I'll handle the adults."

"Okay." Greg pops the last of the toast into his mouth and washes it down with a glass of water.

"Friday night then," his father confirms.

"Friday night," Greg says in agreement.

Both men glare, each one trying to stare the other down.

Mr. McGregor and Greg stare down

☺ ☺ ☺ ☺ ☺

Mr. Lloyd

Mr. Ralph Lloyd's office reflects the man. Although the room was originally a small, square box, he has managed to transform it into a haven of comfort. Willing to endure the ridicule of "faggot" from the students and "girly boy" from the staff, he keeps a scented candle lit for aromatherapy and relaxation purposes. His wall is littered with self-esteem posters: a kitten looking into a mirror at a lion; a hotdog half way out of its bun with the caption "I Am Awesome"; as well as numerous smiling, proud teens. On his desk are multiple pictures of his wife and children.

Mr. Lloyd is a recent addition to H.E.L.L.'s little community. He was transferred to H.E.L.L. three years ago after working five years as a counselor at Sister Imaculata Nell Middle School (lovingly referred to as S.I.N. by its devlish occupants). Many of the students he worked closely with moved schools with him, so it was very easy for him to settle right in as veteran staff. One student file he carried with him to H.E.L.L. (in his own briefcase—not via courier in a box) was that of Gregory McGregor. Today he still shakes his thick, black east-coast mane at the very mention of the lad's name, and, if his equally thick black moustache wasn't cropped short, it would shoot upwards with the exasperated puff of air that follows every head shake. Mr. Lloyd is short and stocky and has to look up to the majority of the people who surround him—even students—but his stature is not short. His strength of character, his ability to listen and comprehend someone's troubles, as well as his overtly amiable nature creates in him the ultimate diplomat. No quarrel, whether between parent and student, student and teacher, student and administrator, administrator and parent, or teacher and administrator, is beyond this man's notice or concern. His plump face, deceptively idle eyes, and relaxed smile encourage everyone's trust in him. Mr. Lloyd's Midas touch when it comes to helping and healing the wounds of others is legendary, which is why Greg is a constant concern and occupies Mr. Lloyd's thoughts daily. It grates at the counselor

24

that, in the last four years, he has not been able to assist Greg. He is left impotent watching the young man's life decline deeper and deeper into debauchery and decay.

Mr. Lloyd

☺ ☺ ☺ ☺ ☺

Susie Cardinal

Susie Cardinal

Susie is madly in love with Greg. A busty, bubbly, peroxide blonde bordering on anorectic, Susie can screw a tear into a man's heart making him do exactly what she wants. She appears perpetually stunned but knows exactly what she is doing when it comes to the opposite sex. Damp, fluttering eyelashes are her mercurial weapons. Knowing this, she uses them sparingly, thus effectively.

Her finest moment always comes after she skips an exam. With her mother in her pocket and tears in her eyes, she marches into the principal's office both pleading and demanding her right to write her test.

Inside Mr. Willow's office, Susie and her mother are welcomed by the faint scent of lavender oil and the soft, soothing sounds of water trickling and birds chirping. The lavender oil sticks are well hidden behind a series of books, and the sounds are emitted by a small silver gizmo sitting on the top of Mr. Willow's desk. His office is spacious. His desk is in the back left corner; the rest of his office is open and inviting. Front and center is a small, round coffee table hugged by three low, padded chairs. This is reserved for parent/student meetings. On such occasions, Mr. Willow always seats himself in the middle to act as an effective sounding board.

Susie is not seated comfortably and is perched on the edge of her chair. No soothing sounds can quell this young woman's ire. She blurts out the unfortunate news that Mrs. Bird refuses to let her write the exam she skipped out of. She then shoots a glare of warning her mother's way.

Mrs. Cardinal coughs slightly before backing her daughter, "If you need me to excuse her, Mr. Willow, I will."

"That is all well and good, Mrs. Cardinal," Mr. Willow gently reminds her, "but Susie just admitted to the fact that she skipped her English test."

"I wasn't ready," Susie sobs, "Mrs. Bird is making me read a Shakespeare play all by myself."

"Now, as I understand it," Mr. Willow interjects, "it was only one act."

Once again, Susie glares at her mother, who insists, "One act ... one page ... what does it matter if she can't understand what she's reading?" Her face reddens, as does Susie's. "That woman should be explaining the play to her."

Mr. Willow sighs. He knows of Mrs. Bird's daily e-mails to the parents of her students outlining what goes on in her class as she forwards one or two on occasion. And parents do rave about them. "Do you read Mrs. Bird's e-mails?"

"I—I don't always have time to read them," the girl's mother stammers. Susie shakes her head knowing her mother is losing ground here.

"Well." Mr. Willow sighs. "If you did, you would know that she always discusses the act with the students prior to the exams." Fortunately for Mr. Willow, or perhaps more so for Mrs. Bird, she had forwarded him one of these e-mails to stave off parent complaints about her actually making kids read Shakespeare.

"Even still," Mrs. Cardinal insists, "Susie doesn't understand the act. She needs help."

Mr. Willow addresses Susie, "Did you go see Mrs. Bird during her extra help hours?" He also knows how often she sits in her class room after school waiting for students who don't show up.

Fully aware the answer to this question will kill her argument, Susie does what she does best—sheds a tear whilst muttering, "I can't pass if I can't write this test." Then, through a burst of sobs, she wails, "I'm so sorry I skipped that test, Mr. Willow. I swear it will never happen again."

Mr. Willow does what he does best—he bends. "If I let you write this test, Susie, do you promise to go in for extra help with Mrs. Bird?"

"Y—y—yes." Her eyes sparkle with salt water.

"And," he says as he leans forward pointing a finger in her direction, "do you promise to never skip out again?"

"Oh, yes," Susie says with a smile. Then, placing her hand over her heart, "I swear it." And she means it too, until the next time she finds herself unprepared.

☺ ☺ ☺ ☺ ☺

This scene in Mr. Willow's office occurs after an epic battle with Mrs. Bird. Upstairs, in Mrs. Bird's classroom, just fifteen minutes prior to the scene we just witnessed, Susie's mother sits in one of the chairs closest to the door observing, not saying a word. Mrs. Bird remains aloof, leaning against the whiteboard, arms crossed in front of her chest, staring over her glasses at the young woman standing firm footed in front of her. Susie glares at the old woman, her piercing brown eyes as wide as saucers. Tears threaten to burst, but Susie is holding them in … saving them for the one on whom she knows they will have the most effect. Her hair flashes like fire crackling against stormy black clouds as she tosses her head about in righteous indignation. "You're mean," she hisses, her voice like rain against fire. Her head tilts back and her chin juts out, "You *want* me to fail. You *hate* me." Her arms flail in the air pointing a crooked finger at Mrs. Bird's nose before her hands pound down into fists against her hips. She fights back a wince before finally screeching, "You *have* to let me write that test."

Mrs. Bird simply shakes her head and says, "No, I don't."

Here is where Susie lets the tears flow. "We'll see what Mr. Willow has to say about that!"

Mr. Willow

Mr. Willow jogging

Mr. Willow, princi-*pal* of H.E.L.L., is tall and lanky. He has the stringy muscles of a long-distance runner. Every day at five PM, he leaves the school for a run. He is well known through out the community and loved by most students and parents. Horns honk for him all the time, and half his run is spent waving and smiling at people driving by. Having just turned fifty with no pretensions towards maintaining a youthful air, he does not mind that his hair is more grey than black. He keeps it cropped low because of his receding hairline and has even, on occasion, gone for the bald look. When in the bald mode, he sports a goatee. Most often, though, he is clean shaven.

One cannot help but like Mr. Willow. He says good morning to all the staff and knows all their names. He even knows the names of all staff spouses. He always has a smile on his face and a chuckle in his voice even when he reprimands a teacher. "Ah, Bird," he always says, "learn to forgive … learn to let go." Then he grips her shoulders, gives them a shake, and chortles just to let her know he still loves her.

Willow annoys most educators—Bird in particular—when he refuses to exact much-needed discipline on their students. He has absolutely no qualms going against a teacher's dictate if he feels the punishment does not meet the crime. That is not to say that he refuses to allow a teacher to discipline students. In fact, he expects discipline to occur; he just refuses to back a teacher up if a parent or student complains. As far as Mr. Willow is concerned, a teacher can use whatever means necessary within reason to keep order in the classroom as long as no one protests. His staff has come to conclude that what Mr. Willow doesn't know Mr. Willow doesn't care about, *but* one objection from a parent and he will entrench himself firmly behind the student who claims a teacher's method of discipline is demeaning. That student is then removed from the horrors of accepting personal responsibility.

Once again, Susie is a prime example of this. As Susie constantly arrives late to class, Mrs. Bird implements a late policy to quell this behaviour. "The next time you come late, Susie," she warns, "I will assign you cafeteria duty."

"What's that?" Susie asks.

"Pushing around the garbage cart and cleaning off all the tables in the cafeteria," Mrs. Bird responds, smiling.

Susie gasps, "You just want to watch me have to clean up dirty garbage!" Leaping up from her chair and pushing her table forward, Susie shouts, "I will not! I have rights, you know!"

"But clearly no sense of responsibility," Mrs. Bird adds.

At this point, Susie runs downstairs to Mr. Willow's office to register her complaint.

Standing next to the principal's desk, she exclaims, "Mr. Willow, she wants me to touch dirty foodstuff and things. Germs and bugs and spit." Puffing herself up by shoving her arms beneath her breasts, lifting them skyward (causing Mr. Willow's eyes to instinctively rise along with them), she insists, "I am not making myself sick so that woman can get her silly revenge on me!" Sniffing back tears, she adds, "Besides, it's embarrassing."

"Of course," Mr. Willow agrees. He gets up from his computer chair and motions towards the coffee table. "What would you deem an appropriate consequence for always arriving late?"

Susie, watching his hand wave her towards the plush armchairs, finally sits. Mr. Willow sits in the armchair next to her. Susie smiles, scans the ceiling, and lightly taps her tongue against her upper lip in time with her toe, which she is tapping on the floor. "Well," she slowly drawls out as she lowers her gaze to meet Willow, "it seems to me Miss Payne could still use some help with the decorating team." The decorating team is the brainchild of Miss Payne. Not having a background in either sports or theatre, she created a team of students who decorate the school for every festive occasion as well as any of its major events. During the Christmas season, this little group is very busy—especially since they started hiring themselves out to decorate staff parties for local businesses. Most of Susie's friends are on Miss Payne's decorating team, as had Susie been for her grade ten year. After Susie got turned down as the team leader due to her poor attendance record (drastically marred by absenteeism and tardiness), she turned down all other offers to help out. She then spent the first half of the semester watching her friends having fun without her.

Willow smiles. He knows exactly what to do. "The decorating team it is then!"

Susie beams.

Willow's cheeks bulge and his eyes crinkle as he successfully stifles a laugh.

He gives her garbage duty.

Susie doing garbage duty

☺ ☺ ☺ ☺ ☺

The very next day Susie marches back into Mrs. Bird's room and announces for all the class to hear, "I don't have to do your stupid cafeteria duty. Mr. Willow is letting me work with the decorating team instead." After a short sharp laugh, she tilts her head back, raising both nose and chin sky high, exclaiming, "And there is *nothing* you can do about it."

Mary Miller, the quiet, unassuming girl who usually hides behind a wall of silence, ejaculates, "But the decorating team! That's fun!" Susie turns and glares poor Mary back into her shell.

Mrs. Bird's eyes tighten as she glowers at Susie. After class, she walks down to the office to address this issue with the principal. Willow does not change his punishment, though. He knows Susie will be knee deep in garbage even if no one else does. That, he feels, is sufficient punishment even if she does brag about being back on the decorating team to others. Besides, Susie apologized to him about her indiscretion in the classroom. All is well as far as he is concerned.

Mr. Willow's personal mission statement is to love and cherish all students in a Christ-like manner. Forgiveness is his motto, and he extends it at every given opportunity. When Mrs. Bird confronts him with the fact that Jesus was "none too forgiving" the day he tore apart the merchant's tables at the temple, he dismisses her remark by saying, "Christ was dealing with adults, Bird, we are dealing with children." Nor will he listen to reason when she points out that teenagers are no longer children but young adults. "Ah," he replies, "you said 'young,' and *that* is the operative word. No, Bird," he insists, "we are a Catholic school, and we follow in the ways of Christ." There is no swaying Mr. Willow once he has decided to forgive a young adult.

Frank Gibbons

Frank Gibbons

Frank is the boy everyone thinks is gay. According to his peers, his middle name is Faggot. Is he gay? Nobody knows—but faggot, fag, ferry, fembot, Daisy Duke, and fudge packer are a few of the many slurs slung his way. "Gibby" and "Little Girl Gibbons" are the two most common nicknames, and Frank *hates* them. If the other kids liked him, he might appreciate "Gibby," but the fact it is so closely connected to the ridicule "Little Girl Gibbons" convinces him it is not meant to be endearing. Frank has the misfortune of being pretty—girl pretty. He is skinny and effeminate with delicate features and soft eyes with lashes so thick it looks like he wears mascara. He doesn't.

The worst thing in the world that could ever happen to a boy who looks like a girl happened to Frank when he turned fourteen. His left breast started to develop. Before surgery could remove this embarrassing glandular protrusion, Frank became the laughing stock of his peers. Try as he might to hide his "boob" by wearing baggy shirts, he was unable to mask its presence. After the gland was removed, the sunken chest, according to the nasty teenage crew, simply served as evidence of a sex change gone askew.

Perhaps the worst day in Frank's early high school life was the day Damien Headstone, a square-headed fool, asked him out on a date. It is early fall of their grade ten year, and Frank, still uncertain of the high school dynamics (as opposed to those of middle school?) foolishly chooses to eat lunch in the cafeteria. With three long tables extending the length of the room and grey plastic chairs for the inmates, this room looks more like the mess hall of Alcatraz than a high school cafeteria. Wisely sitting at the end of the middle row, Frank is close to the exit. Greg and Damien sit in the middle of the third row. From this position, Damien is presented with the illusion of feminine beauty that is Frank's profile. Being shy and nervous, Frank constantly plays with his hair, periodically exposing his left boob, causing a stir—or shall we say a rise—in Damien. It is love at first sight. After asking Greg who the hot b—ch is, Damien is easily swayed to ask "her" to the school dance. Damien, not having been spawned at S.I.N., does not know who Frank is. So, getting up and crossing over to the center row, glancing back but once for Greg's reassuring thumbs up, Damien seats himself next to Frank.

"Hey, Francine," Damien coos. Sitting on "her" left side, he snuggles in close. Stunned, Frank looks around to see whom this guy is talking to.

"My name's Damien. How's about going to the dance with me, beautiful?"

Realizing he is the one being addressed and that his life is in jeopardy, Frank stands suddenly, quickly mutters, "My name's Frank," and then runs off.

Damien asking Frank out on a date

As there is absolutely nothing Frank can do to summon respect from his peers, he no longer tries. Even his choice of dress screams geek. He is well groomed, wearing pants that don't sag, belted snugly at the waist, and golf shirts always tucked in. He is also the only student at H.E.L.L. who wears Hush Puppies.

Frank takes his education very seriously. One would think he would study the academic stream (for those bound for university) since he is more than capable, but Frank knows that a ninety average in the general stream (usually for future skilled workers) will get him into the college of his choice. His goal is to study computer network engineering at NAIT— Northern Alberta Institute of Technology. As his grade point average is ninety-two percent—the second highest in his grade—he is going to achieve his dream.

All of his teachers love him since he works hard, always has the right answer, and never gives them any lip. Because he has been ostracized from most of his peers, Frank spends much of his free time talking to staff, who listen out of pity. They avoid him, though, when he gets into his sci-fi mode. None but Mrs. Bird is willing to let him ramble on about *Star Trek*, *Star Wars*, and *Battle Star Galactica*. He can be weird, but then again, even nerds need someone to talk to.

Mrs. Bird talking with Frank

☺ ☺ ☺ ☺ ☺

Mary Miller

Mary Miller

Mary is fat. There is no nice way to say it. She is always on a diet, and every month gains more weight. The other kids call her Beluga! She has gorgeous curly blonde hair but that's where the beauty stops. Her harelip scar used to cause her to lisp and still does when she is nervous. Unfortunately, this happens almost every day at school. Boys love to tease her. They know no one will ever date her, and that makes her a prime target. The worst place for her to be is in a classroom when a teacher is late or has to leave to do some business. When this happens, it's as if the rows of desks suddenly open wide their jaws to chomp down and swallow Mary. And, on this day, they literally do as Mary gets trapped between two desks.

"Hey, Beluga," Damien taunts seductively, "I'll bet you don't get many kisses."

Greg laughs. "Anyone ever touch your melons?"

Damien takes this as his cue to grab Mary. "Fat girls may be gross," he says, "but they sure have big melons!"

"Thtop," Mary lisps.

"Did you hear that?" Damien cackles. "Thtop. Thtop." Everyone in the room laughs at Damien's imitation.

Mary, traumatized by the ordeal, says nothing. She runs quickly to her desk and spends the entire class with her face inside her textbook, but she neither sees the text nor hears the teacher's lecture. Mary isn't learning anything in that class.

Boys grabbing Mary

The hallways are always a blur to Mary. She never sees the posters advertising dances, Students Against Drinking and Driving, Writer's Guild, Drama Club penny drives, or any other exciting student group activity she could become involved in. Student lockers are a blend of metallic colours: red, blue, orange, yellow, and green blend together into a garish brown seen only through her limited peripheral vision. As Mary walks, she stares at the floor to avoid looking her peers in the eye. This unfortunate habit often sends her flying, only to land face down on the hallway floor as she trips, yet again, over someone's foot. Laughter always abounds with the sight of her body fat wriggling as she rolls over and struggles to stand up. It doesn't help that she has to grunt to accomplish this task. A chorus of "oinks" immediately follows, echoing throughout the crowd of onlookers. What hurts Mary the most, though, is that she can never tell who the perpetrators are. How can she when she is constantly looking down?

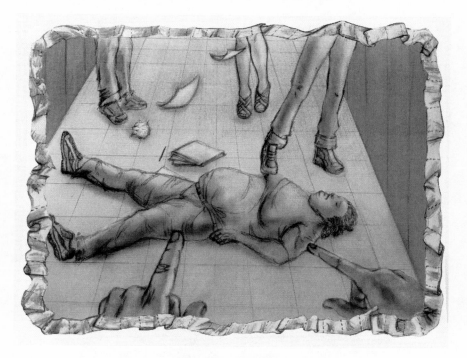

Mary tripped in hall

Mary also suffers from acne. She wants her mom to let her get her skin scraped, but her mother keeps refusing her. As Mrs. Miller—also overweight—is a single mom who works as a custodian at S.I.N. (Sophia

Imaculata Nell Middle School), they can't afford the costly procedure. Mary never gives up hope, though. Every so often, Mary asks her mother if she can get a job, but Mrs. Miller is adamantly opposed. Sitting in the living room of their small apartment squashed together on a love seat built for two (more like one in their case), Mrs. Miller emphasizes her point of view. "Your education is the most important thing in life, Mary. You'll grow out of the acne stage, but your education … that's what really counts. Don't you want to go to university, young lady?"

"I could thave half the money from my part-time job to pay for the procedure and the other half to pay for university."

"Watch your lisp," Mary's mother snaps. "Make an effort to put your tongue behind your teeth."

Mary sighs. Her mother knows just what to say to silence her.

"You let me worry about your education fund." Mrs. Miller sacrifices everything but the basics so she can put a hundred dollars away every month for Mary's education. Placing an arm around her daughter's shoulder to lessen the blow, she adds judiciously, "Besides, your marks aren't good enough. A job will only take away from your studies."

Mary knows her mother is right, but university seems so far off. She is failing all but one class, and, besides, the general stream doesn't qualify her for university.

Mary talking with mother

☺ ☺ ☺ ☺ ☺

Damien Headstone

Damien Headstone

Damien's favourite stance is leaning up against the lockers with one foot crossed over the other and his free hand shoved down inside the pocket of his pants. In this manner, he offers up his profile to the student body. Damien is self-conscious about his appearance. His face, he's told, is square, and he believes he has more a chiseled masculine look when seen from the side. Unfortunately, Damien's face is so flat there is almost no profile at all for anyone to look at. Damien is block shaped and stocky, and no variation to his stance will ever change that. Overly sensitive, Damien is always looking to others for approval, and, as Greg is the most popular among the "tough crowd," he is always looking to Greg for his cue. If Greg were to offer him crack, he'd do it. If Greg were to tell him to shoot the principal, he'd do it. Everything he does, he does to be accepted. Everything he does, he does because he thinks it will make him look cool. Everything he does, he does for approval. Which is why, when Greg says, "Ask Francine there to go to the dance with you," Damien has no qualms. Pointing to Frank, the other unsuspecting victim in this prank, Greg makes the task even easier when he says, "I know she likes you. I've seen her looking at you."

"You bastard," is all Damien can bluster when he gets back to the lunch table. Greg slaps his back, "Man, that was great!"

Now, Damien does not have a great sense of humor when it comes to jokes at his expense, but he buries his humiliation and laughs along with Greg. Regardless, he is determined to get back at Frank. It is *her* fault, not Greg's.

Greg slapping Damien's back

☺ ☺ ☺ ☺ ☺

H.E.L.L.'s Community

H.E.L.L.'s Community

Mrs. Bird's first—and only—teaching job is at H.E.L.L. She came to H.E.L.L. because it was the only school that offered her a position in her area of expertise. All through university, she had been regaled with horror stories of English teachers being hired to teach phys-ed, science—even math! To avoid such a terrifying fate, she applied for every northern job possible, convinced that the more desperate the location, the more likely it would be that she would teach English. She was right. H.E.L.L. sucked her in, and she's been here ever since. And, even though her memories of her first few years at H.E.L.L. are mostly hazed over because of excessive drug and alcohol use, Mrs. Bird has eventually settled down and is determined to love her job and community.

One of Mrs. Bird's favorite pet peeves is the way people like to put down her community. True enough, it is a bustling, oil-rich party town overflowing with drugs and booze. People come for the money and leave after they drink it down (or snort it up their noses). Big trucks at $80,000 a pop line the streets, and houses sell for astronomical prices—$600,000 plus for a great little fixer-upper. A typical lament from shell-shocked first-year teachers is, "There is nothing to do here besides get drunk."

"Not true, people," Mrs. Bird tries to impress upon these impressionable young educators who, after only a few days, are already thinking of packing up and making a run for the south. "Don't believe it for a minute," she reiterates. "Those of us who live here for the long term, like me and Wood, know there are lots of great things to do here."

"Like what?" Justin Pitts, a first-year English teacher, used to a more metropolitan society, is finding life in the northern boomtown rather stifling.

"We have live music, home business markets, festivals, even a great community theatre." Touching each finger as she lists off these advantages, Mrs. Bird starts to ramble, "We've got quad trails for ATVs, cross country ski trails, running trails, walking trails, lakes to the south, rivers to the north, fishing frenzies, hunting extravaganzas, moose eating berries off trees in your front lawn—heck, we've got everything the wild and wonderful northern environment has to offer. And," she says, pointing straight into Pitts's face, determined to prove to the young man that the north is where it's at, "in the winter, we get the most wonderful sky show God has to offer!" Leaning back in her chair, convinced her point has been made, but still not willing to let it go, the old bird adds, "What few people realize, young man, is that, beyond the crime, the hookers, the strip bars, and the drugs, which, by the way, are just as rampant in every other city in North America, our little community is home to authors, playwrights, painters, artisans, musicians, actors, teachers," pointing to herself, "engineers, doctors, lawyers, and countless other decent creative and wonderfully happy people!"

"All right, you win," Justin exclaims. "I'll stick it out until the end of the year. But after that, who knows." As if to support his uncertainty, he adds, "Hell, I can barely afford to pay the rent let alone make payments on my student loan."

"That," Mrs. Bird says, "is why I will buy you kids beer after work on Friday."

The Origins of H.E.L.L.

On the first Friday of every school year, the veterans take the first-year teachers out for beer. The Copper Kettle, affectionately known by the teaching staff as "the library," is a small, dingy pub frequented by educators. Over half the teachers from H.E.L.L. line up like cowboys in an old B western movie, elbows drowning in a Molotov cocktail of spilt liquor, determined to dull the week's edge with rum and coke and beer. Mrs. Bird's mothering instinct always comes into play this time of year. She wants more than anything to help these young teachers transition into their new careers as smoothly as possible and keep them from suffering the same dreadful trauma all first-year teachers go through. Although there is really very little she can do to change the climate of their classrooms, she can at least get them drunk and regale them—in her own eloquent way—about the origins of Father Hubert high.

This year, Mrs. Bird has three budding young educators under her wing: Thomas Wright who will be forever known by Mrs. Bird as Young Goodman Wright—needless to say he is the new religion teacher (she fears the worst for him as religion teachers take the most abuse); Amy Abel, a math teacher (making her completely incompatible with Mrs. Bird); and Justin Pitts, the new English teacher, to whom she is instantly endeared.

"Our little high school," she comments proudly whilst pouring everyone a beer from the communal jug, "is named after the infamous Father Hubert Edmund Lucian Laurence." After a swig of beer, she reminds them, "You'll meet him on Sunday."

"Why is he infamous?" Wright asks.

Completely ignoring the first-year's query, Mrs. Bird continues with her story in the fashion of all good teachers who know exactly what they want to say regardless of the needs of the listener. "His parents were staunch Catholics—they made sure every one of his names was that of a saint." Taking a moment to look as if she is seriously pondering the story, she pauses to sip more of her beer. "They must have been a little daft not to recognize the acronym that ensues as a result of this particular combination of saintly names." She smirks and looks to her little flock of first-years expecting them to be basking in her fabulous sense of humor. Having been told by the second-year teachers that a smile and a nod for the old bird will get them plastered, they behave appropriately. After obtaining the anticipated smiles and snickers, she continues, "One thing is for sure, though, Father Hubert is certainly aware of the irony—he uses the acronym as his signature! I really like this man!"

"Why is he infamous?" asks Wright again, now leaning in closer, enunciating each word.

Mrs. Bird, pleased by the near proximity of such a handsome young man (religion teacher or not, he is still nice to look at), launches into the story. "Well, he grew up in America. He denounced his faith when he was fifteen and joined a group of hippies protesting the American war in Vietnam. After jumping the border to avoid the draft, he ventured quite heavily into the drug scene and found himself on the streets of Vancouver addicted to heroin. Good old Father Hubert finally hit rock bottom when he found himself with his hands wrapped around another man's neck for stealing his fix. It was at that moment—just as he was about to strangle the life out of another human being—that he found God's loving grace, professed himself a sinner, and begged forgiveness. After a long battle to overcome his addiction, Hubert Edmund Lucian Laurence entered the seminary and, as a born-again Catholic, dedicated his life to God, the church, and its followers."

And, like every first-year before him Pitts mutters, "Wow, that's some story."

"Hell, kid, that's only the beginning." Leaning in close enough to smell the musk of his cologne, she lowers her voice to suggest the upcoming scandal, "History aside, perhaps the most infamous story about Father Hubert concerns the fact that he and his parish secretary—a nun by the way—have recently ... actually ..." She pauses for a moment to recollect herself, "Well ... not so recently. It's been close to ten years, but the ongoing scandal over the affair makes it seem like yesterday."

"What scandal? What affair?" a wide-eyed Abel asks.

Mrs. Bird smiles, eager to share this tidbit of community gossip, "The two lovers announced to the world their long-standing relationship."

Wright tightens his shoulders and gasps, whilst the other two, Catholic only by birth, venture a slight chuckle. Frowning at Young Goodman

Wright, Mrs. Bird ponders sadly how such a handsome young man could be such a prude. *Still*, she reasons, *he's willing to suck back a few drinks, so he can't be all bad. There may be hope for him yet.*

Smirking, Mrs. Bird continues, "Neither priest nor nun has any intention of renouncing their ways. They would, both insist, if given the opportunity, marry. Well, let me tell you ..." at this point Mrs. Bird leans back in her chair and claps her hands. She is so taken by her own storytelling that she has almost forgotten the first-years who are listening to her. "Gasps, shudders, and guffaws rippled through the church like shock waves that year." She hoots loudly and slaps Justin, who is laughing along with her. "I swear, if the church was not so damn desperate for priests, Father Hubert would have been excommunicated. But, as we all know, the shortage of young men willing to give themselves up to the church and all hope of future sex—well, okay, not according to Father Hubert—are at an all-time low, so not only was Father Hubert not excommunicated, he is still preaching at our pulpit."

"You mean he's still preaching?" Young Goodman Wright demands.

"What about the nun?" Abel asks. Unbeknownst to Mrs. Bird, Amy Abel studied in the convent for two years before the mother superior determined she wasn't nun material.

Mrs. Bird winks and smiles, "She was ousted."

"Well, that hardly seems fair," exclaims the young woman.

"Whoever told you life was fair was lying to you." Pausing for a moment to recollect an important detail, Mrs. Bird adds, "The last person to say that was Bill Gates." Watching the scowl ripping across Abel's face, Mrs. Bird laughs. "Don't feel so bad for the old lady. Father H.E.L.L. is doing right by her. He has her set up in a nice apartment and she is still his parish secretary." With another deep-throated laugh, Mrs. Bird adds, "I really like the idea of my high school being named after this man." In response to the stunned look on Young Goodman Wright's face, Mrs. Bird explains, "Of course, the high school was named long before the old man and his old lady came out of the ecclesiastic closet—so to speak. Debates still rage over whether or not we should change the name of our high school as a result of the man's scandal." Then, with a wicked gleam in her eye, she challenges Young Goodman Wright. "What do you think? Should we keep the name?"

Pitts saves his colleague from a potential argument by inquiring, "Why did they choose to name the high school after him in the first place?"

"Quite simply," Mrs. Bird replies after another swig on her beer, "after he was first appointed to our church, he was appalled to discover there was no Catholic school district in our community, so he fought for Catholic schools to be opened. Prior to Father Hubert, the only available school board was public. He ensured Christ's message would be made available to our children. As he so aptly put it, 'Catholic schools are the front lines of the Church. It is essential that we run a Catholic school board in our community!'" Looking past the first-years into space as if actually addressing the man, she cheers him on, "Damn straight, Father!" With a coy smile she adds, "Did I mention I like this man?"

Mrs. Bird salutes father and nun

☺ ☺ ☺ ☺ ☺

Mrs. Bird pauses long enough for Justin to turn and address Amy. Before he can utter a word, though, Mrs. Bird dives into another rampage on her school's namesake. "Other aspects of this man's nomenclature …"

Justin Pitts whispers "classification" and then "another word for naming things" to Amy Able and Young Goodman Wright.

This does not stop Mrs. Bird; she just keeps right on with her storytelling: "… that I really enjoy are the various meanings and histories behind the assorted saints he's named after. To begin with his Christian name, *Hubert* means 'bright mind.' It seems appropriate, therefore, that a high school be named after him, since our goal is to poop out 'bright minds' into society. That is, of course, assuming we educators are, in fact, responsible for creating the truly bright minds of the future. Ask any one of your colleagues and they'll say the same thing, 'that bright mind came to me that way' or, 'I lucked out this semester. I've got a class of really bright minds.' And my favorite comment of all times, 'these kids'll do well no matter what we do in the classroom.' I often think these kids make it through despite our best efforts. And, yet, these are the kids who improve our stats and make us look good as educators. So, the question remains, how did they get so smart? We're they born this way? Or did their parents help them? I suspect the latter." Addressing an invisible audience, Mrs. Bird pronounces, "Mommies and daddies, you are the real educators, and, without your support, your child has very little chance at being successful." Turning back to stunned looks, she adds, "I have noticed over the years that those students whose parents read to their children at night and study with them at the kitchen table are the ones who excel."

Motioning to their glasses, she waits long enough for them to nod, then waves the pitcher at their waiter. "Now, *Edmund*," she continues, "the good father's second name, means 'happy protection.' This, too, is another most appropriate name for the patron saint of high schools. All our students should feel that benevolent sense of security. All our students should feel safe. True—oh so very true—but they don't. Bullying does not end in elementary and junior high schools. No sir, it builds with a voracious hunger in the senior years. Watch for it in our school. Keep an open eye, because it's everywhere. The most common attack is a lock covered in bumble gum."

Taking another swig of beer, Mrs. Bird launches back into her repartee. "Sometimes apple cores are slung at the nerds. Sexual harassment— fondling, touching, thrusting abusively against one's peer—is yet another predominant agony suffered by teens, and not just by the girls either. There's name calling; pushing; stealing of books, pens, paper, wallets, iPods, cell phones—ah, the cell phone. Technology has brought forth a new age in bullying. Now students can film their peers in embarrassing circumstances and post the images on the Internet."

"I heard about that," Pitts says.

"Great fun, eh!" Mrs. Bird shakes her head. "Indeed, we need 'happy protection' in our schools."

"What's the good father's third name?" Young Goodman Wright inquires.

"Lucian."

"*Lucian* means light, doesn't it?"

"Good for you! That deserves another drink. Waiter!" Turning back to what Mrs. Bird perceives to be three very eager young ducklings, she offers up a suggestion she knows won't be refused, "Would you like a shooter? Best way to start off a new year. Don't worry, I'm buying." Bird adds this last little bit to relieve them of the concern of over spending an already-too-small budget. Thus, there is no surprise for the old bird when the young teachers readily agree. "Sure," they chirp in unison, "Thanks!"

"No, problem." Mrs. Bird winks. "You'll pay for it by having to listen to me all night. Now, where was I?"

"*Lucian* means light," Young Goodman Wright pipes up.

"Of course." Bird suspects Wright really wants to learn all he can about his new priest. "Now, as you know, as a Catholic school, it is our duty to share the light of the Lord with our students. To this end, we offer a number of liturgical celebrations for our student body, and anywhere from a quarter to a third of this unwilling congregation tries to skip out of any given service. That's why we have to patrol the halls while ushering our kids down to the gymnasium to make sure they don't slip out any of the side or back doors. Some kids don't even bother skipping anymore as their parents will phone in and excuse them." Here Mrs. Bird screws herself upright and imitates a snotty-nosed individual: "My child does not wish to attend a religious service, so I am excusing her from this activity."

"Do they really?" Young Goodman Wright's eyelids open wide and then scrunch in. "Catholic parents really do that?"

"That's right, young man," Mrs. Bird replies sternly. "Not all Catholic parents support their own educational institution. Watching Young Goodman Wright shake his head, Mrs. Bird muses, *Ah, the young and the naïve.* She sighs. *It's not so sweet when there's a long, hard fall ahead for them.* Their shooters arrive, and the four of them clink shot glasses and toss back the first of many drinks.

Mrs. Bird and first-year teachers tossing back shooters

Letting the alcohol buzz settle, Mrs. Bird resumes her narrative. "Still …" She tips her head slightly and looks up over her forehead. "It would be unfair to say only Catholic parents excuse their children from mass. We do have students from a variety of denominations and faiths attending our school."

"What difference should that make?" inquires Young Goodman Wright.

"Oh, I agree completely!" Mrs. Bird exclaims in delight, as she is now free to expound her theory to a like-minded audience. "I've had a few interesting fights with parents over this. I swear I am always dumbfounded when that happens. It's not like I'm a great Catholic or anything, but being that attendance at a Catholic school is a choice, and given that religion is going to play an important role at a Catholic school, why would you send your child to a Catholic school in the first place if you did not want your child to be exposed to this religion? I mean, it's not as if we're abusing anyone's religious freedoms here." Unable to get a word in edgewise, all the first-years can do is nod their heads up and down. "We are what we say we are: *a Catholic school!*" At this point, Mrs. Bird flings her hands open wide in emphasis every time she uses the expression *a Catholic school*. She becomes very dramatic, and her hands start flying about wildly. "We openly profess ourselves as *a Catholic school*. Anyone who registers here knows full well that we will be teaching the Catholic faith at *a Catholic School*. We will be sharing Catholic services in *a Catholic school*. In order to graduate from *a Catholic school* you have to take religion!" Now she addresses an unseen crowd: "What in all of that can you not possibly understand, people? If you don't want your child exposed to the Christian faith, don't send the little rascal to *a Catholic school*. It's as simple as that." She briefly addresses the first-years, "You know what I really want to say to some of these people? By the way, if your kid has screwed up so many times at all the public schools out there and no other school but the *Catholic school* is willing to take the little reprobate, then sucks to be you. The little ruffian blew it everywhere else so, quite frankly, you're stuck with our rules now."

Abel starts to giggle, and Pitts puts an arm around her shoulder. These two, Bird determines, are forming a drunken association that may lead to foolish maneuvers on their part. Mrs. Bird motions to Pitts and offers him whispered advice, "Don't dip your wick in the company ink." Pitts bursts out laughing then leans back and wraps his arm around Abel's shoulder. She giggles some more and rests her head comfortably against his pectoral muscle.

Drunk couple cuddling

Mrs. Bird, recognizing there is little hope for the drunken youth, resumes her story. "Now," she says, her voice slurring and her mannerisms becoming more exaggerated, "this leaves us with the last name of our illustrious priest—*Laurence*. There were two saints by the name of Laurence." Mrs. Bird leans forward and waves two fingers in the air for emphasis. "The first," she affirms as she wiggles one pointed finger, "was martyred by being burned to death—*slowly*. They roasted him over a bed of hot coals. Can you imagine? And, let me tell you, this man had balls. Big, fat, hairy boys—steel kahoonies!" She lifts both hands waving them wide open and out to the sides to help emphasize their grandness. Even Young Goodman Wright snickers at this image. "Whilst he was gradually roasting, he asked his tormentors to turn him over as he was already cooked on the one side. Now, this is a priest I can truly admire! Think about it. Would you be able to spew out humor whilst dying slowly and in the most horribly painful way possible? Absolutely not! You'd be too busy screaming bloody hell and writhing in agony to take the time to think up a quip, let alone shoot it off."

"How do you know?" asks Young Goodman Wright.

Mrs. Bird rolls her eyes … another teacher who can't take a joke. As far as Mrs. Bird is concerned, every good teacher needs a robust sense of humour. *No doubt*, she reasons, *I am too brassy and bold for his liking*. "Because," she answers smugly, "that is what I would be doing."

St. Laurence roasting over a bed of coals

"So, who was the other Saint Laurence?" asks Young Goodman Wright.

"The other Saint Laurence was a military captain, and," she adds with emphasis, "he was a teacher, spreading the faith around the world!" All four teachers clink glasses. "So, there you have it." Mrs. Bird smiles before slamming back her last shot. "The origins of H.E.L.L."

The Battle With Greg Begins

(Greg's perspective)

Greg McGregor enters Mrs. Bird's classroom for the first time in September, at the beginning of the school year. Mrs. Bird is standing at the whiteboard, her back to him. She appears unaware of his presence. He is the only other person in the room. He takes a moment to inspect his surroundings. Mrs. Bird's classroom is on the second floor of Hubert High. Students call it the cell since it is in the center of the building and has no exterior windows. With no window light, this room gets pitch black when the lights go off—it's a great room for showing movies. Looking up at the TV hanging front and center, suspended by an iron casing, Greg laughs. *Damien's been in this room.* His touch is everywhere. A red gummy bear sticks to the TV screen. Spitballs litter the walls. One brand-new HB lead pencil sticks in the ceiling, its dangling shaft tempting Greg to leap up and grab it. He fights off temptation. Too much is at stake. He doesn't want the old bird to know he's there.

No worries there, he realizes. The teacher is still working at the whiteboard. Things look good. She hasn't noticed him yet. *She's not as alert as the average teacher,* he ponders. Although he knows she is not a new teacher, she appears to be acting like one. Even better—an old teacher who hasn't forgotten what it means to be a teacher. *Yes ... Mrs. Bird. Good. She'll be roast turkey before long.* Greg has heard a lot about her. She's a weird one, they all say. She used to do drugs too. Apparently she had to take a leave of absence in order to quit. To top it all off, they say she studied mime. He notices the poster of Marcel Marceau on the back wall. *Good God! Who studies mime?* From what he's heard, she does a pretty good gorilla imitations and a damn fine robot. *The odds are I'll miss that little show.* Greg's attendance is slim to none, but, when he is in class, the teacher really knows he's there! *Oh, well,* he figures, *it hardly matters if I miss her performance since I already caught the act on YouTube.* One of Mrs. Bird's students from the previous semester downloaded the show, and it's a five-star video clip with lots of nasty comments. One calls her a "f—ed-up b—ch," and another (Greg's personal favorite) says she is "an embarrassment to her school." *I might just get along with her, you never know.* He takes a moment to cogitate on this possibility, but then reconsiders. *Nah! She's a teacher. It's my job to ruin her.*

A more in-depth study of the room is in order. Greg likes to know every inch of his surroundings; he's like a good general studying the battlefield before a war. The floor's linoleum is off white with a grey mottled design. The grey mottle is advantageous as the added dirt and scuffmarks tend to blend in with it. In the far right corner, behind three filing cabinets (*What teacher has three filing cabinets? This woman is excessive*, he concludes) and next to the back door there should be a spittoon! Unfortunately, there isn't one. *I'll bet Damien sat in that corner*, Greg laughs to himself.

Greg decides he likes this room. It has two doors—one that leads out into the hallway and another that leads into a computer lab! *An escape route. I love it!* The bulletin boards sport their original beige cork. This he sees as another interesting character trait of his teacher. *That is something I can definitely capitalize on.* He smiles. Not only has she not added bulletin board paper, she can't even be bothered to apply a few layers of paint. Most teachers at least paint their bulletin boards to make the room look inviting. He notices that she still puts in some effort, though, as there are a few posters on the walls. This room is definitely an English teacher's room. There's the Romeo and Juliet poster every English teacher displays: "Boy Meets Girl. Parents don't approve ..." Blah! Blah! Blah! And, of course, one for Hamlet: "He hates his girlfriend. His mother married his uncle. Now that's teen angst!" Greg smirks. This teacher actually wrote graffiti on one of her own posters—"Arrgh! Hamlet is thirty—read the play people!!!!" No student would ever write that! Glancing past the mime poster, he takes a moment to consider the image of a boy sitting at a desk with a closed book in front of him covered in cobwebs. *Is she being ironic or sarcastic?*

Now this is interesting, he thinks as he looks up. Kites hang from the ceiling dangling over the student tables. Kites make the room colorful and friendly—inviting so to speak—without the teacher having to go to any great lengths to ensure a pleasing atmosphere. *So, she doesn't like to work hard*, Greg surmises. *Here is another trait I can exploit.*

Greg hopes he doesn't skip out on Mrs. Bird's famous "create a theme day." Damien explained how, on days when the old bird has nothing to teach, she gets the class to decorate the room for her. "It gives them a feeling of ownership," she has been heard to say by way of explanation to Mr. Willow. *No doubt he sees this as a capital idea.* Greg laughs silently, knowing teachers play on the old man's flaws just as much as the students do. Even though he has only ever seen this woman's back, he believes he knows what she is thinking: *Crap, what am I going to do today?* "Okay, kids, it's time to decorate the classroom. What theme do you want to use?" Greg can't help but laugh at this thought. He freezes. *Did she hear me? It wasn't that loud of a chuckle.* He watches her closely for any sign of awareness. She is still focused on her work. *Damn, she's dedicated.* He deliberates over this for a moment. *So much so, she misses half the picture.* He wants to laugh but only smiles. No point taking any chances.

Feeling secure again, Greg continues his inspection of the classroom. Instead of desks, Mrs. Bird's room is filled with tables and chairs. She has arranged the tables so that students sit in groups of six. Greg grimaces. *Clearly she hopes to encourage cooperative group learning. I hate that sh—.* Cooperative learning is something that seldom happens in accordance to theory. Her classroom is fitted with an abundance of technology. She has a TV, a VCR player, a DVD player, a tape player, a CD player, what used to be a top-of-the-line iMac computer, which is connected to the TV. Everything is sorely outdated. There is nothing worth stealing or Damien would have cleaned the room out two years ago.

Studying the chairs at the tables, Greg grimaces. They are the crappy plastic grey kind that hurt the rump after just a few minutes of sitting. Damien said she used to have cool blue chairs with padded seating. Unfortunately, so little respect was shown that the fabric got torn up and the metal got bent, and Mrs. Bird said, "To heck with it! If you kids can't respect our environment, then you can sit on crappy chairs." So she exchanged padded seating for grey plastic.

She is even more radical with the pencil sharpener. The grey skeleton of the old one is still screwed to the wall as a reminder to the students as to why she refuses to replace it. Whenever a student complains about it, she points to the old sharpener and says, "Since kids continue to vandalize my sharpeners, you will have to bring your own."

When Susie warned Greg about this, he became irate. "To hell with that," he blustered. "What if I can't afford one?"

"Just buy one from the loonie store," Susie replied amicably. "Everything's cheap there."

Righteous indignation burst out of Greg, "I'm not going to some stupid dollar store to buy something the school should be providing for me."

"Well, there isn't one in Mrs. Bird's classroom, and *she* won't be providing you with one."

Good, Greg figures, *the old bird's given me another excuse not to work.*

Now it is time to study the teacher. Greg needs to determine all of Mrs. Bird's weaknesses in order to learn how he can manipulate then control the classroom. Right away he determines this one is going to be easy. He's been in the room for well over a minute and there is still no recognition from her that anyone is around. Stifling the urge to laugh again, he reminds himself to keep quiet. *Watch how she moves. Look at what she's putting up on the whiteboard. Oh my God, it's an essay question. She's going to make the class write an essay on the first day. Hmmm ... maybe her class won't be so simple as all that. She actually expects work on the first day. Well, she'll get it, today—or not.* Greg still hasn't decided if he can take her down on day one. *I might,* he figures, *if the moment strikes.* Greg is a firm believer in spontaneous action. For Greg, keeping a watchful eye on all events in the classroom is integral to his success. Teachers can never do this. They have far too much on their plates to keep up with every individual act that happens in the classroom. Greg knows this and knows how to take full advantage. You see, Greg does not pay attention to the teacher as much as he pays attention to everything else that goes on around him. This gives him the edge. Class lessons—irrelevant! What the teacher is doing in one corner and what his peers are doing around him—*very relevant indeed*!

Mrs. Bird is clearly engrossed in what she plans to teach. So engrossed, in fact, she doesn't appear to hear or see Greg. Clearly, she wants to impart real education to her students. Greg laughs silently. *A teacher who's ripe for the picking. So ripe, she's practically pulling the branches to the ground.* Greg chuckles again to himself.

Greg studying Mrs. Bird's classroom

☺ ☺ ☺ ☺ ☺

The Battle With Greg Continues

(Mrs. Bird's point of view)

What Greg fails to realize, though, is that Mrs. Bird is fully aware of his presence. She has heard all about his in-class antics and is watching him with her peripheral vision to determine what his initial plan of attack will be. Typical of day one, Bird and Wood had scanned each other's class lists, giving each other the rundown on unfamiliar names. Wood, having taught Greg one time too many, had plenty of stories to share about him.

"So you got Gregory McA—hole McGregor, eh. Holy sh—."

"Why do you call him that?" Bird inquires.

"Because he's an a—hole." Wood, as always, is blunt. "Don't grimace, Bird. You know me. I call a spade a spade. There's no nice way of putting it."

"All right." Bird sighs, knowing she too would have used such language before William entered her life. "Tell me what he's like."

"He'll come early for the first week. He'll be Little Mr. Perfect. He'll listen, he'll even do work. He'll lull you into thinking he's okay, and then he'll start skipping. If that's all he does, everything will be fine, but, when he does come to class, he is a major nuisance. He will contradict every thing you try to teach. To put it bluntly, he's a pr— ... a waste of skin, as useless as tits on a bull, and, in my estimation, a sperm that should have been swallowed."

"Ouch, that's harsh."

"Wait till you've taught him, Bird. It won't be long before you're agreeing with me." Then he adds with a laugh, "He's the little sh— who decorated the school cross with toilet paper." Greg's toilet paper décor of the school cross, made matted and muddy by spring wind and rain, made for quite the scandal at H.E.L.L.

Staring down at her class list as if observing a revelation, Bird says, "So, that's him, eh?"

"Yup." Wood smiles slyly. "And now it's your turn to teach him." After a menacing laugh, he adds, "Take my advice—do nothing when he skips, and, when he shows up, kick him out at the first sign of trouble. The less you have to deal with him, the better."

Mrs. Bird, on the other hand, has another strategy in mind. Cynical she may be, but, ironically, that cynicism makes her even more determined to get as many kids through the system as possible. She will make certain that Gregory McMiscreant McGregor (as she determines to call him) comes to class even if it means phoning home every single day and bombarding his old man with a dozen e-mails.

Oh yes, Gregory McGregor will be attending English 30-2, and he will graduate! Mrs. Bird smirks as Greg chooses a seat in the front row, smack dab in the middle. *So you think you can fool me into thinking you're a good little boy. Ain't gonna happen, buddy boy. Even if I have to rout you out of the cafeteria at the top of every class, I'll do it!* Smirking, she remembers she won't have to. Willow, she figures, will be more than willing to follow up on this. *He'll be an eager aid as long as he believes it is all being done for the little kiddie. Oh yes,* Mrs. Bird determines, *this one will be a challenge. I am so looking forward to kicking his scrawny little butt into a pass!*

Mrs. Bird's evil eye

☺ ☺ ☺ ☺ ☺

Class Begins

So class begins. The bell rings and Mrs. Bird patiently waits the extra five, which ends up being more like fifteen—minute leeway required of staff on day one. After attendance is taken (and readjusted ten times to accommodate latecomers), Mrs. Bird begins, "Welcome to English thirty-dash-two, your core curriculum diploma class—the class you need to pass in order to graduate." Behind her on the board, she has written all the disciplines this class is required to study: poetry, modern drama, the novel, short stories, essays, visual communication, the business letter, the speech, and literary appreciation. She reads the list aloud, enunciating each category clearly to emphasize its importance. Inevitably, as she reads out this list, someone asks, "Do we have to study Shakespeare?"

"No, Susie, Shakespeare is not a requirement in thirty-dash-two. However, if you want to …"

Before she can finish, a chorus resounds across the room. "*No!*"

"Of course not." There is no surprise in her response. "Well, don't worry, it is not required of you."

"Thank God," Susie replies.

Damien mutters, "I think I'd kill myself if I had to study Shakespeare again."

"Don't tempt me," Mrs. Bird replies. The class laughs thinking she is just being jocular. Although she would never say it, Damien is the one student she agrees with Wood about. *He is the sperm that should have been swallowed.* But she always fights to push that thought out of her brain. *Find something good about him*, she keeps telling herself, but to no avail. For the past two years now, she has been trying to find something good about this boy, but he simply refuses to cooperate. *Why*, she laments every semester, *does counseling keep sticking me with him?* Damien has failed English every single semester since the first term of grade ten, but, being in the dash-two stream, he only has to fail each course twice before he just gets pushed ahead. *God,* Mrs. Bird prays, *let him please pass thirty-dash-two the first time 'round!*

"For every unit," she continues, determined to get back on track and not give Damien the opportunity to do something stupid, "you will be evaluated two ways. Some units will require more evaluation than others, but every unit will end with no less than a reading comprehension test and a timed essay, both in the style of your diploma."

"What's that again, Miss?" Damien asks thinking he's being funny.

Mrs. Bird shakes her head. *No wonder you failed every class prior to this one.* "Your final exams," she explains as if talking to a monkey. "The departmental. The exams made up by the Alberta government."

"Oh yeah, those," Damien adds with a little laugh. He blushes, sensing no one else is laughing with him.

After rolling his eyes at Damien, Greg verbally attacks his teacher, "I signed up for the easy class, not this sh—!"

Mrs. Bird is stunned by this interruption. "Pardon me?"

"I think you got us mixed up with thirty-dash-one."

"Yeah," Damien adds, following Greg's lead. "This is the dummy class. You can't expect us to do all that."

"The what class?" Mrs. Bird asks incredulously.

"The dummy class," Damien reiterates. Tapping Greg on the shoulder, hoping to make up for his previous guffaw by showing his friend how cool he is. "The old bird's deaf too."

Marching over to Damien's table, she looks the young man in the eye. She is having none of this. "So you think you're stupid, do you?"

This abrupt inquiry stuns Damien. Greg turns around and fills in the awkward gap. "We're only in dash-two. It's supposed to be easy. That's why we're in here. If we could do the hard stuff, we'd be in dash-one."

"So you want an easy class do you? One with no work?"

"That's right," Susie pipes up. "We can't read or write like the dash-ones. You have to go easy on us."

"Yeah." Damien is finally over his shock. "They're smart and we're stupid."

"Well, I'm very sorry to hear you say that." Mrs. Bird's sigh is deceiving. Returning to the front of the class, she turns and faces the entire brood. "Let's think about this. The general consensus of this class is that you are all stupid." Looking at them, she insists on clarification, "Is that right?" With the exception of Frank and Mary, the entire class nods yes. "So, by *your* definition, dash-two students are illiterate morons."

"Whoa!" Greg sputters sitting upright. "Did you just call us morons?"

"No, I didn't—you did."

"I never used the word moron." Waving to his classmates he adds, "None of us did."

"Not that exact word, no," Mrs. Bird agrees, "but, just as one plus one plus one equals three, can't read, can't write, I'm stupid equals illiterate moron." Glaring at her class, Mrs. Bird hisses, "Now, is this what you truly believe about yourselves?" Not giving them any chance to respond, she barges on, "Because I don't." Turning a burning eye on all her students she explains, "English thirty-dash-two is a core curriculum class. That fact that you have made it here is evidence that you can read and write and you are not stupid! I will not treat you like a bunch of boobies!"

Greg bursts out laughing. "Did you just call us 'boobies'?"

"Yes, I did. Boobies. Foolish children who would rather play dumb than do the work necessary to graduate!" Walking around the classroom to ensure every student has her attention, she continues, "Every semester I have to start up the dash-two classes battling this fallacy. Granted, dash-one classes are more difficult as they are designed to prepare students for university, but that in no way diminishes the expectations placed on you, the dash-two students." With her chin jutting back and forth like a woodpecker's beak, she announces, "Yes, dash-one will get you into university if you have a high enough average. But," she says, pointing her finger in the air for emphasis, "did you know that a 90 percent in the dash-two stream will get you into the college of your choice? Not everyone has to be a doctor or a lawyer. The world needs plumbers, pipe fitters, electricians, computer technicians, and all of these people need to be smart to do their jobs. Now I want you to think about this. I am a dash-one graduate, and every year I help hundreds of dash-two students graduate and go on to obtain successful careers in trades. Many of these students now make ten times my salary. Does that make me smarter than them? Does that make you stupid—you with that potential future ahead of you?" Frank nods his head in agreement. Ruffled with anger, Mrs. Bird walks to the front of the class. Facing her students, she pronounces, "I do not teach dummies." She pounds her fist on her table for emphasis. "I am going to teach you!"

Mrs. Bird glaring at her students

☺ ☺ ☺ ☺ ☺

Why are so many students failing?

You can always tell it is the beginning of a semester when Mrs. Bird begins whining about the state of education. Today's lunch hour is no different as Mrs. Bird screeches, "Why are so many students failing these days?" The June diploma marks have just arrived and Mrs. Bird is distressed. The hardest part about teaching grade twelve is having to wait until Alberta Learning finishes grading all the diplomas. Then it will still take weeks before the results are sent back to the school and into the waiting hands of the teacher. To not know if your student has passed or failed, or if you prepared them properly is grueling, agonizing suspense. Then when the marks finally do arrive the inevitable disappointment sinks in.

Wood instantly groans, "Not today, Bird, please."

"No," Bird insists. "I have to ask. Look at last semester's diploma marks. They're deplorable. I actually had two dash-one students fail!"

"Gasp! The horror!" Wood cries out. Payne laughs. Bird, Wood, and Payne meet every lunch hour (when not on supervision) to visit, grumble, whine, tell dirty jokes, and share lunches. These three are the veterans of H.E.L.L., Payne having survived her first three years of teaching here; Wood, his first twelve; and Bird—well, suffice it to say Bird has been at H.E.L.L. the longest of anyone on staff. The time had been when she had been the same age as most of the staff, but all the others have long since fled the sulfurous pits.

Just like the old girl, the staff room is ancient. It is the only room in the building that has never seen any renovations. The ceiling is grimy, and the linoleum is lifting up off the floor against the walls. The faucet in the sink drips, and the drain continually clogs (a toilet plunger is kept underneath the sink at all times). The stove no longer works. Only the refrigerator is new—comparably speaking. Bird donated it a few years back when she and William decided to upgrade to a fridge with an icemaker and water dispenser. There is a ragtag collection of grey and blue plastic chairs stolen from the students' cafeteria, and there are three wooden chairs with loose legs. These surround a large, round table set in the middle of the room. Mixed in with these is one metal chair with a paddled bottom left over from the seventies when the school was first built. It's always a race to score the one metal chair with a padded bottom. Wood is notorious for winning as he lets his block-two class out two minutes before the bell so he can be first in the staff room. He always laughs on the days he wins, spouting the old adage, "They just don't make 'em like they used to!"

Even winning the best seat in the house hasn't made Wood more amiable to Bird's current lament. Continuing with his ridicule he adds, "I guess it's time to retire."

Purposely ignoring Wood's sarcasm, Bird persists, "It gets worse. Eighteen out of twenty-eight thirty-dash-twos failed their first test. Four others have low fifties, and the rest have only sixties." Emphasizing with her index finger, she points out, "And only one student has a ninety."

"Let me guess," Wood interjects, "Frank Gibbons?"

"Thank God for Frank," Mrs. Bird exclaims.

"It's a pity he's gay," Payne adds.

"There's no evidence of that," Bird says in the young man's defense.

"Just look at him," Wood explains, "he is stereotype gay."

"Even if he is gay, what would it matter?" Bird is determined to defend her favourite.

"It matters to Christ and the Church," Payne answers.

Wood laughs. "Love the sinner, hate the sin," he chants.

"Can it, Wood. You don't believe that piffle anymore than I do. You're just trying to change the topic, and that's not going to happen."

Wood groans. "It's lunch hour, Bird. Bring it up at the next staff meeting."

"You know that will never happen. No one wants a decent debate at a staff meeting. All people care about is how fast we can get out of there. And," she adds with emphasis, "the last thing admin wants to do is deal with the real issue." Shaking her head, Mrs. Bird persists, "No, I need to hear what you guys think. This question has been on my mind for a number of years now, and I can't seem to find any viable answers."

"Look, Bird, give it a rest." Wood really is tired. Every lunch hour Bird wants to talk about the declining state of education. "There are too many circumstances beyond our control: drugs, alcohol, part-time—hell full-time—employment, fetal alcohol syndrome, the fad telling us to view kids as 'clients.' Christ, woman, with all this sh— thrown our way, all we can really do is try to help our students in the classroom."

"I know that," Bird complains, "but it's gotten so bad I feel like I can't do anything for them even in the classroom."

"I don't know what you're getting on about," Miss Payne says. "There have always been students who can't grasp some of the most basic concepts presented to them."

"Yes," Bird exclaims, "but, in the past, these students have been the minority not the majority. As we advance as a society, with technology moving faster and faster providing new modes of communication for them, students' minds seem to be draining. Why is this?" Pondering the situation deeper, she concludes, "Technology has compacted everything into instant gratification. They expect everything *now* without ever having to work for it."

"There you go, you just answered your own question. Now let's get on with lunch."

"Not yet," Bird insists.

Wood grimaces. "Lunch hour is for resting, Bird, not whining about students and the state of education. You know, what you really need," he says with a smirk, "is to get laid."

"Aroint thee, witch."

"That's Shakespeare for *p— off*," says Payne. "Though she is a math teacher, she is able to interpret for Wood because she was stuck teaching English in her first year on the job."

"Shouldn't I be a warlock?" Wood inquires.

"That's not what Shakepseare wrote," Bird adds. "But enough of that. You're just trying to change the topic again."

"You got me, you 'rump-fed ronyon.'" Unbeknownst to Payne, Wood, too, got stuck teaching English in his first year.

"Uh-uh. Back to the topic."

"Like I said," Wood continues with a sigh, "you answered the question yourself."

"I know the answer seems obvious," she persists, "but the irony of the situation is too much! With so much technology at their disposal, with so many means of improving the intellect available to our students, why is the collective mind dumbing down? Are technology, mathematics, science all moving too fast for the average person? Is that stupid movie with Luke Wilson, *Idiocracy*, really coming true? I mean here at H.E.L.L.—"

"Don't say that!" Payne always reacts when anything negative is spoken about her school.

"Say what?" Bird inquires innocently.

"Quit playing the teenage bada——, Bird. You called our school *hell*."

Acting like her worst student, Bird laces innocence with treachery. "I was just using the acronym."

"Well, don't," Payne insists, falling deeper into the annoyed teacher role. "I find it offensive."

Rolling her eyes, Bird apologizes, "Sorry. Now where was I?"

"Talking about stupid movies," Wood ventures.

Bird refuses to take the hint and barges on anyway. She really wants her colleagues to help her understand what she sees as a relatively new and increasing phenomenon. "*Idiocracy* … stupidity, yes. Thanks, Wood." He grimaces and Bird smirks. "It seems like fewer and fewer students are able to keep up with higher-level thinking—even in language arts. I mean, this is an area that allows for freedom of imagination, leastwise in English—yet so many students are failing to accomplish even a simple sentence—and these are not mentally retarded students, either."

"That's ignorant," Payne insists. "Do you use language like that with your students?"

Rolling her eyes and tossing her head to the side, Bird instantly counters, "Look, I'm sorry. I'm not trying to be politically incorrect here. I'm simply trying to be honest. What really frightens me is just how many of today's students require individual personalized planning."

Catching Bird in a brief pause, Wood flicks his fingers in exaggerated quotation marks coupling his sarcasm by crossing his eyes. "*IPPs*," he intones.

"Individual personalized plans are necessary," protests Payne. "They help each student learn at his or her individual pace."

"IPPs do no such thing," Wood protests. "All they do is make more work for teachers allowing for less focused time in the classroom. Besides, who the hell wants a doctor on an," rolling his eyes, making quotation marks with his fingers and stretching out all the vowels and accenting all the capitals, "an *Individualized Personal Plan?*"

Before Payne can counter, Bird jumps in, "Hold on, you guys. You're both right, in a way."

"We can't both be right," Wood interjects. "Either they're good for kids or they're not." He pauses to look sternly at Payne. "All IPPs do is demand that we spoon-feed education to our kids. No more teaching them, no more expecting them to think for themselves. No more learning, no more copying notes, no more having to read tests, no more having to even write—" Noting the look of discontent on Bird's face, he adds, "Don't look at me that way; you've said all of this yourself."

"I know," replies Bird with a sigh. "That's what's so gosh darn frustrating about them."

Wood laughs. "'Gosh darn,'" he mimics. He knew Bird back when she swore worse than a jarhead.

Bird chooses to ignore him. Shaking her head in consternation, she adds, "This IPP thing is a serious conundrum."

"There's nothing confusing about it at all," Payne says in defense of the program. "There are students who really need the extra help—"

Before she can finish, though, Bird leaps back in, "Yes, students with an honest-to-God disability like the deaf, the blind, the physically handicapped. They deserve—no, they need—accommodations. But, my God, we have *way* too many kids on these things. I mean, last semester I had fourteen IPPs in a class of twenty-two. How ridiculous is that!"

"*And*," Wood adds aggressively, "the bulk of these *special kids*—and I'm not talking about the *real* special-needs kids—the bulk of these kids use the IPP as an excuse not to work."

"I suspect," Bird interjects, "that the IPP phenomenon is the result of double-income families."

"How so?" Panye asks.

"No one parent has the time to sit down with the child. Students today have not been trained to do nightly homework and spend time studying. Kids needs supervision in order to study effectively. Kids need help to assimilate the knowledge they are given at school, and today's society places all expectations on the teacher when what is really lacking is the home study environment—and we can't replace that."

"Okay, I admit there is logic to your argument, but not all the kids failing are on IPPs."

"Good point," Bird agrees.

Even Wood is willing to accede the point. "It is more than mollycoddling—so many students are skipping out, and a lot of kids fail simply because they refuse to do the work."

"They're just lazy," Bird states. "They admit it themselves. Yesterday, out of frustration, I asked my block-four kids why they and so many students today are failing."

Payne smiles. "What did they say?"

Even Wood appears intrigued. "This should be interesting."

"They said things like 'we don't care,' 'we're too lazy,' 'we just don't want to do the work,' 'it's too easy for us to get drugs'—"

"That last one's the truth," Wood adds.

"They also said we rush through the curriculum."

"That we can't help," Payne replies grimly.

"I agree. Math teachers can't slow down," Wood states. He taught math in his first year, too. "But even the rest of us are limited by time."

"That is a tough one," Bird agrees.

"What else did they say?" Payne asks. This conversation is turning out to be better than any enforced professional development.

"They said they can't take notes and listen to us lecture at the same time. It's too confusing for them."

"That's a good point," Wood adds. "I'm definitely guilty of that one."

"Me too," Payne agrees.

"Me three," says Bird. "Well, I guess that's one thing we can all change."

"Did they say anything else?" Wood inquires.

"They said some of them come to class loaded. They have too many after-school activities like work and sports and dance and things—oh, yeah, and video games. And they said some teachers don't know what they're talking about."

"Well, Bird, you'll have to work on that," Wood says laughing.

"Hardy har har har."

"What I hate," Payne says, "are the kids who leave everything to the last minute. They skip, they skip, they skip, they won't do their work, and then—"

"And then," Wood adds, "in the last two weeks of school, they figure they can make it all up."

"Just enough to pass," adds Bird.

"And we have to let them do it," Payne laments.

"To hell with that," Wood complains.

"Not me," Bird agrees.

Payne is stunned. "But," she sputters, "Willow says you have to. They have to have fifty percent of the course work complete in order for—"

Before she can finish, Bird explains, "He says you have to let them finish, but you don't have to give them everything at once. Give the kid one assignment at a time. When the first assignment is complete, then—*and only then*—do you give him the next one. You don't go all the way back to day one and find everything he missed. One assignment at a time, kiddo, and only when the kid is finished does she get another."

"That's the only way to do it," Wood agrees. "Otherwise, you spend hours retrieving old material—work the kid never does anyway. Nope, Bird is right ... one assignment at a time. You can't kill yourself because some kid wouldn't work all semester."

"But these aren't the means by which we need to help these kids. Letting them play catch-up at the last minute doesn't teach them anything. What we need is a way to get them into class, to keep them there, and to help them understand that education means something ... that it's important to their lives. It's like that old Latin phrase—don't ask me to say the Latin, I can't—but the one that goes 'Education is a possession no man can take away from you'—or something like that."

"That's right," Wood agrees. "These kids need to learn that education is power, and without it their lives are nothing—well, not nothing ... that's too harsh—but empty, destitute ... humph ..." Wood slumps over, his fists opening into the crooked claws of an eagle; his face scrunches up.

Bird finalizes Wood's thoughts with every teacher's favourite jest, "Would you like fries with that?"

"Exactly," Wood replies. He opens his hands and raises them as if in praise to the ceiling.

"So we've got to get them back into class, but how?" Payne interjects.

"Who knows." Bird shakes her head in wonder at the enormity of the task. "But when we do—if we ever do—" Bird is feeling dejected at the moment, the task at hand too daunting to perceive as possible.

"We need to make them understand that they need to do the work," Wood emphasizes. "We can't do it for them."

"You are so right," Bird concurs. "The fact is, the more we feed education to them with a silver spoon in an attempt to shove it down their throats, the less we—*no*, the less *they*—get in return for our efforts."

"So what do you suggest we do instead?" Payne asks.

Motioning with her own (plastic) spoon to illustrate, Bird explains, "I don't know, but one thing is for sure—in order for them to truly learn anything, they have to lift the spoon themselves."

Staff room banter

☺ ☺ ☺ ☺ ☺

Cheater's Remorse

As the day's lesson is complete and English class is almost over, Mrs. Bird has given the class a simple synonyms crossword puzzle to work on—the ultimate time filler she can justify since it teaches an element of grammar seldom taught in high school since the onset of holistic learning. Her current occupation is making up a new unit for the novel *The Hound of the Baskervilles*. Her favorite teaching tool is a crossword puzzle computer program that enables her to make crossword puzzles quickly and effectively without a lot of spelling errors (it even has a spell check, thank God!). She can easily dismiss the whines and cries from some students of "Another crossword, Miss?" since other students are more than willing to shut them up for her. "Are you kidding? Crosswords are easy! Keep 'em coming, Miss." Mrs. Bird's studious efforts toward producing ever more crosswords as time fillers in her class, however, keep her attention off the students, thus allowing for a wide variety of activities to go unnoticed. Thank God for stooges!

On this particular day, Greg turns to see Mrs. Bird working studiously at her computer desk, which is at the back of the room. His glance around the room shows most students working quietly on their crossword puzzles. Turning to Susie, he asks, "Why not cheat?" He points to Mrs. Bird's desk at the front of the room. "Her mark sheet is right out in the open." Pointing to the back, he adds, "And, look, the old bird is occupied at her computer. She'll never see a thing."

Susie begins biting her nails. Greg leans in and whispers "Don't be scared, baby girl. It'll be easy."

"I don't know, Greg," Susie says as she chews down hard on her thumbnail.

"Come on," he says, leaning in closer, "It'll be fun."

"This just doesn't feel right."

Greg winks suggestively. "I'll give you what feels right, if you help me."

Susie tilts her head briefly before shaking it. "I don't want to Greg."

"Oh come on!" Greg grimaces.

"I'm scared, Greg. What if we get caught?"

"Don't be such a pussy."

"Don't call me that! That's gross."

A cruel smile forms as Greg whispers in Susie's ear. "What, you don't like your pussy?" Susie starts to blush. She shrinks in her chair. Greg whispers conspiratorially into her ear, "I like your pussy."

Beginning to shiver, Susie cries out, "Stop it!"

Greg is relentless. "Pussy, pussy, pussy," he whispers.

Although she cannot hear Greg's voice, Mrs. Bird definitely heard Susie ask him to stop. Gregory McGregor is up to something, and it's making one of her students uncomfortable. Mrs. Bird grimaces. *If only it was someone other than Susie—she always lies to defend him.* Standing up from her computer desk, she addresses the young man, "Greg!"

Leaning back in his chair and rolling his eyes at the ceiling, Greg answers, "What?"

"Stop bothering Susie."

"Susie's my girlfriend. I'm not bothering her, am I, Susie?"

Like a lost kitten, Susie looks first to Greg then to her hands before she finally comes out with, "He's calling me names, Miss."

Banging the front legs of his chair back onto the floor, Greg looks askance at Susie.

Mrs. Bird releases an exasperated sigh and asks, "What kind of names?"

Turning to look the old bird straight in the eye, Greg loudly pronounces, "Pussy."

Mrs. Bird frowns. "Greg, we've talked about this before. That kind of language is unacceptable."

With impeccable logic, Greg launches into his defense. "I wasn't saying it out loud. It was just to her."

"Irrelevant, Greg. You are in my classroom, and you are making one of my students uncomfortable. In fact, your very actions can be construed as sexual harassment."

"Sexual harassment, my a—." Greg gives Susie a look that suggests she won't get any after school if she doesn't start defending him real fast.

Susie caves. "Oh, Miss, I don't feel harassed. I just don't like being called that name."

Greg smiles but still adds, "Man, you girls can't stand your own bodies." Then, smiling sheepishly, he inquires, "Why is that, Miss?"

Not willing to entertain one of Greg's inappropriate conversations, Mrs. Bird responds, "That will be enough out of you."

But Greg doesn't want to let Mrs. Bird off the hook. "Guys aren't afraid of their c—s," he tosses out.

Mrs. Bird, having already turned away and headed back to her computer desk, spins back around on her heels and glares at the young man. "I said that's enough of that kind of language."

Once again, Greg pushes the envelope. "I'm sorry, Miss—" Mrs. Bird nods and is about to accept the young man's apology when he adds, "I meant to say *penis*." Smiling at the frustrated look on Mrs. Bird's face, Greg counters her upcoming objection. "Now, you can't get mad at me for saying *penis*; that's the scientific term describing a body part."

Mrs. Bird grimaces. *Why does the little rake have to be so smart?* "Are you finished?" she inquires curtly.

"I think so."

"Then get back to work." Mrs. Bird returns to her computer and resumes her work.

With the old bird out of the way, Greg returns to his initial plans. "So, whadda ya say? Her mark sheet is right there. Come on. Let's change a few grades."

"No," Susie whispers in a whine. "My dad'll kill me."

Greg smiles. "Don't worry, I'll do it for you. You'll not've done anything, and she'll have no way to prove you did. It's the perfect scam. Come on, whadda ya got to lose? You're failing anyway. I'll do you and you do me." He sticks out his tongue and gives it a little wiggle. Susie can't help but giggle. "Shh," says Greg looking back to Mrs. Bird's desk to make sure she's looking down and working hard. "She'll know something's up." Then he returns to his original argument: "Like I said, if I do you and you do me …" he explains, this time only tossing in a wink, "… then we're both innocent."

Tantalized by Greg's tongue wiggling, Susie acquiesces. "All right. But you'd better make sure she's not looking."

"Easy. I'll go over and talk to Gibby. That'll p— her off. One little snip about his stupid haircut and she'll freak."

"Just don't call him a fag again. She hates that!"

"Since his new haircut and dye job, the dork's emo." Greg laughs as he gets up and crosses to Frank's desk.

As soon as Greg starts to move towards Frank's side of the classroom, Mrs. Bird looks up from her computer desk and fires a query Greg's way. "Greg. What are you doing?"

Playing defensive, he responds, "What? I'm just borrowing a pencil."

Mrs. Bird is not fooled. "You already have a pencil."

Snapping his pencil in half, he exclaims, "It broke. I need another."

Annoyed by this intrusion to her work, Mrs. Bird points toward Greg's desk and demands, "Go back to your seat—now."

From the corner of his eye, Greg can see Susie still muddling away at the marks sheet. "I said I need a pencil." Continuing to harass Frank, Greg demands, "Hey, Gibby, gimme a pencil?" Greg tries to grab the pencil out of Frank's hand, but Frank puts a grip on it like a vice.

"No!"

"F—, you're cheap."

Mrs. Bird stands up from her desk. "Greg, watch your language."

Greg immediately apologizes, avoiding the daily routine of being kicked out of class. "Sorry, Miss, it won't happen again."

Never one to look a gift horse in the mouth, Mrs. Bird accepts his apology. "Fine, now let go of Frank's pencil and go back to your desk."

As Susie has returned to her desk, Greg's little bout with nonsense comes to an end. "Whatever you say, Miss." He returns to his spot and asks Susie, "Did you do it?"

Susie smiles sweetly. "Yup. I changed your three zeros." Susie raises her eyebrows and licks her lips. "I gave you a sixty-nine for the essay, a sixty-nine for the reading test, and a sixty-nine for the timed short story."

"Awesome!" Greg leans in to kiss her, but, as Mrs. Bird is still watching him, he simply nods and says, "Your turn. Go ask her for help on a question."

Susie does as she is told and crosses over to Mrs. Bird's computer desk. "Mrs. Bird, can you help me please?"

Mrs. Bird is delighted that Susie is asking for help. She has taken a liking to the poor girl (she calls her that because she knows she is dating Greg). Since Susie quit coming late and skipping out, she is almost passing. Mrs. Bird wants so much to see her graduate. "Of course, Susie. What is it?"

"I can't figure out seven down."

"Well, let's see. *Portly*. Did you look it up in the dictionary to see what it means?"

Looking a word up in the dictionary would never have occurred to Susie. "No."

"Head on over to the shelf, get a dictionary, and bring it back to me."

"Yes, Miss." As Susie walks over to the bookshelf, Greg gives her a wink. He has finished the deed. Susie thumbs through the book for a moment before shouting, "Oh, I get it. Thanks, Miss."

Pleased that the girl was able to figure something out on her own, Mrs. Bird smiles sweetly, "You're welcome, Susie."

Susie runs back to her desk and asks with bated breath, "Did you do it?"

"Yup. I fixed your last test mark. You got a hundred percent now."

Susie beams, just like a little burst of sunlight. "Awesome! I love you!"

Greg leans in and gives his girl a deep wet kiss.

Catcalls and chuckles alert Mrs. Bird to what's happening. "Stop that nonsense. I will not have you canoodling in my classroom."

"Canoodling?" Greg asks jocundly. "What's canoodling?"

"It is what the two of you were just doing."

"So canoodling means sticking your tongue down someone's throat?"

Susie reddens and punches Greg hard in the shoulder. He grunts, and Mrs. Bird smiles. "You deserved that, young man."

Before Greg can retort, Mrs. Bird looks out at him over her glasses. She knows Greg is attempting to steer her down a road of inappropriate discussion. Refusing to accept the bait, Mrs. Bird resorts to acceptable teacher student banter. "Get back to work, Greg." The bell rings, and Mrs. Bird breaths a sigh of relief as another class with Gregory McGregor has come to an end. Smiling at the students as they exit her class, she calls out to them, "See you tomorrow."

Susie chimes out, "Good-bye, Mrs. Bird."

Mrs. Bird looks up, smiles, and waves. "Good-bye, Susie."

Greg looks incredulously at his girl. "What are you saying good-bye to her for?"

Susie smiles. "She likes me, Greg. If I can keep her that way, maybe I can get you out of trouble."

Greg wraps his arm around Susie's waist. "I like the way you think." And the two exit the classroom arm in arm.

After the class empties out, Frank crosses over to Mrs. Bird's computer desk. "Mrs. Bird?"

She looks up from her work. "Yes, Frank?"

Looking around the room before he speaks, Frank starts to tattle, "Don't tell anyone I said this, but I have reason to believe that your mark sheet got changed."

"Ah." Mrs. Bird thinks over recent events in her classroom, and a light starts to dawn. "Thank you, Frank. Say no more. I will have no trouble figuring out who the perpetrators were."

Frank smiles. "Do you think they'll finally kick him out?" he asks expectantly.

Mrs. Bird grimaces. "Now, Frank, I hope you're not telling me this just to get someone kicked out of school."

"Oh, no, Miss," Frank blubbers, "I just don't like it when kids cheat."

"Neither do I, Frank." Her grin is wicked. "I'll figure out who the perpetrators are, and, when I do," she laughs fiendishly, "I know exactly what to do with them."

"You're pure evil, Miss."

"I try to be. See you tomorrow, Frank."

"Bye, Miss." Frank's wave goes unnoticed as Mrs. Bird is already plotting her revenge.

As soon as Frank passes through the door, Mrs. Bird gingerly leaps across the room to the front desk where she keeps most of her work. She can't help but smile when she picks up the folder for her thirty-dash-two class. From it she retrieves her mark sheet and heads back to her computer desk. As she sits herself back down at her computer, she quickly pulls up her marks program and opens up the file for her block-four class. Comparing the computer entries to the hard copy, she quickly determines who the perpetrators were—Greg and Susie. She knew even before she looked it up, but having the evidence in front of one is always useful. Greg, who has skipped nearly every test written in class so far, magically receives a plethora of sixty-nines. *Sixty-nine!* Mrs. Bird rolls her eyes—*and Susie earning a hundred percent! Give me a break. Talk about your classic neon sign!* Smirking, she picks up the phone and begins dialing a number. She has this one memorized.

"Hello, may I speak to Mr. McGregor please?" There is a short pause giving her a moment to grin. "Hello, Mr. McGregor? This is your son Greg's English thirty-dash-two teacher."

Mrs. Bird on phone—evil smile

☺ ☺ ☺ ☺ ☺

The Wall

That the staff room is dingy only adds to Bird's foul mood. With her chin to chest, her arms wrapped tightly under her breasts, and a scowl ripping across her forehead, Bird is the countenance of doom.

"Don't look so glum, Bird." Although Wood appears to be comforting the old girl, his grin suggests he is really laughing inside. "Look at it this way," he says, his smile widening, releasing more of his mirth, "A five day suspension, Bird. He got five days for his little escapade. That means five full days for you without Gregory McA—hole McGregor."

"Must you call him that?" Payne inquires.

"Must you always defend every student?" Wood replies.

"It's unprofessional to refer to our students in that manner." Payne slouches. There is a downturn to her mouth.

"Give it up, Payne," Wood responds defensively. "Don't pretend you like him. Or have you forgotten the way he treated you in your first year?"

Vehemently shaking her head, Payne cries out, "No one could ever forget that. I had him in three out of four classes one semester: math, English and religion. It was hell!"

"I don't know what counseling was thinking when they did that to you," Bird remarks.

Cynical as ever, Wood remarks, "Counseling never considers things like that."

"He was only in grade ten," Payne replies. "I'm sure they had no idea what kind of lad he was."

"Ha!" Bird ejaculates.

"That was second semester, Payne," Wood insists. "They knew all about his shenanigans by then."

"Oh well." Payne sighs in relief. "He's not my problem anymore." Smirking, she taunts Bird, "He's your student now."

Both Wood and Payne let out a long-held-in laugh.

"Har, har, har! Neither of you would be laughing if he had drawn *your* face on the school wall!"

"Five days of respite, Bird," Wood reminds her. "Just remember that piece of graffiti got you five days of respite."

"Five days ..." Bird finally smiles. "Thank God Willow suspended him." Pondering for a moment, she concedes the point. "Maybe it is worth being associated with that damnable song for five days free of Gregory McGregor."

Wood smirks. "If you didn't crack down so hard on his skipping out, you wouldn't see him at all."

"That's true," Payne admits. "I hate to admit it, but I used that strategy during my semester from hell."

"So unprofessional of you!" comments Wood.

"P— off, Wood!"

Bird grins. "He may be making my life miserable, but I assure you I am making his infinitely more so."

Leaning across the lunch table, Wood and Payne burst into song, "Hey, teacher, leave those kids alone!"

Her feathers ruffled, Bird points roughly at the two. "Never—and I mean *never*—sing that song in my presence again! Not if you know what's good for you."

Both Wood and Payne suffer from a choking fit due to laughing too hard. When Wood finally regains control, he adds, "Just imagine Bird and Pink Floyd in the same room together."

Payne, unable to regain control, barely manages to stutter out, "It wouldn't be pretty."

Bird softens to their humour. *Oh hell*, she figures, *if you can't beat 'em, join 'em.* "UFC eat your heart out!"

The staff room shakes with raucous laughter.

Greg spray painting graffiti on school wall

☺ ☺ ☺ ☺ ☺

Mrs. Bird's Youth

It doesn't take long for the students to learn about Mrs. Bird's youth. Rumours abound at H.E.L.L., and last year's students are always ready and willing to regale the newcomers with stories of Mrs. Bird's unique talents. Everyone loves to talk about the fact that the heinous hag once did drugs. Cocaine, to be exact: the straight line, the razor's edge, nose candy, brain balm, that smooth sweet silky sensation. Ironically enough, she didn't get into this "sport" until after she started teaching. All warnings aside—throwing caution to the wind—an early-thirties Priscilla needed something to take the edge off teaching. When you're a type A anal-retentive workaholic, no years are worse than those first few years as an educator. By the end of her first year, Priscilla was binging alcohol. By the end of her second year, she was smoking dope. By the end of her third year, she had snorted her first line of coke. Priscilla managed to keep her illegal usage to a moderate level for a number of years, but, as so often happens, time and an addictive personality made for a deadly combination. By the time she met William, she was an addict. The night he figured what it was all about, they were at a house party hosted by another teacher. Priscilla disappeared for a few minutes only to return and sit on his lap—facing him. She then proceeded to give him a lap dance (to the cajoles and jeers of onlookers). Now most men are not adverse to a lap dance, but there are those who prefer such acts to happen in a strip bar or the privacy of one's home (or a hotel room at the very least). And William A. Bird is a very private man. As he was attempting to stop this fool woman from further embarrassing herself (and him!), he noticed her nose was bleeding.

Perplexed and staring at her, he blusters out, "You're bleeding!"

"Huh?" Priscilla's inquiry is accompanied by a sideways thrashing of her head. Blood splatters onto William's face.

"Stop!" he yells as he grabs hold of her shoulders.

Finally stationary, Priscilla notices the blood on William's face, "Oh my God, you're bleeding!"

As she is about to wipe his face with her sleeve, William grabs her hands and claps them between his own. "Not me. You! *Your* nose is bleeding."

Looking down in horror into William's eyes, Priscilla knows he's figured it out. He releases her hands, wipes away some blood, and asks in a whisper, "Coke?"

Her cover blown, Priscilla falls face first into William's chest and bawls.

"Come on," he says standing up whilst carrying her in his arms, "let's get out of here."

William carrying Priscilla out

Students, of course, don't know this side of the story. They only know the old bird used to do drugs. "Too bad she quit," is the most often replied comment. "If she had kept up with it," many a teenager laments, "she might not be such an old b—ch today." In fact, she'd probably be dead! But quit she did when William told her he could never live with her addiction. Faced with the choice between life with William Bird and no drugs or a life with drugs but without William, she wisely chose William.

Sound easy? It wasn't. William supported her through a six-month leave of absence during which she endured rehab. Priscilla really didn't believe she was addicted until she had to stop cold turkey. After she had been straight for a full year on her own, Priscilla and William were married. Often times, when snuggled tightly in William's arms, Priscilla expresses the wish that she had never touched drugs in her life.

"Never regret, my love," William always says. "Had your life been different, we would not be married today." Priscilla's heart glows as she thanks God for bringing this incredible man into her life.

Getting her old job back wasn't as hard as she had anticipated. Priscilla was most fortunate, being an unofficial member of the good ole boys club. Willow, then the vice-principal of H.E.L.L., pulled a few strings and got her back into the high school. Rehab seemed easy compared to having to teach multiple subjects (science, social studies—even phys-ed) until a full-time position in language arts opened up again, but she swallowed her pride and stomached the load. Perhaps the finest trait of the woman is her willingness to pay up. She accepted full responsibility for everything—her drug addiction and losing six months of work, as well as her honored position in the language arts department. Upon returning to H.E.L.L., she worked long and hard to win back staff and student respect until she was finally able to resume her role as a full-time English teacher.

After talk about her drug-induced days becomes old, students inevitably start talking about the one quirk she has that they actually *love*. Old Mrs. Bird used to be a mime. If pressed, she will eventually perform a couple of mime routines for her class. She makes them beg and plead for a good month before giving in, though.

"Will you mime for us today, Miss?" Susie bats her eyes and sticks out her chest. (The kids also say she's a lesbian. They think her husband's real name is Wilhelmina.)

Mr. Bird in drag

"Not today, we've got too much work to do."

"You say that every day," Frank puts in. Everyone turns and looks at the boy. Frank blushes. He doesn't normally join in on class rants. He somehow manages to mutter, "I wanna see a mime show."

"I'm sorry, Frank." Mrs. Bird is beginning to melt. She really likes Frank. Even still she apologizes, "I'm just not dressed for it."

Greg turns to Susie. "Good God, she turned down Frank! This is never gonna happen."

The rest of the class, having heard Greg's lament, bursts into choral song, "Please! You promised."

"I can't. I'm in a skirt."

"You always have an excuse, Miss," Greg points out.

"Be reasonable, people. Perhaps tomorrow."

"But I won't be here tomorrow," Greg says, hoping this will encourage her to act now.

"Why not?" she asks. "Are you planning on skipping?" The class laughs. Greg used to be a notorious skipper before Mrs. Bird cracked the whip and put a fire under Gregory's (and his father's) posterior. "I can't do mime dressed like this. I need to wear sweat pants."

"I got a pair in my locker," Damien belts out.

Mrs. Bird's face squishes up like she just bit down on a kumquat. "Ah, no thank you." Again the class laughs at her response. *It is time*, she decides, *to give in*. "I will wear sweatpants tomorrow. You have my word."

The class cheers, and Greg announces, "I won't be skipping out tomorrow."

The next morning, Mr. Bird smiles when his wife walks into the kitchen in sweatpants. "I thought you swore you would never mime again. You told me last year—"

Before he can finish his reprimand, she jumps in, "I know, I know. I say this every year. But they always manage to talk me into it."

"And you always manage to come home with a bad back," Mr. Bird politely points out.

"I'm not going to crawl on the desks this year."

"Of course not, dear." Mr. Bird chuckles as he sips more of his coffee.

"I mean it."

A nod and a wink from William proves she will do the routine exactly as the students are hoping for, with Mrs. Bird climbing all over the desks chasing them around the classroom.

☺ ☺ ☺ ☺ ☺

The Gorilla

It's a simple mime routine. Mrs. Bird didn't even make it up. She saw Shields and Yarnell perform it on the *Tonight Show* (back when Johnny Carson was the host—yes, she is that old!). It was either Shields or Yarnell, whichever one was (or maybe still is) the man.

First Mrs. Bird moves all the tables back to give herself plenty of room. She clears off the table directly in front of her, too, since she will climb onto it. She then removes her glasses claiming that gorillas don't wear them, but it's really so she doesn't have to see the looks on her students' faces. Then, after a brief moment of hiding her face in her hands, she asks herself—yet again—*Why am I doing this?* Sighing, she gets into position. Reaching up with her right arm, she grabs for an imaginary branch. Her body slumps and arches to the right as she leans into her right hip. Her knees bend. Her face squishes up as she mimics a gorilla chewing and sticking out its tongue. Her left hand scratches her side and tummy. Mrs. Bird's gorilla scans the class judiciously as if selecting the tastiest looking head of hair from which to collect lice, bugs, and other potentially juicy foods. Tired of the onlookers, she glances around her imaginary cage and spots a bunch of bananas to the right of her on the floor. Finally the gorilla has something to eat.

Releasing her grip on the branch, she drops down into a crouch. Her butt lifts into the air. Her hands form fists upon which she struts over to the bunch of imaginary bananas. She rips one banana off and begins to peel it. Then she notices the students watching her. She eyes them suspiciously as if they are plotting to steal her meal. After the peeling process is over, she throws away the peel and stuffs the entire banana in her mouth.

But this gorilla is still hungry. She scratches her head, picks a parasite from her head, and eats it. She picks her nose, pulls out some snot, and eats it. Scratching her butt, she plucks something off of it and eats it, too. All the "ewes" and "that's gross, Miss" catch the gorilla's attention, and, once again, she stares angrily out at them. Their heads look greasy enough to hold something good to eat. The hungry gorilla stands, pounds her chest, and lets them know she is watching them. Pacing her cage, she decides she wants to eat their head lice. Crossing to the front of the cage, she grabs for the bars. Jumping from bar to bar while sporadically pounding her chest, she lets them know she is queen. She finally decides it's time to break out of her cage. Pulling the bars to no avail, she leaps to another part of the cage and tries again. Still the bars won't budge. On her third try, she decides to move one bar at a time. Having doubled her strength, she is able to finally spread the bars wide enough to squeeze through. Once free from her cage, she grunts and pounds her chest.

She then starts attacking the students. Waving her arms above her head and dashing towards various students, she elicits a series of screams as teenagers leap up from their desks and run away from her. Greg just sits there laughing. Grabbing the insolent young man in a headlock, the gorilla begins picking out and eating his head lice.

A stupid, simple routine, but the kids love it. Mrs. Bird always ends those classes with a deep bow and saying, "Nothing like watching your teacher make an a— out of herself." This is the one time Mrs. Bird decides it is okay to swear.

The kids absolutely love it when she says that, and the class booms with, "Miss, you swore!"

Mrs. Bird doing the gorilla

Mrs. Bird wisely performs her gorilla act during the last ten minutes of class. This routine always inspires extreme bursts of energy in her students. The clamour of the classroom reaches new levels, and to start a day in this manner would simply be foolish. On this particular day, Greg deems this display as the perfect opportunity to perform his animal imitations. He is really quite good. He does not jump up on any desks or wave any arms, but his whale song is so accurate the class suddenly turns into the ocean. Mrs. Bird nods her approval.

The Teenage Boy's Obsession

As Bird plops herself down on the couch in the staff room, she declares, "I give up!"

Wood looks up from the photocopier. "Aw, Birdie, don't do that."

"I mean it!" Bird exclaims.

"Give up on what?" Payne inquires. She has just entered the staff room. Seeing Bird in a state of distress, she sits down next to her on the couch.

"Trying to teach those little—" Bird pounds her fist on her thigh to avoid swearing. "you-know-whats some manners!" Bird is on another rant. "What is it with teenage boys and their penises?"

Wood, laughing, joins them at the couch. "This could turn into an interesting b—ch session."

"My goodness," Bird laments, "women are constantly accused of penis envy if they so much as show a modicum of strength in the workplace, but, when it comes right down to it, penis envy is way more prominent in the teenage boy!" Payne bursts out laughing. Even Wood smirks. "One can't even begin to count the number of phallic symbols boys draw all over my tables—even all over each other's faces."

"What?" a stunned Payne inquires.

"Yeah," Bird nods her head up and down in rapid succession. "Yesterday I went to the bathroom only to return to Greg drawing a penis on Damien's face."

"And Damien let him?" Wood asks. "I know the kid is stupid, but come on."

"I guess he told Damien to close his eyes and guess what he was drawing."

"Yup," Wood confirms, "Damien is that stupid."

Bird pauses briefly to reflect. "Why did I ever show them *10 Things I Hate About You?*"

"Behind on marking again?" Wood asks.

"I wish I still taught English," Payne laments. "I miss being able to show all those movies."

"Yeah, it's kinda hard to justify a movie in math," Wood adds sympathetically.

"Hey, its curriculum based!" Then shaking her head violently, "No, no, get off the movies, people. I had a crappy day!" Emphasizing the severity of her distress by pounding two fingers into her chest.

"What did McA—hole do this time?" Wood inquires. Everyone knows that, whenever Bird complains about a crappy day, she is really complaining about Gregory McGregor.

"He was drawing phallic symbols all over his table."

Wood starts to sing, "Here a penis, there a penis—" Payne follows his lead and joins in on the song, "everywhere a penis, penis. Old McBirdie had a class, *ee-eye, ee-eye, oh.*"

Completely ignoring their warped sense of humour, Bird rambles on, "You haven't heard the best of it. On one of his penis drawings, the scrotum had eyes and the shaft had a runny nose."

Wood cackles, "This kid's creative."

"Oh, he is a creative little wisecracker. Another penis spanned the length of three tables. And, of course, they were all erect. Well, I finally had had enough, so I asked McGregor what he was trying to prove by drawing all these penises."

"What did he say?" asks Wood.

"Well, look at you," Bird comments sardonically, "you'll never talk about the state of education, but mention one word about the crazy antics of students and suddenly your all ears."

"Yeah, yeah, whatever." Wood rolls his eyes. "Just answer the question."

"Nothing," a distressed Bird replies. "He just laughed." Wood and Payne laugh too.

"What did you do next?" Payne asks.

"I crossed over to my desk and grabbed my hand sanitizer—"

"Good thinking," Payne adds, "that's stuff's like acid—it'll cut through just about anything."

Without even a pause, Bird carries on with her story "—then marched back over to Greg's table where I started to squirt gobs of the stuff all over his graphic penises." She mimes every action as if she were still in the class with her arms pumping at her side for the marching, her right index finger pumping up and down for the hand sanitizer. Then, suddenly, she puts her hands up on each side of her head with palms open. Her jaw drops open.

"What does that look mean?" Wood asks.

Bird drops the stunned expression—and her hands—to explain, "The hand sanitizer goop looked like semen!" Wood and Payne burst into raucous laughter, Wood starting to show his age by rasping and coughing. "To make matters worse," says Bird, also enjoying the humour, "I started frantically rubbing away at the penis as fast as possible succeeding only in animating Greg's art work and increasing the vociferous laughter in the classroom."

"How the hell did you keep from laughing yourself?" Wood asks, practically in tears.

"I couldn't." Bird admits defeat. "I ended up laughing with the rest of them."

"No doubt that only made matters worse," Payne suggests.

"Well, it certainly didn't help," Bird agrees whilst shaking her head. "So, Greg looked up at me and smirked, 'You did that on purpose, didn't you Miss?'" All three teachers burst into laughter. Bird winks, "Susie topped the whole thing off, though, when she stated most emphatically, 'I am never using hand sanitizer again.'" Wood and Payne resume laughing, this time at Bird's imitation of the prissy young woman.

Mrs. Bird washing image of a penis off the table

☺ ☺ ☺ ☺ ☺

"When sorrows come they come not single spies but in battalions"

Claudius to Gertrude, Hamlet, Act IV, scene V

The Penis Game

As if drawing images of their genitalia isn't enough for them, the boys also like playing the penis game. Greg begins to utter the word that their stolid, matronesque teacher most ardently hates, then Damien repeats the word one octave higher. This, they are certain, will elicit the desired outburst from their teacher. What better button than the word *penis*. Giggling under their breath, each one practically gagging every time it's his turn, the boys bounce the word back and forth, successfully uttering the scientific term for male genitalia five times each before poor Damien is heard. Having put up with more antics from these boys than could fill the volumes of the Britannica Encyclopedia (all editions past, present, and future), Mrs. Bird merely looks up and says, "Damien, get out."

Greg stands up, smirks, and confesses, "I guess I'd better leave, too, since I started it."

"Well, now," Mrs. Bird replies dryly, "aren't you just the honest little jackal." Not being one to complain when a wisecracker willingly leaves her room, Mrs. Bird nods curtly then smiles as both backs pass across the threshold of her door.

Greg following Damien out the door

☺ ☺ ☺ ☺ ☺

The Erection

"Mrs. Bird?" Greg's hand is actually raised.

Although suspicious, Mrs. Bird has no reason to ignore the boy, so she must ask, "What is it, Greg?"

"Have you ever had a kid in your class with an erection?"

Her eyes blink, her mouth gapes, and then Mrs. Bird grimaces. She should know better than to trust this smart aleck by now. "What?" she sputters as she alternately clenches and then opens her fists.

Greg, looking his most studious, asks again, "Have you ever had a kid in your class with an erection?"

She forces herself not to look at the young man's groin as she is certain this is his little game. *Some kind of trap no doubt*, she thinks. Turning away from the boy, she mutters, "I've never looked."

Not having been sanctioned too harshly yet, Greg begins to explain his question, "Well, we had this kid in block two with a boner on him. He didn't even try to hide it or nothing."

"Greg," Mrs. Bird turning back to face him states sternly, "this is an inappropriate discussion."

"His pecker was sticking out, and he was walking around like he was proud of it." Greg sneers at Frank. "Too bad you couldn't have seen it."

Frank blushes and puts his head on his desk. He had foolishly shown interest in Greg's story.

"Greg," Mrs. Bird insists, "please stop this topic of conversation."

"Why?" Greg asks in his most innocent tone. "You should have seen it, it was so gross. He had this little dick, and he thought he had something special."

"That is enough, Greg. I will not allow you to continue this conversation."

"I just don't understand why he didn't try to hide it. Man, if I had a woody, I wouldn't be showing the whole world. Maybe he's a little faggot like Frank here and was hoping to turn some guy on."

"That's it! One more word about this ridiculous topic and you will go downstairs to the office and tell your story to Mr. Willow."

Greg, acting confused, inquires, "Why would I want to tell this to Mr. Willow?"

Mrs. Bird, sincerely confused, blurts out, "Why do you want to tell it to me?"

Greg laughs, "Because you freak out over everything."

"Fine, I've had my little freak-out. Are you finished?"

No, Greg is definitely not finished. He has only pushed this button half way. "What would you do if a boy had an erection in your classroom?" With this wry little request, Greg pulls out an old nylon stocking stuffed with brown socks. It flops over his leg. Damien howls, as does the rest of the class.

Greg with stuffed sock on leg

Mrs. Bird stares down at the fake appendage and smirks. "My dear, dear, *little* boy. What is your obsession with male genitalia, Greg? Tell me, are you having some issues? Would you like to go speak to the school counselor?" And on that note she waves elegantly towards the door.

Frank laughs the loudest of anyone in the class.

Even Susie is enjoying this. "Burn! She got you good, Greg."

Finally, Greg shuts up.

When Greg Awakes

Greg very hung over

Greg's bedroom is on the third floor of the old condominium. His room is L shaped and has the oddity of having two doors. It used to be two smaller rooms, but, after his mother left with his little sister, Greg and his father tore the one wall down to enlarge the room. Containing the typical teenage boy's mess, Greg's room is now crusted over with the aftereffects of a weekend-long party. The festivities had started Friday night around ten PM and ended around half past four early this Monday morning. When Greg awakes, his mouth feels like it is glued shut. Scrunching his face up, he slowly opens and closes his mouth a few times before rolling over to reach for the glass of water he had preset by his bed. Flailing his hand about, Greg manages to knock the glass over, spilling all of the needed water. Muttering a low guttural "F—," he rolls over onto his back. This is not a good position to be in as his stomach starts to rumble and roll. Darting out of bed, Greg races down the hall to the bathroom spewing up half of last night's booze and potato chips on the tile flooring before he manages to get his mouth over the toilet bowl. Hurling chunks is a good way to describe what Greg is doing at this moment. His whole body contorts, and his knees jerk up and down off the floor. He is loud enough to wake his father who growls out his discontent. "Jesus Christ, kid, shut the f— up. Me and my lady are trying to sleep."

Ignoring the old man, Greg gets up to wipe off his face and take a look at himself in the mirror. After a brief inspection that shows him a gaunt face, stubble, and a few drops of puke remaining on his chin, Greg drops his head towards the sink and once again mutters, "F—."

"Hell of a party last night, eh, kid?" Old man McGregor laughs until he chokes. A scratchy, high-pitched voice screeches out, "Shut the f— up already. Jesus, you two, what time is it?"

"Go back to bed, b—ch, it's only nine o'clock."

"What the f— are we doing up at this hour?" There is the sound of a slap. "Don't call me b—ch."

"Quit hitting me," McGregor booms. "'Sides," he mutters, "the kid's gotta go to school. Hey," he yells at Greg, "what time's your first class?"

"Eight," Greg responds as he exits the bathroom and heads down the stairs towards the kitchen. In the distant background, he hears his father laugh. "Looks like he missed that one." Kicking beer cans out of the way, Greg spills beer, cigarette butts, and a quarter of a joint at his feet. Greg picks up the doobie and groans, "What a f—in' waste." Tossing the soaked and stained joint back to the floor, he stumbles into the kitchen. He opens the fridge and grimaces. Something in there doesn't smell right, and it attacks his stomach. Once again he races for the bathroom. This time he is able to make it to the toilet in time as the downstairs bathroom is right next to the kitchen. All he can summon up is dry heaves. After his stomach has finally settled, Greg manages to make his way back into the kitchen to prepare a cup of instant coffee and two pieces of dry toast. "F—," he mutters, "I need McDonalds." Considering his options through a bleary head, Greg decides that walking to McDonalds and then catching the bus to school is out of the question. He would never make it in time for fourth block. He can get away with skipping out of every other class but not that old b—ch's.

"Dad," Greg foolishly yells. The resounding boom echoes through his head causing him to stagger on the spot. When he gets no response, Greg pulls himself back up the stairs clinging desperately to the handrail. His father's bedroom reeks of sex, booze, cigarette smoke, and pot. There's a crack pipe on his night table. Standing in the doorway, Greg tries again to get his father's attention. "Dad."

A redheaded woman with vicious grey roots moans and rolls over exposing two of the largest breasts Greg has ever seen. They are so perfectly round there is no way they can be real. Right now, Greg doesn't even care. They're big, they're breasts, and they're exposed. Two long nipples are pointing skyward. He can't help but stare.

Noticing his son gapping at his woman, the old man growls out his displeasure, "Quit staring at my b—ch's breasts." Before he has a chance to cover the woman up, the woman's fist slams into his chest. He grunts, curses profusely, and sputters out, "Stop hitting me!"

"Stop calling me b—!"

Greg, too tired, too hungry, and too hung-over to want to stand and witness his father fight with yet another woman, interjects, "Dad, I need the car."

"What the hell for?"

"I'm late for school."

"Take the goddamn bus. I pay for that f—in' bus pass ... you can f—in' use it!"

"The bus takes too long. I'm already late."

"What if I need the car?"

"You got your lady here," Greg says, smiling. He knows how to charm his father. "It looks to me like you'll be laid up all day."

The old man laughs, thinking he and his son have just bonded. "What the f—, take the car." He reaches for the keys on his night table. "Here," he says as he tosses them at Greg, "be back by four, though." Looking at the woman at his side, he says, "I plan to take my b—ch ..."

Before he can finish, there is another smack, this time upside his head.

"F—, b—ch quit hitting me already!"

"My name's Julia! *Julia!* You godd— well f—ed me. The least you can do is remember my name!"

Turning on his sheepish grin, he finishes his sentence: "... Julia here out for supper tonight."

"Sure thing, Dad," Greg says as he heads towards the stairs. Before he can start down, though, his father calls him back.

"Greg, wait. Come here, son."

"What?" Greg asks annoyed. A grumbling stomach is not good on top of a hangover. What he needs right now is grease; nothing cures a hangover better than grease.

"You're Uncle Ambrose is coming up for a visit. He's arriving on the midnight bus. I'm working night shift, so you have to pick him up."

Now maybe it's the hangover, maybe it's the coffee and toast ... but, as soon as his father mentions Uncle Ambrose, Greg turns and runs back into the bathroom to puke.

Susie's Place

"Psst, Susie," Greg whispers through shudders. Greg is cold. He's wearing a stout winter jacket, but he has been outside for over four hours, and even his jacket isn't keeping him warm anymore. He needs to get inside before his innards freeze. When she doesn't answer, he taps on her bedroom window. *Surely she's in her room by now,* he thinks hopefully. Looking at his watch, he reaffirms it's already half past ten. "Come on, Susie," he says a little louder, careful though not to be heard by Mr. Cardinal. Mr. Cardinal spent five years in the army and always takes the opportunity to remind Greg of his commando war training. As a joke, Greg calls him Commando Joe. Susie finds it funny. Mr. Cardinal does not. Greg taps a little louder hoping to wake Susie up. The lights are off in her room so Greg assumes her to be asleep. Suddenly, her bedroom door opens and Greg ducks behind the bush in front of her window. Light glares in his eyes and then he is able to see Susie entering her room. "F—," he whispers, "took you long enough." Once again he taps on her window, this time catching her attention.

Greg climbing in Susie's bedroom window

Susie's room is in the basement, which puts her window at ground level. Susie, though, has to jump up on her bed in order to open it. The house they live in was built in the sixties, and the window winds open and closed with a small hand crank. Greg backs up to let the window open wide enough for him to fit in. "Thank God!" he mutters when he's finally crawled through the window and has landed down on Susie's bed. "Where the hell have you been?" he asks without ceremony.

"I was upstairs watching TV with Mom and Dad," Susie responds defensively. Greg's tone is harsh and accusatory, but she continues, "Don't make this my fault. I wasn't expecting you, you know." She looks around tentatively and quickly shuts her bedroom door; her voice lowers to a whisper, "If Dad catches you down here, he'll kill you first—then me."

"Don't tell him," Greg replies flatly.

"What are you doing here?" Susie asks.

"Aren't you glad to see me?" Greg asks as he moves in for a kiss. Susie, with nose upturned, presents him her cheek. "What?" Greg asks defensively.

Susie repeats her whispered query, "What are you doing here?"

Greg slumps down on the bed. "I need a place to sleep."

"Here?" Susie almost shrieks but catches herself in time to keep her voice low. "My dad'll kill me."

"He'll do me first, though, remember," Greg adds with a grin, hoping humour will calm Susie down.

"You can't stay here," Susie says whilst grabbing Greg by the shoulders to try to move him back towards the window. Greg gets up and closes it. "Sh—, it's cold in here."

"Of course it's cold," Susie retorts. "The window was open."

"It's f—in' more than twenty below out there." Greg points to the window. "You want me to go back out in that?"

Susie relents, "Look, warm up first and then go home."

Greg slumps back down on the bed. "I'm not going home. I'll freeze in hell first." Greg takes a moment to register his surroundings. "So this is your bedroom?" He had only been to the Cardinal's once. He had never even made it past the front foyer. Mr. Cardinal had smelt the dope on Greg and ordered him out. He had then ordered his daughter to never see that young man again. Susie has spent a wild eight months lying to her dad and seeing Greg behind his back.

Greg laughs as he looks around. Susie's room is pink. The wallpaper is a light shade of pink with dark pink flowers dotted across it. The shag rug on her floor is a creamy pink; even her bedspread is pink. "I take it you like pink."

"We've been dating for eight months and you just noticed that now!"

"Well," Greg retorts defensively, "it's not like you're always wearing pink."

"My mom won't let me." Susie begins to pout but starts suddenly at the sound of footfalls upstairs. Her eyes shift from side to side. "Are you warm enough now?"

"Yeah, I'm warmer," Greg replies. He is angry. Susie is actually going to kick him out. *So much for love!* "But I'm not going home." Pointing to the window, he threatens, "I'll go if you want me to, but you'll be throwing me out in the cold and the snow."

"Why do you always blame things on me? It's not like it's my fault, whatever it is." Pausing to study her man, a little sympathy enters her voice, "What *is* the matter anyway? Why won't you go home?"

"My Uncle Ambrose is there." Greg shifts his eyes upward to avoid looking Susie in the eye and takes this opportunity to change the subject. Forcing a jovial mood upon himself, he laughs. "God, Susie, you even have pink flowers painted on the ceiling."

"So what!" Susie responds angrily. "Stop changing the subject." Softening her voice, she asks again, "Tell me what's wrong."

Greg looks down to the floor. He shuts up tighter than a clam covered in barnacles.

"How can I help you if I don't know what's wrong?" Susie laments.

"Let me stay here." Greg answers. "You're dad doesn't have to know." I'll sneak out the same way I came in." There are almost tears in his eyes. "Please," he begs.

Susie caves. With Greg so close to tears, she lunges forward and holds him in a bear hug. "Of course you can stay, but please tell me what's wrong. Why are you so afraid of your uncle?" This inquiry angers Greg, and he shoves Susie off him. "I'm not afraid of him." He states this far too venomously and a little too loud for both their safety.

"Shh!" Susie points to the ceiling to remind him of her father.

"Sorry." Greg quickly lowers his voice. "I never said I was afraid of him. I just—I just hate him. He's a pr— that's all."

"Your dad's a pr—," Susie reminds him. "And that's never stopped you from going home."

"Well, you don't know Uncle Ambrose."

"Tell me about him," Susie says kindly.

"I already told you, he's a pr—." Then he tries to change the subject. "Can I sleep in bed with you, or—" He tries to toss in humour to defuse the conversation, adding, "Do you want me hiding in the closet?" Before Susie can answer, he leans in and kisses her. Susie succumbs to Greg's seductions, and they lie down on the bed together.

Intervention

Greg hates the counselor's office. Every week he gets called down there—when he's not being harassed in the principal's cell that is. Mr. Lloyd sits, his arms stretched across his desk, his hands clasped.

"Greg." He sighs. "Your father is worried about you. And Mr. Cardinal is not impressed that you've been hiding out at his house."

Greg snorts; he knows how unimpressed Mr. Cardinal is. He was there for the uproar. It was bad enough being found hiding out in his basement ... but to be found naked in Susie's bed. No, Mr. Cardinal was far from impressed. Greg and Susie won't be dating for a while. Mr. Cardinal has grounded Susie for the rest of her life!

"Where are you staying now?" Mr. Lloyd asks compassionately.

"At the Salvation Army." Greg clips off his answer. He wants to keep everything short and sweet—reveal nothing!

"They don't open the doors until nine o'clock. What do you do until then?"

"Soup kitchen."

"That's it?" Mr. Lloyd asks. "Surely they don't let you sit there all night?"

"I walk."

"Greg, please," Mr. Lloyd implores. "Open up to me. Why won't you go home?"

Greg just shrugs his shoulders and studies the floor. "You're carpet is gross."

"I know," Mr. Lloyd replies, "but that doesn't solve your problem."

"I don't got a problem."

"You're living on the street."

Still avoiding eye contact, Greg declares, "I come to school. I'm doing my homework."

"Are you getting enough to eat?"

113

"I eat."

"How?"

"Soup kitchen."

"Supper only, Greg. What about breakfast? What about lunch?

"Susie shares with me."

"You're lucky to have her."

"Yup." Now staring at the wall, Greg mutters, "God you're posters are stupid."

Mr. Lloyd looks concerned. If they do as required, they will be depriving the boy of a meal. "Mr. Cardinal insists we keep you and Susie apart."

Greg rolls his eyes, "Whatever."

"We have a lunch for kids program. Are you interested?"

"F— off."

"Where did that come from Greg?"

"I'm no f—in' charity case."

Sitting upright, Mr. Lloyd sighs. "I'm not thrilled with your language." Waving his hand to keep Greg from interjecting, he continues, "But, that aside, I think you need to face facts."

"What facts?" Greg demands roughly.

"As long as you walk the streets, eat at the soup kitchen, and sleep on the floor of the Salvation Army, you *are* a charity case." Stopping to study the effects of his words on Greg, and seeing the boy slumped over, Mr. Lloyd leans forward to make another offer, "Let me help you."

"No need," Greg responds. "I'm going home tomorrow."

"That's great, Greg." Mr. Lloyd releases a sigh of relief. "But why tomorrow? Why not today?"

"Tomorrow," Greg says standing. "You can tell my old man I'll come home tomorrow."

Mr. Lloyd leans back in his chair and motions to Greg's seat. "Greg, sit down, we're not done."

"We're done," Greg says as he walks to the office door and opens it. He walks out of the office and closes the door quietly behind him knowing it will still sound like a slam inside Mr. Lloyd's head. Mr. Lloyd closes his eyes and shakes his head before picking up the phone. "Birdie." He pauses briefly to sigh. "Send me Susie Cardinal. Maybe she can help."

Greg talking with Mr. Lloyd

☺ ☺ ☺ ☺ ☺

Jaywalker

Another boring day at school is more than Gregory McGregor can take. Math with Miss Payne was so mind numbing that Greg spent the entire block with his head on his desk. During the break, and after a little necking in the hall, Greg is able to convince Susie to skip the rest of the day.

"My dad's at work," he whispers, "we'll have the whole house to ourselves."

"I don't know, Greg. I've been skipping too much lately."

"Oh, come on," Greg persists, "We'll experiment." He winks. "You can have a pony ride."

"Cowgirl!" Susie giggles.

"Backward cowgirl," Greg smirks. "We'll do anything and everything except missionary." They kiss.

Susie is easily coerced. "If you weren't the hottest stallion at school …"

Within minutes, they are racing through the school parking lot making their way towards the Pizza Palace, which is two blocks from H.E.L.L. Greg doesn't bother to look for oncoming traffic before running across the street. He never even sees it coming. Tires screech, Susie screams, and Greg is thrown face first onto the pavement. A car door opens, and a gaunt, middle-aged man jumps out hollering, "What the f—?"

Mr. McGregor had been at work—just as he had told his son—but his boss had sent him home for being stoned. Staring down at the injured boy at his feet, he is too stunned to recognize Greg. Susie's piercing wail brings him to his senses, and he finally recognizes his own son lying inert on the pavement.

"F—!" He elongates the word to a mournful cry.

Mr. McGregor hits Greg

Greg does not die. Mr. McGregor hadn't been driving that fast. All Greg suffers is a bruised hip. The accident, as well as providing him with great prescription drugs and oodles of attention from his peers, has dramatically changed his father's attitude towards him. Greg can't believe his good fortune. Mr. McGregor is behaving almost like a real father.

When he finally returns to school, Greg spends the whole day retelling the same story to everyone who asks. "The old man is so wracked with guilt he never even yelled at me for skipping. Sh—, it's great! He drives me to school every day, gives me lunch money, picks me up, and takes me out for dinner. F—, man, it's almost like having a real father!"

He is so elated about his current winning streak, it doesn't even bother him when Mrs. Bird struggles to stifle a laugh as soon as she sees him as she walks down the hallway. She really tries hard not to guffaw; unfortunately the more a person tries not to do something the more she is apt to do it.

"That's mean, Miss," Susie blurts out indignantly.

"I'm sorry—I j—just—can't seem—to help myself." She stutters as she chokes back the laughter. "Did your father really hit you while you were skipping out?"

"Yes, Miss," Greg smirks.

"Well …" Mrs. Bird's eyes start to glisten. Turning quickly, she heads towards her classroom. Her body starts to shake as she desperately tries to hold back the laughter.

Even Greg can see the humor in this situation, but he isn't going to let Mrs. Bird know that, so, he shouts, "Ha, ha, ha, Miss!" as she races down the hall.

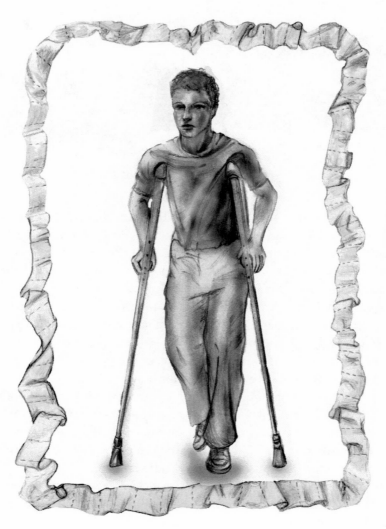

Greg on crutches

☺ ☺ ☺ ☺ ☺

Regrets

Mrs. Bird typing on computer

From: PBird@hell.ab.ca
Subject: I really blew it this time!
Date: October 12, 20— 11:32AM MST
To: EFlett@hell.ab.ca

Oh, Livy, I really blew it this time! There I stood in the hallway desperately trying not to laugh at Gregory McGregor hobbling around on crutches. Oh it was horrible. It was so unprofessional of me. I actually had to turn and run away from the boy to avoid splitting a gut in front of him. Even his girlfriend could tell I wanted to laugh. She told me I was being mean. She was right.

From: **EFlett@hell.ab.ca**
Subject: Re: I really blew it this time!
Date: October 12, 20— 11:38AM MST
To: PBird@hell.ab.ca

I know, I heard. Susie was complaining about it in art class. Look, don't let it get you down. You're human. I mean we all can't be perfect. You try too hard, you really do. Really, when you think about it, it is very funny. I saw Greg at the end of block 2 when he came to meet Susie, and he wasn't upset. I asked him if it bothered him that you were trying not to laugh, and he said, if he'd been you, he would have laughed so hard you'd've been showered in spit. He won't make any trouble for you. I doubt Susie will either.

From: PBird@hell.ab.ca
Subject: Re: Re: I really blew it this time!
Date: October 12, 20— 11:52AM MST
To: EFlett@hell.ab.ca

I know I try too hard to be perfect. It sucks, Livy, it really does. Damn those Hollywood movies that make teachers think they have to be a super cool and hip with the kids.

From: EFlett@hell.ab.ca
Subject: Re: Re: Re: I really blew it this time!
Date: October 12, 20— 2:58PM MST
To: PBird@hell.ab.ca

Don't get me started on Hollywood teachers. I just finished watching Freedom Writers. *Was that woman for real?*

From: PBird@hell.ab.ca
Subject: Re: Re: Re: Re: I really blew it this time!
Date: October 12, 20— 3:00PM MST
To: EFlett@hell.ab.ca

Or the one with Michelle Pfeiffer. The karate chick! She's freakin' lucky no one caught her, that's all I've got to say about that.

From: **EFlett@hell.ab.ca**
Subject: Re: Re: Re: Re: Re: I really blew it this time!
Date: October 12, 20— 3:01PM MST
To: PBird@hell.ab.ca

No kidding. And then there's the one with buddy what's-his-name—that math teacher dude who pulled off miracles in one semester at his school for Latino kids. Didn't he die of a heart attack or something?

From: PBird@hell.ab.ca
Subject: Re: Re: Re: Re: Re: Re: I really blew it this time!
Date: October 12, 20— 3:03PM MST
To: EFlett@hell.ab.ca

I don't think so. I'm not even sure he had one. Fifty bucks says he quit teaching and joined the speaker circuit.

From: **EFlett@hell.ab.ca**
Subject: Re: Re: Re: Re: Re: Re: Re: I really blew it this time!
Date: October 12, 20— 3:05PM MST
To: PBird@hell.ab.ca

Isn't that what happens to all these teacher gurus? They teach for a few years and then become professional speakers telling the rest of us how we're supposed to do it. If they really believed in all that piffle, then why aren't they still in the classroom?

From: PBird@hell.ab.ca
Subject: Re: Re: Re: Re: Re: Re: Re: Re: I really blew it this time!
Date: October 12, 20— 3:10PM MST
To: EFlett@hell.ab.ca

They know full well they'd burn out. No one can withstand that kind of momentum for more than a few years.

From: **EFlett@hell.ab.ca**
Subject: Re: Re: Re: Re: Re: Re: Re: Re: Re: I really blew it this time!
Date: October 12, 20— 3:15PM MST
To: PBird@hell.ab.ca

That's right, girl. You remember that! You and I, we're lifers. We can't afford to be whole hog forty-eight hours a day, ten days a week. Not if we plan to keep at this job for thirty odd years.

From: PBird@hell.ab.ca
Subject: Re: Re: Re: Re: Re: Re: Re: Re: Re: Re: I really blew it this time!
Date: October 12, 20— 3:22PM MST
To: EFlett@hell.ab.ca

Nor can we afford to do malarkey like buy these kids textbooks out of our own pockets!

From: **EFlett@hell.ab.ca**
Subject: Re: Re: Re: Re: Re: Re: Re: Re: Re: Re: I really blew it this time!
Date: October 12, 20— 3:40PM MST
To: PBird@hell.ab.ca

Oh no, they don't pay us enough! But, admit it, you did buy them stuff in your first year, didn't you?

From: PBird@hell.ab.ca
Subject: Re: Re: Re: Re: Re: Re: Re: Re: Re: Re: Re: Re: I really blew it this time!
Date: October 12, 20— 3:47PM MST
To: EFlett@hell.ab.ca

Didn't we all? I still buy them pens and pencils and loose leaf paper.

From: **EFlett@hell.ab.ca**
Subject: Re: Re: Re: Re: Re: Re: Re: Re: Re: Re: Re: Re: Re: I really blew it this time!
Date: October 12, 20— 4:02PM MST
To: PBird@hell.ab.ca

See! That means you really love these kids regardless of all their mischief. Face it. We all do stupid things from time to time. Trying not to laugh at Gregory McGregor sure beats the heck out of actually laughing at him.

From: PBird@hell.ab.ca
Subject: Re: Re: Re: Re: Re: Re: Re: Re: Re: Re: Re: Re: Re: I really blew it this time!
Date: October 12, 20— 4:50PM MST
To: EFlett@hell.ab.ca

Thanks, Livy, you always know just what to say!

☺ ☺ ☺ ☺ ☺

That's Bullsh—, Miss!

Technology has finally advanced to the stage where a teacher can now print out a student's attendance record. A document that identifies how many classes a child has skipped or arrived late for is a very powerful tool indeed. One-third of the way through the semester, Mrs. Bird decides to take advantage of this technological wonder and hit her tardy and absent students where it hurts. To add to the elegant grace of this convenience, Mrs. Bird decides to print out the reports and accent all unexcused absents and late days with highlighters, using pink for a skip and yellow for a late. This document, coupled (or should I say tripled) with a homework contract (purple on all incomplete assignments) and a mark report (orange for all failing grades), makes for quite the effective—and colourful—letter when sent home to mommies and daddies.

Needless to say, very few modern-day teenagers appreciate having such intelligence sent home and will often refuse to be courier. Mrs. Bird, knowing this, plans ahead by e-mailing all parents telling them to expect this series of documents.

Grinning with delight at the upcoming misery she is about to impose upon her students, Mrs. Bird announces gaily, "All right, class, I have a little present for you all today—or rather, I should say, a little present for you parents."

"A present?" Susie chirps. "I love presents."

Greg is not so easily fooled. "If it's a present from Mrs. Bird it's going to be a nasty one."

Pleased to no end, Mrs. Bird replies, "Right you are, Greg. How right you are." Waving the fat bundle of missives emphatically, Mrs. Bird begins explaining, "What I hold here are your interim reports. These lovely little packages include an attendance report highlighting all absenteeism and tardy arrivals this semester." Ignoring the communal groan, her smile widens and she continues, "It also includes your homework contract that lists all your unfinished homework." Damien groans and puts his hand on his head—as well he should since his current homework mark is zero. "And the last little form," she accents her point by giving the bundle a little shake, "is a list of all tests and essays that have been averaged into your current grade."

Greg says out loud what everyone else is thinking (and fearing), "Are you serious?"

Completely ignoring the young man, Mrs. Bird barges on, "I have taken the time to highlight all unexcused absents in pink and all tardy arrivals in yellow to help your parents identify your bad habits. All incomplete assignments are in purple, and all failing grades are in orange."

Mrs. Bird handing out reports

Once again, Greg expresses the communal disgust, "You're f—in' insane, Miss."

Mrs. Bird gives him what her students have come to refer to as the *evil eye*. "Watch your language." She would kick him out for this, but Mr. Willow has asked her to *cut him some slack*.

Greg, on *thin ice* with Bird, apologizes, "Sorry—but come on." He drags the vowels out expressing the class's concerns about such an extreme measure.

Susie lets this woman know exactly how she feels by over annunciating, "You have way too much time on your hands, Miss."

"True, I have one free period this semester, which is to my—or rather, I should say to your—advantage as it gives me more time to focus on your needs." With a grin and a chuckle, Mrs. Bird passes back and forth among her students handing out the reports.

Greg freaks when he gets his. There is yellow slashed all over his attendance record. There is also a plethora of purple and way too many orange streaks. There will be a fistfight if his dad ever gets his hands on this. "There is no f—in' way I'm showing this to my dad. He'll f—in' kill me."

Mrs. Bird grimaces. She would *so* like to kick Greg out right now, but visions of Willow dance in her head. Turning on Greg, she growls, "Watch your tongue."

"I can't, Miss," he says as he pulls at it with his fingers, crossing his eyes and shaking his head in a feigned attempt to "look at" it, "it's in my mouth."

Battling the urge to smack Greg on the back of the head, Mrs. Bird grimaces. *Oh, for the good old days when corporal punishment was legal.* For a brief moment, she ponders, *Technically, it is still legal here—God love Alberta. But,* she reminds herself shaking her head, *It is now frowned upon.* Bending forward, her hands on her hips, Mrs. Bird reiterates her order, "You are showing these to your father." Turning to the entire class to ensure they all understand, she informs them, "I have already e-mailed your parents to let them know these documents are coming home. I warned them that I want them to look them over, discuss their contents with you, sign them, and send them back to me, *tomorrow!*"

Frank, the only one in the class likely to show his parents his report chimes out, "You're pure evil, Miss."

As it is evident Frank meant that as a compliment, Greg turns on him, "What do you care, snot rag? You never skip." Then, with a squished up face, he adds, "You always do you homework!" And, as if this somehow proves his point, he adds, "Fag!" Damien's laugh cackles over the rest.

"Greg," Mrs. Bird demands, "you apologize this instant!"

"I'm not apologizing to that squid freak."

"That's it," Mrs. Bird exclaims, "I've had all I intend to put up with from you. Go to the office. This instant."

"Whatever." Despondent, Greg starts to mutters as he crosses the room, "Go to the office. Go to the office. Like I give a sh— about that! If only I could delete dad's work e-mail," he groans. "Why does that b—ch tell him every goddamn thing I say and do. After one of her f—in' e-mails, he thinks he has to play the old man. His voice rises in intensity the closer he gets to the door until he blurts out, "F—! I hate you."

Mrs. Bird, choosing to ignore this outburst, still responds in thought, *I'm none to crazy about you, either.*

Just as Greg walks through the door, he turns around to toss Frank a warning, "Watch your back, faggot."

Mrs. Bird crosses over to the phone, picks up the receiver, and dials three quick numbers. "Yes, is Mr. Willow in his office?" *Great,* she mutters, *he's never there when you need him.* "Well, Gregory McGregor is on his way down." Her eyes roll, as, on the other end of the line, an office lady expresses her displeasure. *No doubt,* Bird figures, *they want him there about as much as a mouse wants to sit in a box with a boa constrictor.* Feeling no mercy, she insists, "I am sending him to the office. Have him sit there until Mr. Willow returns." She grimaces. It's the same question with the same answer every single time. "The usual: swearing and ridiculing and threatening his classmates. Thank you." With concerted effort, she hangs the phone quietly even though she'd much rather slam it down.

Mrs. Bird's Day Off

Mr. Bird has just arrived home from work. He has just put in his last night shift and, as is his custom, he treated himself to a hearty breakfast before going home. Knowing that he needs to stay awake much of the day so that he will be able to sleep that night, he has just consumed a half a dozen cups of coffee. He is wired and ready to sit on the couch and watch a stupid movie. The first thing he hears when he enters the front door is his wife hacking up a lung. "Priscilla, why are you home?"

"Why do you think, dimwit." Now Priscilla isn't normally rude to her husband. She loves him to distraction, but, when she is sick, she is a miserable woman. Her students refer to her as the heinous hag from hell—actually, she taught them to refer to her that way. The average teenager simply asks, "Why are you being such a b—ch today?" As a result, Priscilla has learned that, when she is sick, she is better off at home—for her sake and her students'.

"I know, stupid question. What's wrong?"

"Good Gawwww—Oh for crying out loud, William, isn't it obvious? I'm sick!"

"I know you're sick. With what? The flu, a cold, the runs?"

"All of the above!"

"That sucks!"

By this point in the conversation, William has reached the bedroom. He peers inside to find his wife sitting up in bed with a pile of marking on her lap. "What are you doing?"

"What is this?" Priscilla is in no mood for trite conversation. "Act like a moron day? You can see what I'm doing!"

William remains undaunted. "Why are you marking if you're sick?"

"I'm behind on my work."

"So you're not sick then. You just stayed home so you can mark." William knows he is walking along the precipice, but he risks the abyss anyway. Leaning against the doorjamb, he crosses his arms and feigns a relaxed attitude.

"Look," Priscilla utters indignantly, "you can tell I'm sick. Just look at me." She hasn't figured out yet that William is playing with her. She's also a little daft when her head is mired in snot. In fact, it feels as if the upper half of her head has been cemented shut.

"Oh, I'm looking at you," William says smiling. When Priscilla is sick like this, he can string her along for hours. "It looks to me like you're sitting up in bed marking." Grinning sardonically he adds, "You taking a Ferris Bueller day?"

Priscilla is completely taken in by her husband's tomfoolery. Her red nose immediately blends into the rising scarlet of anger on the rest of her face. "Ferris Bueller can go suck a raw egg! And so can you!" William bursts out laughing. He has pushed all the right buttons. Priscilla is too busy ranting on to notice that she is the brunt of his joke. "Like any teacher is able to ever take a day off, go out in public, and act like an idiot! The only time I ever take a day off is when I'm *sick*—" She has to stop at this point to cough and hack up a greenish gob. She proudly presents this ghoulish image to her husband as concrete evidence. "*Sick—and* then I mark. Like Ferris Bueller'd ever stay home to study when he was sick!" She ends her indignant rant in another coughing fit; one so serious William crosses over to the bed to slap her back. He hands her more tissue for her to spit into.

"Come on," he says, smiling as he picks up the pile of papers from her lap, "put that away." Kissing her forehead, "No fever, that's good." Sighing he asks, "Would you like me to make you a tea?"

Priscilla turns weepy, another unfortunate trait when the old girl is sick. "Please," she whimpers.

William gets up and leaves the bedroom. At the door he turns and smiles. "I only meant you need to take time to rest."

"I know," Priscilla replies. "I'm sorry I got so wacky."

"That's okay." William blows her a kiss. "I love you."

"I love you too!"

A sick Mrs. Bird marking in bed

☺ ☺ ☺ ☺ ☺

Mary's Lament

It is Friday the thirteenth. God, what a horrible day! Mary knows there is no truth to the superstitions about this day. She has read *The Da Vinci Code*. According to Dan Brown, her favorite author, Friday the thirteenth is only significant because, in 1307, that was the day the French king and the Catholic Church hunted down and arrested the Knights Templar. Yet Mary is sure that her classmates will use this day as the perfect opportunity to do something miserable to her. Oh, how she wants to stay in bed and forget all about school! The only problem is, she is a terrible faker. Her mother always seems to know when she is lying. "Get out of bed! Quit trying to skip out. Education is important, you know. Don't you want to go to university?"

Mary knows her mother is right, but university seems so far off. Even though she is in grade twelve, she is only taking the general stream *and* failing half her classes. But her mother's better judgment always seems to win, which, quite frankly, is the distinguishing feature between Mary and the majority of her classmates.

Scanning her room through bleary eyes, Mary wishes her mother made more money or would at least let her work part time. Every day they have the same argument.

"You're job is school!" her mother continues to insist. "And," she reiterates, "with the marks you are getting, you don't have time for part-time work. Besides," her mother always adds, to Mary's chagrin, "I'm afraid that if you got too much extra cash in your hands you'd just spend it all on junk food. You've got to lose weight, you know."

There's no doubt in Mary's mind that some of that money would go to feeding her addiction, but what she really wants this time is a new dresser. Mary's room is simple—old furniture consisting of an old oak mirror, desk, dresser, and a four-poster bed, without draping, of course. All of her furniture has been handed down from her grandmother who, as Mary figures it, probably got it from her grandmother. Mary wonders what it would be like to have a dad who works for a living instead of just a mom barely breaking minimum wage. *Oh, well,* she figures, *at least we have our own apartment.*

Standing in front of her mirror, she inspects her face. *D——, two new pimples. Should I pop them?* This is always a difficult decision. Popping them means red welts and maybe even scabs, but leaving them means exposing whiteheads to her peers. *My peers!* Mary can't help but scoff. *More like mortal enemies.* Tough call. Mary opts for popping.

This Friday the thirteenth does indeed prove to be a dark day for Mary. Anticipating the usual trip in the hallway, Mary is taken aback when someone makes a grab for the hand-knitted toque her mother made for her. "My toque!" Mary screeches. Looking around at the students who are walking past her and laughing, she asks the air, "Who took it?" When no one answers, Mary pleads, "Please, my mother made it for me." Mary is dejected. *How am I going to tell mom someone stole the toque she knit me?*

Being in class isn't that much safer. Mary's only hope of avoiding in-class ridicule is to sit as close to the teacher as possible. Her teachers seem to be aware of her suffering and do as much as they can to help lessen the abuse. But, as Mary has learnt the hard way, teachers can only see and do so much. More things happen in the classroom than even the best of teachers know of.

Thank God for Mrs. Bird. At least in English class no one picks on me. Mrs. Bird always stamps down hard on bullies. Mary smiles remembering how Mrs. Bird confided in her last week about having been picked on in high school, too. "Mary," she'd said, "whatever you do, don't let these other kids drag you down. I know it's tough right now, but, believe me when I tell you it does get better." Although what Mrs. Bird said is hard to believe, Mary likes her English teacher and feels safe in her class. In fact, English is the only class in which Mary excels. Granted, her marks are only in the seventies; still, it feels good to be doing well in something. Mrs. Bird attributes Mary's success to her unusual appetite for reading and insists that, if Mary continues to read as much as she does, her writing skills will eventually improve. As far as Mrs. Bird is concerned, anyone who can read and understand *The Da Vinci Code* as well as Mary has done is going to be all right in the end.

Lunch hour is always brutal. Mary has taken to hiding behind the back stairwell. It is dark and dusty, a very lonely place to eat that always aggravates her allergies, but Mary desperately needs to avoid her peers.

The back stairwell seems like the safest place until today. Greg and Susie, looking for a place to make out, find her there. They jeer for the longest time, and word spreads through out the student body like a prairie fire in August.

Mary caught eating behind stairwell

After racing away from Greg and Susie, Mary decides to try hiding in the library. There is always a teacher there doing supervision, and, even though she can't eat lunch in there, she can at least do her homework. Choosing a cubicle in the back so no one can see her, Mary calls her mother on her cell phone and explains what is happening. Her mother is a very understanding woman and knows how hard the teenage years are. She, too, had been harassed by her peers and always allows Mary to vent her frustrations. When Mary has finished her lament, her mother tries hard to reassure her that Mary is better than "those other kids" and that she will be stronger in the future for all this current strife. "Remember, Joaquin Phoenix has a harelip scar. I'm sure he used to lisp too."

"Mom!" Mary responds in exasperation. "I'm not Joaquin Phoenix. And, besides, he's a boy!"

"I know, dear, I know. Just try to hold on. It will get better after you graduate."

"But, Mom, that's not going to happen this year! We both know that. I'm failing everything but English." A tourniquet starts to tighten around Mary's throat. "Look, Mom, I gotta go."

"Are you all right, dear?"

"Yeah, the bell's about to ring."

"Okay, sweetie, just be strong."

"Whatever, Mom."

The last class of the day is the proverbial final straw. (So much for being safe in Mrs. Bird's class!) Nothing so big as what happened at lunch occurs, but it is enough to throw Mary over the edge. Because it is Friday the thirteenth, it makes sense that Mary is having a bad hair day. Cowlicks stick up everywhere. That morning, every attempt to comb, curl, even re-wet it did nothing to correct the tangle. God, how she hates her hair! Fortunately, or perhaps not so fortunately, her mother had tried to rectify the situation by giving her a scarf to wear. Mary had taken the scarf begrudgingly and shoved it in her pocket. She insisted on wearing her toque instead. After having had her precious hand knit hat stolen, though, she had little choice but to wear her mother's stupid scarf. Well, Susie decides it would be funny to pull the scarf off Mary's head and see what kind of a mess is hidden underneath it. Mary screams in horror as her tangled mass of curls is exposed. She runs out of the classroom, straight for the bathroom where, through a gurgle of tears, she calls her mother on her cell phone and tells her what happened.

Mary running out of the room; Susie holding up scarf laughing

"That's it," her mother says. "I've had enough of this. I have informed the school of this abuse and still it happens. You come straight home. We are going to register you in another school."

Hearing her mother say this makes Mary feel more loved than she has felt in a long time. For some reason, just knowing that her mother is willing to do anything to protect her makes Mary feel stronger. "Thank you so much, Mom. I don't know what I'd do without you. If you weren't around, life would be unbearable."

"Oh, sweetie—"

Before her mom can finish, Mary cuts her off.

"No, Mom, listen. You're the only person right now who believes in me. Without you, I'd have nothing. I've no friends here. I'm so alone at school, but when I come home you're there for me. You don't let me get away with stuff, but, the truth is, you're my only friend and I need you."

"Oh, Mary, I'm sure—"

"No, Mom, there are no friends here for me, but I don't care because I have you!" Mary knows what she has to do now. "Mrs. Bird is right. Those other kids don't mean anything." Mary smiles. She knows the truth now. The other kids pick on her because she lets them, because she is always afraid. *Well*, she says firmly to herself, *I am no longer afraid!*

"Mary," she hears her mother say. "I want you to come home right now. We are going to register you in another school."

"No, Mom," Mary says firmly. "I want to stay here."

"I don't understand," her mother replies.

"This is life, Mom. And, it's like you're always saying: I have to face it, I have to deal with it. So I'm walking back into that classroom. They can laugh if they want to. I don't care anymore."

Mrs. Miller bursts out, *"I love you!"*

Mary, feeling the full weight of the compliment, replies meekly, "Thanks, Mom."

Mary talking to mother on cell phone in girl's washroom

And Mary does just that. She walks back into her class with her head held high. Her hair is still a mess, her scarf is still lying on the floor underneath her table, but she does not even bother to pick it up or put it back on. The other students do laugh at her. *No doubt*, she ponders, *they think it quite the joke.* The big difference, though, is that Mary doesn't care anymore! She has survived the scourge of Friday the thirteenth. Now she is strength and steel; her peers can no longer torment her, they can no longer hurt her inside. Love is her armor. Tomorrow is a new day, and she will face the fourteenth with pride. *Let the worst come. With Mom on my side, I know I can survive high school.*

The Big Bomb!

the mushroom cloud

Sometimes events occur that are so outrageous that even the most seasoned teacher can't help but stare dumbfounded at her students. Poor Mrs. Bird. Echoes from numerous battles continuously bombard her brain, but nothing compares to Gregory "Napoleon" McGregor's well-laid-out massacre.

Today's target is Frank. Sitting next to his victim, Greg attempts to engage him in friendly conversation.

Seeing Greg seated out of place—and next to Frank—sets off an alarm in Mrs. Bird's brain. Being determined not to allow any student to suffer ridicule and shame in her classroom, Mrs. Bird judiciously hovers close to that side of the classroom during her lesson.

Greg, observing his teacher's movements angrily blurts out, "Don't stand so close to me."

Unimpressed, Mrs. Bird turns to face the young man. "Excuse me? Don't stand so close to me? The Police?" Then with a high-pitched mockery she begins to sing, "Don't stand, don't stand, don't stand so close to me." Shaking her head, looking sorrowfully at Greg, "I hardly think so, little boy!"

Greg reddens, attempting an explanation. "You're invading my personal space."

"This space, young man, is *my* classroom." Determined to prove her point, Mrs. Bird stations herself immediately next to Greg's desk. Leaning over, within inches of his face, she states matter-of-factly, "And, as I am the teacher, I shall stand anywhere in *my* classroom that I choose."

Greg immediately recoils from the old buzzard's coffee breath. Satisfied Greg is now willing to behave for a time, Mrs. Bird begins the day's lesson. "All right, class," she says, turning to face the rest of the students, "yesterday we finished watching the movie *Mean Creek*. So, students, who can give me a brief synopsis?"

Frank, Mary, and Susie raise their hands. As tempting as it is to support Susie in one of her rare offerings, Mrs. Bird judiciously selects Mary to respond, as she wants a clear, concise summary of the movie's events.

"A group of teens plot revenge on the school bully. Their plans go awry, though, and the bully dies."

"*Awry?*" Greg snorts. "What the hell kinda word is *awry?*"

"*Awry*, Greg," Mrs. Bird replies curtly, "means not in keeping with the original plans. Things go askew."

"Oh, well, that explains a lot. Things go *askew*. Thanks, Miss."

Damien snorts and guffaws.

Rather than be pulled into Greg's sarcasm, Mrs. Bird simply sighs and moves on with her lesson. "So, students, what does the movie *Mean Creek* suggest to you about taking responsibility for our actions?"

Although Susie is not the brightest bulb on the tree, a rare moment of intellectual enthusiasm seems to be overtaking her, and she thrusts her hand eagerly back into the air.

Encouraged by Susie's zeal, Mrs. Bird turns towards the young woman and asks, "Susie, what do you think?"

"Susie think?" Greg blurts out. "Don't let your brain explode from the effort, little girl."

"Greg," Mrs. Bird shoots back instantly, "that was rude and uncalled for. You owe Susie an apology."

"Yeah," Susie agrees indignantly. "Apologize to me," she demands, with a look that suggests he won't get any after school if he doesn't.

Greg turns to Susie with a look that implies he has ways of manipulating her. He then turns his gaze on Mrs. Bird. Her glower indicates that Greg has just made a fatal error. The only way to get the old bird off his back now is to apologize as contritely as he can. "Gee whiz, Susie." *Gee whiz*? Mrs. Bird scorns internally. *Like Greg ever uses the phrase* gee whiz! "I was only kidding. I'm real sorry."

Mrs. Bird, stunned by this sudden act of contrition on Greg's part but not being one to look a gift horse in the mouth, decides to use positive reinforcement to encourage this type of behavior. "That's good, Greg. Thank you."

"Now, Susie," Mrs. Bird continues, "what does the movie *Mean Creek* suggest to you about the idea that we must take responsibility for our actions?"

Beaming, Susie says, "Don't the kids turn themselves in?"

Asking a question isn't actually a response. This indicates to her teacher that she doesn't really know the answer. Greg lets out a massive guffaw and snort.

Casting a quick glare Greg's way, Mrs. Bird replies as positively as possible to Susie. "Yes, they do, Susie." She can tell that Susie feels confident in her response, and she doesn't want to shatter the poor girl's illusion. Besides, there is a hint of insight in her question. So Mrs. Bird decides to steer Susie's question towards a more correct response. "So what does the fact that the kids turn themselves in suggest to you about the idea that we must take responsibility for our actions?"

Susie slumps back in her chair. The more Mrs. Bird persists in questioning her, the lower she droops until her chin is practically resting on the table. Regardless of Mrs. Bird's delicate attempt not to crush Susie's fragile self-esteem, the girl is clearly devastated. "I dunno," is all she can mutter.

Now, Mrs. Bird is a good teacher, which is why messing up in her class is always a challenge for the worst of students. If she is studied carefully, though, her vulnerabilities can be exposed. The best time for a jackal to strike is when she is concentrating on helping out one of the slower students. If that slower student's feelings have been hurt, Mrs. Bird always offers that child a little bit of extra attention. This "little bit" is just the opening any good rapscallion needs to enact a deadly plan! Smiling, Greg watches as Mrs. Bird leaves her perch next to his desk and strolls over to comfort poor Susie. Leaning over, he taps Frank on the shoulder. "Hey, Frank," Greg whispers in conspiratorial tones, "how's it going?"

"Fine," Frank whispers through gritted teeth. He turns back moodily to stare at his desk.

Fortunately for Greg (not so fortunately for Frank), Mrs. Bird is determined to re-instill confidence in Susie. The biggest problem with Susie, she figures, is the poor girl's lack of self-esteem. "Now, Susie, don't be discouraged," Mrs. Bird responds in her sickly sweet way. "No question is a bad question." Discouraged by the rolling of Susie's eyes, she rattles out even more feel-good, face-saving statements: "Your question was excellent. What I'm trying to do is get you to expand on your thought. You're not wrong; there is just more to say about the issue."

Pouting, Susie pounds her foot on the floor insisting, "I'm too stupid."

"No you're not," Mrs. Bird insists. "Try."

"I don't know!"

"Let me rephrase," Mrs. Bird says kindly. "What does the fact that these kids turn themselves in suggest to you about the idea that we must take responsibility for our actions?" Mrs. Bird's fixation on helping Susie will last a good two or three minutes until Susie parrots some appropriate answer. Perhaps longer, as pitiable Susie will never produce an answer sufficiently good enough to satisfy Mrs. Bird.

Greg smirks. "So, Frank," he whispers, "go to any wild parties this weekend?"

"No," Frank spits out. Alas, poor Frank is always on the receiving end of a cruel joke. Frank raises his hand and clears his throat to get Mrs. Bird's attention.

"Yes, Frank?"

"Marty didn't turn himself in."

"Good point, Frank. But we'll look at his situation after."

Turning back to her current project, Mrs. Bird persists. "Susie, why did the others turn themselves in?"

Susie burns crimson. Greg watches as Susie slouches even deeper in her chair, eyelashes fluttering. Susie always acts this way just before crying.

Susie slumping in her chair, half hidden by table

A rare moment of compassion bursts out of Greg, as he tosses out the answer Mrs. Bird is looking for. "They were scared they'd get caught."

Pleased that Greg is actually participating and not picking on someone, Mrs. Bird allows for the interjection. "Really?"

Susie perks up. Greg's answer is simple and clean. She repeats its main idea, "Yeah, they felt guilty," she adds.

While Mrs. Bird is praising Susie for her response, Greg turns back to harass Frank. "I went to a real puke fest this weekend."

Rolling his eyes in disgust, Frank responds, sarcasm dripping of his tongue, "Sounds like lots of fun."

Now that Mrs. Bird has opened the floor to others, Mary raises her hand. "But, Miss, didn't Sam ask what life would be like for them after they graduated from college?"

Mrs. Bird smiles. Here is the direction she wants the class discussion to take.

"Good question, Mary. Can you answer that?"

"Well," Mary says thoughtfully, "Sam wondered about the future consequences of their actions. He thought about what their lives would be like if they carried this awful secret with them. He thought about the burden of carrying that guilt through life."

Greg, still leaning in close to Frank, persists. "I partied like an animal."

"You are an animal," Frank retorts.

Greg stands blurting, "Stop trying to come on to me, you stupid little faggot! You fudge-packing freak!"

Damien howls with laughter.

"Greg!" Mrs. Bird wheels back in his direction. "Apologize this instant!"

For a brief moment, student and teacher stare down. Suddenly, contrary to all teacher expectations, Greg apologies, "Sorry, Frank. I didn't mean it."

What? Mrs. Bird wonders. *No cursing, no walking out, no rant on how I favour the nerdy kids?* Although stunned by this sudden shift in Greg's character—kindness to Susie is one thing, but to Frank?—Mrs. Bird knows better than to trust him. She decides then and there to engage Greg in the lesson. Looking the young man (*rascal, runagate, whoremonger*) squarely in the eye, she asks, "So, Greg, why do you think it was important for the kids to tell George's mother what they had done?"

Shaking his head, he says, "Sorry, Miss. I'm with Marty on this one." Immediately turning back to Frank, he said, "I got sh—tered man. You ever get sh—tered, Frank?"

"No. Leave me alone." Frank is leaning forward in his desk, using his hand as a wall, a feeble barrier between himself and Greg.

Frank hiding behind his hand

Mrs. Bird, noticing Frank's posture, starts moving back toward that side of the room. Greg perks up instantly with a comment effectively stalling her return. "Marty chose to avoid taking responsibility, Miss."

"That's very true, Greg." Greg frustrates Mrs. Bird to no end. This boy is smart but he refuses to do any work and always ends up failing!

"So, Greg, what happened to Marty as a result of his choice to avoid responsibility?"

"Easy! He got a car and a gun."

Trust Greg to boil things down to petty materialistic gain. "Thanks for that amazing insight, Greg. Let me rephrase. What direction did Marty's life take as a result of not accepting his responsibility in George's death?"

"George's death was an accident. It wasn't Marty's fault."

"Yes, that's true, it was an accident, but ..."

Frank groans. "This is so stupid." Not even bothering to raise his hand, he just blurts out, "But they covered it up. They didn't tell anyone. They buried the body. They were gonna leave his family never knowing what happened to their kid."

"That's right, Frank. The other thing you have to consider, Greg," Mrs. Bird adds, "is whether or not the accident would have ever occurred if Marty hadn't insisted on carrying through with the original plan."

Steadfast with his argument, Greg insists, "Marty was right. The little twit deserved it."

Frank explodes. "George had an anger management disorder. He couldn't control it."

"Frank is right," Mrs. Bird agrees. "George was unable to control his anger."

"Quit making excuses for him," Greg retorts. "The fact is, George was an ignorant little twerp."

"What about the fact that Marty insisted on telling George the truth?" Mrs. Bird is determined to make Greg see the light, even if it kills her. "That is what caused George to react in such an extreme fashion. Would the accident have still happened if the truth had not come out?"

"Yeah, because he's a freak. Something else would have caused him to blow his fuse."

Fatally turning to face Greg, Frank asks indignantly, "So, you think Marty is completely innocent then?"

"That's right." Greg smirks in response.

"All right, wise guy," Mrs. Bird demands, "why did he run away then?"

"Easy," Greg replies. "He wanted to live the cool life."

"A life of crime?" Frank's face is squished up to comic proportions.

"That's right, Gibby." Greg smiles. "Grab a gun—" Greg stands, smirking. "Load 'er up—" He turns his back to Frank. "Take aim—" He bends so his rear end is within an inch of Frank's face. "Fire!" He explodes a trumpet blast of foul, pestilent air in Frank's face. "And blow a few faggots away!"

Greg farting in Frank's face

Greg leaps up into the air, arms in the air, as if he's just scored the winning touchdown (*for Saskatchewan!*) in the last few seconds of the Grey Cup. And the crowd goes ballistic!

"What the—?" Before Frank can even finish, he begins to gag. He jumps up from his seat and frantically waves his arms through the air. Although the sulfur-laden odor was intended for Frank's nose only, the left half of the classroom instinctively stands and leaps in unison. A collective groan ripples across the entire classroom. Instantly, students leap away from their desks with arms shielding their faces as they dash toward the opposite side of the room. Even Mrs. Bird instinctively steps back in disgust.

After he regains composure, Frank turns to face Greg and takes a swing at him. Greg ducks in time to avoid contact with Frank's fist. Turning indignantly to his teacher, he cries out, "Did you see that, Miss?"

Mrs. Bird, having recovered momentarily from her shock, points a finger towards the door and whispers in a menacing tone, "Greg, get—out—of—my—class."

"Weren't you watching?" Greg inquires, still pointing a finger at Frank. "He just tried to hit me!"

Thunderstruck by Greg's inability to accept personal responsibility for anything he does, Mrs. Bird roars, "You just farted in his face! If you had done that to me, I would have tried to hit you too. No—" she adds crossly, "I would have *successfully* hit you!" Pointing a finger towards the door for emphasis, she repeats, "Now, get out of my class!"

"Oh, sure, the little faggot gets away with everything."

If eyes could bulge out of one's face from anger, Mrs. Bird's would be all the way across the room. "Stop calling him that! And, for the last time, *get out!*"

Mrs. Bird's eyes bulging out

Greg's smile widens. By farting in Frank's face, he has managed to push all the right buttons to make his teacher go nuclear. "I'm leaving. Don't have a *Bird*!" With a laugh and a snort, Greg does a little Irish jig out the door.

The Fallout!

In situations such as this, some teachers feel compelled to contact the parent instantly. This tactic works only if the perpetrator is still in the classroom. If said blackguard has already been removed from the room, an astute teacher usually refrains from making any phone calls home until after school.

Mrs. Bird, too stunned and shocked by Greg's juvenile and premeditated act, is determined to set in motion a series of consequences that will force this young rapscallion into accepting personal responsibility for his actions once and for all!

Within seconds, she is at the phone dialing the all-too-familiar sequence of numbers. Tapping her toes and ripping at her fingernails with her teeth, Mrs. Bird learns that Mr. McGregor is not at work on this day. Inhaling deeply, Mrs. Bird begins dialing the other memorized sequence of numbers. As she taps out the last digit, she slowly releases her breath until every ounce of air is expelled from her lungs. As her foul temper builds, Bird's fist starts pounding out a rhythm on her desk.

"Will someone please answer the phone?" she mutters under her breath. All eyes are honed in on her, and all ears are tuned for the pending telephone conversation. Just as she is about to hang up, someone picks up at the other end. "Mr. McGregor? Good. This is Mrs. Bird. Yes, again. Today's incident is far more serious than any committed yet. What has he done this time? I'll tell you what he's done." (It should also be noted that, prior to such a phone call, the teacher really should take whatever wait time is necessary to calm down. Perhaps the cliché of counting to ten would help! Unfortunately, Mrs. Bird isn't feeling too wise at this particular moment—ah, for the day when robots become teachers!) "Your son, sir, purposefully stood up, aimed his buttocks into another boy's face, and passed gas! *That* is what your son did." Mrs. Bird's face begins to twitch. Her entire head shakes. From it, flakes of dandruff scatter over her desk. "Excuse me, Mr. McGregor, this is no laughing matter." Mrs. Bird holds the receiver away from her face and stares at it in disbelief, unable to conceive that there is actually a human being at the other end. Heavy laughter can be heard all the way to the back of the room. Stifled snickering echoes throughout the classroom as students try desperately not to laugh along with him. Frank drops his head on his desk effectively smothering it with his arms. "That is enough, Mr. McGregor! No, sir, you are not my student. Your son is, and his behavior today was both vile and despicable." Once again, Mrs. Bird's head shakes in utter disbelief. "Boys will be boys? I am *not* getting carried away! Surely you jest? Where is your son now? I removed him from my classroom and will not allow him to return until he apologizes to his classmate." A frown emerges. Her eyes squint. Her mouth tightens. Her voice lowers. "You want to know why can't I discipline my class? The real question here, sir, is why you can't discipline your son!" Incredulity ripples across her brow. "You're not interested? You're not *interested*? You don't care what your boy is up to in my class?" Suddenly, she raises her palm and slaps it against the air. "Whoa, what did you just say? Did you just say 'don't F'n phone me anymore'?" Her palm clenches into a fist. "I know you used the whole word. I heard you. And don't worry, I won't!" She slams the receiver down.

An angry Mrs. Bird on the phone

The class is silent for a full minute, which, under such circumstances, feels more like five hours to Mrs. Bird.

"Was that wise, Mrs. Bird?" Mary asks in a tentative voice.

"No, Mary." Mrs. Bird sighs. "It was not. In fact, it was likely the most foolish act I have ever committed as a teacher. It's just, that da—" She bites her tongue at the last moment to avoid swearing. "It's just that Greg … well, he makes me so crazy sometimes."

"Y—yeah," Mary stutters, "but now his dad is just going to blame it all on you." The poor little girl is almost in tears. "What if—what if—he gets you fired?"

Mary looks away as Mrs. Bird responds a bit too curtly, "I'm not going to get fired, Mary."

Turning to observe Frank for the first time, Mrs. Bird agonizes over the sight of the young man slumped over his table with his head hidden beneath his arms. "Class, I apologize. Frank, to you I apologize the most."

Refusing to lift his head up from his desk, Frank mutters, "It's okay, Miss."

In an attempt to regain some sense of normalcy in her room, Mrs. Bird forges ahead with her daily lesson. "Shall we get back to our discussion about accepting personal responsibility for our actions?"

Mary lets out a quip: "I think it's evident that some people never will."

"So true, Mary." Mrs. Bird sighs. "So very true!"

With rising hostility, Susie exclaims, "What about you, Mrs. Bird? Are you gonna accept responsibility for what you just did?"

Ironically enough, Mrs. Bird smiles. This is the smartest thing she has ever heard Susie say.

Ain't gonna happen!

Needless to say, Mrs. Bird's phone call home only leads to further measures being taken—not against Greg, the infamous fart bomber, but against her. Before she even has a chance to inform administration of what has occurred in her classroom, Mr. McGregor phones the administration office to complain. He, too, fails to calm down before he makes his famous phone call. He ends up uttering such profanity into Mr. Willow's ears, that the principal insists the man call him back when he is ready to speak in a calm and rational manner. So, instead of dealing effectively with Greg's inappropriate behavior in the classroom, Mrs. Bird finds herself on the hot seat in Mr. Willow's office. And they don't sit around the coffee table either. Willow is his high back-desk chair purposely pumped up to its fullest height, and Bird is seated in one of the low, cushioned chairs, which dramatically diminishes her in size.

Mrs. Bird sitting in the principal's office

Willow sighs, then asks, "Bird, Bird, what am I going to do with you?"

Unfortunately, Mrs. Bird has calmed down only slightly since her phone call, so finding herself the accused instead of the accuser is a bit too much to bear. "Me? Why aren't you asking Greg what you're going to do with him? He's the fart bomber!"

Mr. Willow can't help but laugh. Sometimes Bird's expressions, though delivered quite seriously, are comical. Managing to restrain himself, he turns a serious eye onto Bird. "Your mid-class phone call to his home makes that little incident moot."

"I highly doubt Frank thinks so!"

"Look, Bird, I know what you're saying." He waves a hand to silence her intended interjection. "*And* I know that what Greg did was wrong. But I can't kick him out of your class."

153

Mrs. Bird had known this was coming, but she has to fight anyway, for Frank's sake. "Why not? The boy is a hindrance to the educational process as well as a clear danger to his peers."

Mr. Willow opens his hands and shakes his head. "He never actually hurt anyone."

"On the contrary, Mr. Willow. Farting in someone's face is an abusive and offensive act. It is harmful. It leaves the victim in a state of physical discomfort and emotional distress. On top of that, he called Frank a faggot. You know full well we cannot tolerate that kind of abuse in the classroom!"

"However true that might be, Bird, the father insists his son was only joking. He says Greg is willing to apologize—which is what you demanded over the phone—and promises never to do *it* again."

Leaning forward, which causes her to sink even lower into her chair, she laments, "This is so wrong, and you know it!"

Willow rubs his hand over his head. Sighing, he places his hand over his mouth. Lifting his eyes up into his brow, he glares at Bird. He shakes his head. "If you hadn't tied my hands by making an irate phone call to Greg's home, I might have suspended Greg for his behaviour."

"I know I messed up with that phone call, but why does the focus have to be shifted onto me? Why can't we focus on what Greg did?"

Pleading, she cries, "Come on, my reaction was normal. I was incensed by the cruelty and utter barbarity of the act committed against one of my students. Surely you would have flown off the handle over that one too!" Mr. Willow's only response is an elongated sigh. Sputtering, she continues, "I'm right and you know it. Who wouldn't have reacted badly to something like that?"

"No doubt I would have," he concedes. "I have, in fact, lost it many times in this office as well as in the classroom. But the fact remains, Bird old girl, when we lose our cool, we lose our credibility."

With a mind fluttering like a trapped bird, she ventures, "I swear to you, Willow, that man was stoned." Grasping at straws, she adds, "The kid too, probably."

"No doubt. But Mr. McGregor is threatening to take this to the school board if we try to withdraw his son. If that happens, what you did—your little phone call—will be what is called into question—not Greg's fart."

Mrs. Bird drops her head into her hands and shakes her head back and forth as she speaks. "What is wrong with the world today?" Staring up at the principal, she begins to lecture him. "You know what we're teaching that boy, don't you? We are telling him he can act like a fool and get away with it. Why? Because his inane antics are so outrageous, so crude, that people cannot help but explode in anger over them. If he can light a fuse and explode a bomb big enough, the teacher will take the blame, and he will get away scot-free."

"Look, Bird, you need to learn not to lose your cool no matter how outrageous the circumstances. If you can step back from these bizarre incidents and give yourself a little breathing space, you'll discover just how much more effective you can be at dealing with extreme behaviour."

"You're right. I know. It's just hard, especially when he does something like that." Pausing to wipe the tears from her eyes, she asks, " What about Frank? Why does he have to put up with Greg's antics every single day? All the e-mails, phone calls home, and detentions Greg never shows up for in the world won't change this boy's behaviour or attitude. How can I protect my students when this kid gets away with everything because nothing I do seems to have any impact?"

Feeling her frustrations, Mr. Willow begins to relent. "Look, here's what I will do for you—"

"For Frank!" she interjects. "You're doing this for Frank!"

"Of course, for Frank. From this day forth, Greg is on a permanent daily suspension. If he even looks at Frank in a threatening way, you can kick him out of your classroom. I'll have a cubicle set up in the main office just for him. Does that work for you?"

In a pout to rival that of Susie's, Mrs. Bird mutters, "I guess it'll have to do."

"It's the best I can do considering everything that's happened."

A disgruntled Mrs. Bird gets up to leave.

"And, Bird," Willow calls before she can pass through the door, "the next time this kid messes up, wait a few hours before phoning home. Understood?"

"I won't be phoning home again. The father told me not to 'F'n' phone him anymore, remember?"

Wood emphasizes his point through reiteration, "Understood?"

Grumbling as she closes the door, she admits defeat. "Understood."

☹ ☹ ☹ ☹ ☹

Intervention—Again!

Looking across his desk at the all-too-familiar face, Mr. Lloyd sighs and begins, "All right, Greg, why?"

"Why what?" Greg replies with a smirk.

"Don't 'why what' me." Mr. Lloyd interlinks his fingers and places his hands on his desk. "You know full well what!"

Still feigning ignorance, Greg shrugs his shoulders, wanting to hear Mr. Lloyd say it.

"Fart in Frank's face, all right! Why?" The alliteration is too much even for the stolid counselor to bear, and a quick smirk touches his lips. Having succumbed to Greg's sense of humour causes Mr. Lloyd's face to flush dark crimson.

Greg's laugh is a raucous repetition of hah, hah, hah, with a heavy emphasis on this initial 'h'. He even lifts his head back to belt it out. "Because it was funny."

Leaning his head into his right hand, Mr. Lloyd lets out a long exasperated sigh. "Greg, you're not in grade two anymore."

Greg rolls his eyes in response.

"Look, we really need to get to the root of what's bothering you."

After a slight harrumph Greg, spits out, "Nothing's bothering me."

"Yet you always act out in class." Rifling though a pile of papers on his desk, he starts reading from the list of Greg's notorious exploits: "Swearing in science class, swearing in English class, pouring glue over Frank Gibbon's collage in religion, gumming up Mary Miller's lock. And now this!" Mr. Lloyd takes a moment to breathe before pronouncing, "Come on, Greg, people don't fart in other people's faces. You are acting out. There is something wrong. Let's talk about it." Greg shifts in his seat. "Tell me about your mother."

"My mother? Who the f— do you think you are, Freud?"

"Watch your language, Greg. I'm here to help."

"Maybe I don't want your help."

"You may not want it, but you certainly need it."

"I don't *need* your help."

"I know what happened."

Greg tenses in his chair. "That was five f—in' years ago."

Softening his tone as he leans over his desk, Lloyd continues, "I know it happened in the past, but it may still be colouring your—what I mean is, it couldn't have been easy for you walking in on her like that."

Greg grips the armrests and clenches his eyes shut desperately trying to erase the image of his mother sitting naked on top of a stranger, her boobs flopping up and down as she rocks back and forth crying out 'oh baby, oh baby.' Memory of the little-girl squeal he emitted at the sight floods him. "Oh, *f—!*"

"I understand why you want to swear," Mr. Lloyd says soothingly, "and it's okay."

Greg opens his eyes and glares at the counselor. "Will you just f— off?" He takes a moment to wipe his face and erase the tears from his eyes. "I don't want to talk about my mother anymore."

"How about your uncle then? Why did you run away when he came up for a visit?"

Greg leaps out of his chair swearing, "Bloody f—in' *hell!*" His fists are clenched and pounding against the air with every word, "Just—leave—me—alone!"

"I can't Greg. I ca—"

Before he can finish, Greg shrieks, "Don't say you f—in' care." Then he spits out with venom, "You don't even f—in' *know* me!"

Leaning back in his chair, Mr. Lloyd points out, "I know you very well Greg. We've had countless visits in this office. Every time you pull a stunt like this in the classroom, I have the privilege of meeting with you. In fact, I've been meeting with you ever since you were in grade eight, back at Sister Imaculatta Nell."

Once again trying to avert the conversation with humour, Greg laughs, "Ah, S.I.N.! The good old days."

Ignoring Greg's use of the acronym, Mr. Lloyd continues, "We came to the high school in the same year. You're in grade twelve now. I'd say I've had ample opportunity over the past five years to get to know you."

"What the f— has all this talking done anyway?" Greg spits the words derisively.

"It could do a whole hell of a lot if you'd let it." Sighing, Lloyd takes a moment to observe the boy as Greg stands, legs apart, fists clenched, his face the countenance of anguish. Mr. Lloyd asks softly, "Will you sit back down if I promise not to mention your mother or your uncle again?" Greg sits. As the chair swivels, he tosses his head back and begins to spin in a circle. Mr. Lloyd grunts momentarily before ordering the young man to sit still. Greg stops but continues to stare at the ceiling. Scratching his forehead, Mr. Lloyd asks, "Does your father beat you?"

"No."

"Do you still do drugs?"

"No."

"Would you be willing to let us test your urine?"

"No."

Mr. Lloyd shakes his head, looking impotent.

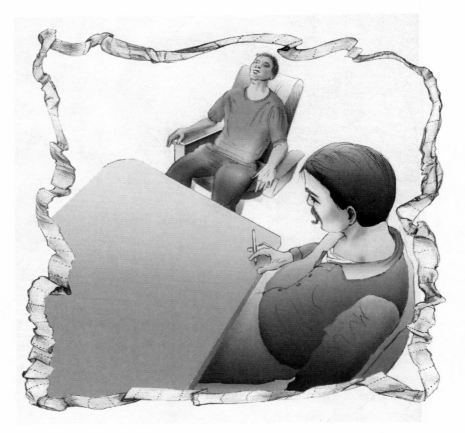

Greg staring at ceiling—Mr. Lloyd shaking his head

"All right, Greg." he sighs.

"Is that all you ever do—sigh?" Greg asks.

Opening his hands mid-air, Lloyd says, "Greg, I can't help you if you won't let me." His fingers clasp and he rests them on his chest.

Greg finally looks the man in the eye. "Can I go now?"

"Not yet."

"F—."

Mr. Lloyd leans forward and points his finger at the boy. "The bottom line is this—"

Greg bursts into raucous laughter. "The bottom line." Sarcasm drips from every word. "Do you know how many times I've heard *that*?"

Mr. Lloyd looks sadly on the boy. "One of these days you're going to hit rock bottom, Greg." He releases a long drawn out breath. "I'll be there to help pick you up. I promise."

"Can I go *now*?"

Mr. Lloyd puts his hand on his forehead and closes his eyes. Speaking to his desk he recites, "Promise to apologize to Frank."

"Whatever."

"No, Greg." He looks Greg in the eyes. "'Whatever' doesn't do. You will apologize to Frank."

"Fine. I'll apologize."

"Then you will apologize to Mrs. Bird."

Greg leaps out of his chair. "No f—in' way!"

Lloyd gestures for the young man to sit back down. "Yes ...," he says, biting his tongue, "... way."

"She should apologize to me!" He points his finger into his chest so hard he almost grunts. "And to my old man." After a feigned spit, he adds, "I'm not apologizing to her."

The two stare down for a moment. Knowing he is on the verge of being kicked out, Greg capitulates. "Fine. I'll apologize to her, too."

"And lastly—"

"For f—'s sake," Greg interjects, "isn't that enough?"

"And lastly," Mr. Lloyd reiterates, "you will stop making fun of Frank in the classroom, in the hallway, or anywhere else for that matter." Greg ponders that a moment. He is not sure he is willing to give up a favored form of entertainment. He looks up to the ceiling, squinches his face, and taps his toes. Mr. Lloyd's finger points directly at Greg's nose. "There's no compromise on this, Greg." One single flick of the finger emphasizes his next point. "You are to leave Frank alone."

"Fine, I'll leave the little faggot alone."

"And stop calling him faggot."

Again the eyes roll. Again the response, "Whatever."

"All right, then—" Lloyd begins, but Greg has already harped his meaning and is out of his chair and out the door, slamming it behind him.

"God d— it, Greg," Mr. Lloyd mutters to himself. "Why won't you let me help you?"

Mired in Woe

From: PBird@hell.ab.ca
Subject: advice, or just venting
Date: December 5, 20— 3:15 PM MST
To: EFlett@hell.ab.ca
Cc: **pelicanbird@shaw.ca**

Oh, Livy, I feel so poopy darn useless these days. Alas, what I can I do to improve myself as an educator? (This is a sincere e-mail, by the way—not a silly, sarcastic one. It's just that my tone seldom changes anymore.)

With that said, here's the latest crisis. I thought that The Hound of the Baskervilles *would be a fun novel for my 30-2 students. I mean its filled with all the essential ingredients teenagers love: crime, suspense, a slavering dog from the pits of hell intent on devouring human flesh. I thought for sure they'd get right into it. I mean, hey, its gruesome and gory, just like all that crap they watch on TV or play on those stupid video games, but packaged inside a decent book. I thought I could give them what they wanted and teach them good literature at the same time. Unfortunately, Sir Arthur Conan Doyle's literary classic is so far above their heads that they cannot understand enough to get into it. Perhaps teenagers today are so singular, so much the "individuals," they can't transcend above the teenage experience and relate to something other than their own lives. I really should have done a different novel, but all the other options—*King Rat *("that's too long") or* Fahrenheit 451 *("this is so stupid"), or, worse yet,* The Bean Trees. *With a class of mostly boys, I'd have to listen to "this book is so gay" a hundred times a day—and there you go, I've exhausted all the titles in our book room. But at least those books would all be easier for the kids read. So many words in* The Hound of the Baskervilles *are antiquated as are many of the ideas, such as honour, decency, and a moral code. So few students can get into it.*

Alas, I am mired in woe (okay, I'm being a little sarcastic and cynical here!) The one series of activities that I did discover to be of great use throughout this novel were the vocabulary crossword puzzles. They're an excellent way to get students to understand words from context. I give the definition and the page number of the word, and then students have to scan that page for the word that best fits the definition. As so many words are unfamiliar to them, they must find the word based on its contextual meaning. I was amazed at how many students were successful with this and actually enjoyed doing it. So, I guess there is at least one little success in teaching this novel that I can hold on to. Perhaps I will make vocabulary crossword puzzles for other units.

Other areas I feel pathetic in are attendance and arriving on time. I have to admit, I do nothing in terms of getting students here on time and that is due to a lethargic attitude that I blame Willow for. He kept circumventing my punishments for coming late—I used to make kids do cafeteria duty, but they would go to Willow and complain, and he would change their duty or simply let them off the hook. So now all I do is e-mail parents a few times. When the behavior does not change, I stop e-mailing, as it's a waste of time. Skipping out is no better. Hell, I do nothing about that anymore, either. All I do is e-mail or phone three times, and then I give up! Arrrgggghhhhg! ☹

Then there is homework. Even with all my e-mailing, I still have over two-thirds of the kids not getting their homework done or handed in. What's even more frustrating is how little or how poor the work is when it does get handed in. This is not simply an ailment of the non-academic stream either, anymore. Academic kids are beginning to fall ill as well.

In the end, the only battle I have left to fight with my students is making them work when they are in the classroom. Oh, Livy, I feel as useless as tits on a bull.

I teach the concept of existentialism to my thirty-dash-one students—the belief that we are all responsible for the choices we make and the circumstances we create as a result. So, in many ways, my current classroom environment is my responsibility. I need to change something in the way I teach to bring kids back into line with learning.

From: EFlett@hell.ab.ca
Subject: Re: advice, or just venting
Date: December 5, 20— 3:25 PM MST
To: PBird@hell.ab.ca

Prissy, darling, I know just how you feel. We all get frustrated at times, but please, darling, don't let it get you down. You're a fabulous teacher. The kids love you. Truly they do. Why, just last week one of my grade ten students came up to me to tell me how happy she was in your class. She said you really had a way with Shakespeare that made her understand it better. Think of all the good things you've done for the kids. Every year I hear your students say they never understood Shakespeare until they had you! And then there's the Alcoholism and the Family unit you put together. I just love it! I always know when you're teaching it. The kids always talk about it! I learn so much just listening to them. So The Hound of the Baskervilles *didn't work out like you expected. Sometimes it just goes that way. But remember—this is just one class. Try it again. What one class hates another class inevitably loves. It happens to me all the time. Once semester the kids are high on pencil drawing, the next semester they are all claiming its gay. Don't give up, dear. Try the unit again with another group of kids. You may find it works better for you next time.*

From: PBird@hell.ab.ca
Subject: Re: Re: advice, or just venting
Date: December 6, 20— 7:36 AM MST
To: EFlett@hell.ab.ca
Cc: pelicanbird@shaw.ca

Livy, you're the best. You have no idea what torment my mind is going through these days. I want so much to teach these kids, to get them through high school and on with their lives, but lately it seems I'm fighting battles harder than I ever did in my first year of teaching. Why is this? Why does it feel as if I'm going backwards in time?

From: EFlett@hell.ab.ca
Subject: Re: Re: Re: advice, or just venting
Date: December 6, 20— 7:52 AM MST
To: PBird@hell.ab.ca

I wish I knew, kiddo. I wish I knew.

☺ ☺ ☺ ☺ ☺

Swearing Rules

Mrs. Bird used to swear like a trooper in the classroom. She never did use the *F* word or any of "those horrible genital words" but she did say things like sh——, damn, bullsh——, and you're really starting to p—— me off. Albeit these are all considered soft swears today, they are swearwords nonetheless.

When Priscilla met her loving husband William A. Bird, she encountered a unique phenomenon: the man did not swear—*ever*—shattering all her preconceived notions of the construction worker. Nor did he approve of the use of foul words, or *taboo language*, as he preferred to refer it. To quote the man: "Swearwords are for morons."

When they first started dating, William was stunned at how foul Priscilla's language really was. Yet, in other ways, she was witty and highly intelligent, and the primal call of the groin overwhelmed his natural prejudice toward inappropriate word choice. The guys at work took great pleasure in teasing him once they learned that his wife swore worse than a drunk in a bar and William wouldn't even utter the word sh——. "With a little effort," he reassured them—and himself—"I can help her wash out her mouth." Delicately, and as often as possible, he would explain to Priscilla that swearing is the lowest, most vulgar means of communicating and requires no intellect whatsoever. He even referred to numerous studies on the brain and swearing. Listen to one of their many conversations:

"These," he often says, "identify what part of the brain is used to create swearing." Then, pointing to the computer screen for emphasis, he shows her the image of a brain. "Look here." He stops long enough to point to the left hemisphere. "This is the area of the brain that is in charge of language, the cerebral cortex." He emphasizes the words *cerebral cortex* every time as if they are magical words and somehow prove his point.

William showing Priscilla a chart of the human brain

"Language," he continues, "requires much higher-level thinking skills than swearing." Frowning at her he adds, "You of all people should know this—you're an English teacher!" At which point Priscilla's upper lip curls up under her nose exposing teeth and tongue in silent mocking as her head tilts side to side. Ignoring her completely, William barges on with his lecture, "Swearing, on the other hand," he says, now pointing to the right side of the brain, "is controlled here where your emotions are. Emotions require no intellectual skills at all." When the scholarly approach fails,

William tries embarrassing her. "Aren't you ashamed at the hypocrisy of your actions?"

"Excuse me," she blurts out in response, "what are you talking about?"

"You are a teacher you know, an English teacher, in a Catholic high school."

"Trust me, those little 'bleep, bleep, bleeping bleeps' swear a lot more than I do. And what they say is by far more inappropriate."

"But," he counters, "how can you possibly encourage appropriate language usage in your students if you persists in swearing?"

"But I don't really swear in the classroom," she reasons. "I only say things like sh—, d—, p— me off and bullsh—."

"Those are still swearwords, my dear."

Rolling her eyes like a pampered child, she mutters her students' favorite response, "Whatever!"

Failing with both reason and intellect, William decides to use Priscilla's carnal lust against her. "Sorry, dear. I am no longer prone toward intimate relations. All that blaspheming has extinguished my desire."

Changing her language habits proved to be a serious challenge for Priscilla. In fact, she'd had an easier time coming off cocaine. Suddenly, she had to seriously start watching what she said. She had to come up with other emphatic expressions. The average thesaurus does not give alternatives to swearwords since taboo language is not commonly listed. So Priscilla made a list of all the swearwords she used and began her search for appropriate, forceful replacements. For every swearword, she considered the context in which it was spoken and decided on its specific meaning. From there, she looked up the proper word and obtained a more appropriate word to use while trying still to maintain the same level of shock value. Soon her cheat sheet was created. She keeps its kept hidden in the top drawer of her desk (the one with a lock on it).

Mrs. Bird's cheat sheet

Cheat Sheet

F— - blast it, confound it, cripes

F— off - avaunt thee witch, vamoose, abscond

H— - Hades, infernal, inferno, blazes

A—hole - lout, miscreant, rascal, runagate, scoundrel, wisecracker, ruffian, reprobate

Bulls— - malarkey, hogwash, balderdash, blather, bunkum, claptrap, drivel, piffle, poppycock, rigmarole, rubbish, tomfoolery, twaddle

J— C— - Jiminey Cricket, cheese and crackers, geez Louise, gee willikers

P— me off - aggravate, gnaw, irk, pester, peeve, plague, perturb, rankle, vex

B—h - bedlam, crone, hag, harpy, necromancer, she-devil, shrew, termagant, vixen

B—d - bantling, mongrel, phony, scoundrel

A— - birdbrain, blockhead, buffoon, clod, cretin, dimwit, dolt, dumb ox

Jacka— - Johnny Knoxville, dunce, dunderhead, halfwit, ignoramus, imbecile, lamebrain, nincompoop, ninny, nitwit, numskull, oaf, turkey, twerp, twit

This list could go on and on and on ad nauseam, but Priscilla limits it to her most commonly used foul words.

The upshot of this transformation is that William is now disposed to entertain Priscilla in more ways than mere intellectual conversation. The downside is that her students complain they no longer understand her as she uses far too many big words.

Needless to say, the fact that Mrs. Bird used to swear in the classroom means that the reputation still hangs over her like *le guillotine.* And, like the ex-smoker who cannot bear the smell of smoke, she cannot handle having to hear the same language she is no longer allowed to utter. Thus, every day has become a trial, and, every so often, *le guillotine* comes slicing down to send her head rolling down the hallways of H.E.L.L.

The F Bomb

F this, f that, frick, frak, fudge. If only kids today would use the euphemisms, but … no … it's f—! F— this! F— that! F— me! F— you! F—in' A. Don't have a f—ing bird! F—ing right! F—ing nonsense! F—ing bullsh—! F—ing great! F—ing awesome. F— off. You f— off. Not f—ing likely. Motherf—er. Dumb f—. Don't f— with me. Don't f— with him. Don't f— with her. F— wit, f— bomb, f— nerd, f—ing hell, f—ing dick, f—ing pr—, f—ing a—hole, f—ing b—ch. Where does it end? Not there. There's also f—ing 'ho, f—ing brilliant, f—ing stupid, and f—ing hard. That last one gets used a lot! Greg, needless to say, is the most notorious offender.

☺ ☺ ☺ ☺ ☺

As Mrs. Bird presents her class with yet another old synonyms crossword puzzle, Greg instantly spits out, "This is too f—in' hard, Miss. We're only in high school, you know."

Mrs. Bird counters with, "Please don't use the *F* word," and, unable to resist the impulse of tossing out a sarcastic slur, she adds, "It's a synonyms crossword puzzle designed for the eighth grade."

Staring dumbly, Greg blurts out, "What the f—? No f—in' way! What were they, f—in' grade-eight geniuses?"

Having been warned by Mr. Willow not to lose her temper, Mrs. Bird politely asks, "Please do not use the *F* word in my classroom." Mrs. Bird would give anything to kick Greg out right now, but Willow wants her to bend. *Bend over is more like it*, she thinks cynically. "Give the boy some slack," he keeps saying, repeating over and over about troubles in the home but refusing to go into any details.

Greg, of course, isn't listening to Mrs. Bird. He ejaculates a "Holy f—!" This causes the class to burst into laughter. "How could a bunch of grade eights know what this sh— is all about?" He waves the crossword puzzle in the air for emphasis. "This is old f—in' English." After a brief pause, he looks Mrs. Bird in the eye. "Why the f— not?"

Mrs. Bird is astonished. The boy's ability to spew verbal diarrhea at breakneck speed whilst simultaneously questioning her authority is mind numbingly staggering. "I'm sorry?" she utters in stunned confusion.

"I forgive you," Greg responds wryly, clearly loving every minute. Not only is he holding all the cards this day, he has the whole class enraptured (which is something Mrs. Bird is seldom ever able to accomplish!). Once again shaking the crossword puzzle, Greg exclaims, "… but not for this." The class rewards his victory with more explosive jocularity.

Annoyed that Greg is playing her against herself, Mrs. Bird retaliates by explaining the obvious. This does absolutely nothing to help her regain her position of respect and authority in class; rather, it simply helps cement Greg's stature as the class clown (Mrs. Bird's favorite expression when it comes to describing Greg to her fellow professionals). "What do you mean by, 'Why …'" she pauses to avoid the curse Greg had uttered earlier '… not?'"

Mrs. Bird is definitely off her game today. The head cold she woke up with is worsening, and her body aches. Timing is everything when battling with Greg, and only lightning-fast wit can keep him in his place. Today, when she can barely stand for swaying, is not Mrs. Bird's day for lightning-fast wit. Greg, like a bloodhound sniffing out the scent of a rabbit, is sniffing out her weakness, and constantly setting her up for his abrasive humor. "Why can't I say f—?" His earnest approach to the question and the expression of shock and horror on Mrs. Bird's face causes the class to erupt in laughter. Greg is definitely winning the day.

Knowing Greg's intent, yet somehow trapped in his little game, Mrs. Bird answers the rhetorical question without even thinking. "Because it is inappropriate language. You know that, Greg."

"I don't see why," Greg comments most studiously. "When you think about it, f— is the most useful word in the English language." Leaning back in his desk, placing his hand thoughtfully on his chin, Greg tosses out grammar terms that even Mrs. Bird doesn't know, expounding on the values of the *F* word. Oh, he has set this woman up real good. "The word *f*— is every kind of verb and adverb out there. It can also be a f—in' transitive, f—in' intransitive, even a f—in' linking verb. It's also a f—in' participle—hey," he utters as if a light bulb just went off in his head, "and listen to how many times I just said f—*ing*!" Smiling victoriously, he adds, "It clearly works as a gerund."

Gerund? Mrs. Bird can't believe her ears. *This boy knows what a gerund is?*

"Oh, yeah, I almost forgot, it's also a f—in' infinitive. And the word *f*— definitely establishes voice and mood. It fits in with every f—in' type of phrase—"

Mrs. Bird's head is now spinning with Greg's impeccable logic, and her voice squeaks out, "Stop it."

It is easy to ignore a teacher when her voice cracks, so Greg rolls right on over her words, "And, to top it off, the word is now an integral part of the teenage vernacular. Everyone uses it today."

Teenage vernacular? Mrs. Bird stands stunned. *This little*—Mrs. Bird has to bite her tongue even in her thoughts to keep from using foul language herself—*this* reprobate *actually used the word* vernacular? Even though she is floundering, Mrs. Bird is determined to regain class control. "I don't care if everyone uses that word. It is inappropriate to use it in the classroom." Before Greg can interrupt her, she waves a hand in his face to shush him. "There is a time and place for everything, Greg. Using the *F* word at a party, for example, is acceptable. At the work place, on the other hand, it's inappropriate."

All of Mrs. Bird's attempts to regain class control (and her own composure) are in vain. Greg is now holding the reins and whipping these horses into a gallop. "I swear at work all the time, Miss. F—, my boss swears all the time. Yesterday he called me a f—in' idiot."

Once again the class roars in laughter.

No longer in control of anything, anger and frustrations tossing her into the ring of instinct, Mrs. Bird says what every teacher wants to say at a moment like this, "Why am I not surprised? Where do you work? In a garage?"

Poor Mrs. Bird. If Greg was the hunter and she the prey, he'd definitely have this duck flying in circles above his head with nowhere to turn ... the dumb bird constantly landing herself in the crosshairs of his sights. "No." Greg smirks. "At Kelly's Kitchen."

"That's impossible." Mrs. Bird flusters. "Do you work in the back or out front at the counter?"

"At the counter." Greg no longer has to try to set the woman up. Every word out of Mrs. Bird's mouth gives him another easy shot.

"And your boss lets you swear?"

"F—, yeah!"

"Well, this is my classroom, Greg, and I do not let you swear. If you persist in using the *F* word, I will have to ask you to leave."

"F— that," Greg chimes. As this is the twenty-first time he used the *F* word in Mrs. Bird's class, Greg leaps out of his chair and shouts, "Blackjack!"

"Sh—!" Damien curses whilst tossing Greg a toonie. Greg kisses the two-dollar coin, bites it like they do in the movies, then turns a beaming face towards his teacher. "You can kick me out now."

"You two were betting!" She is obviously dismayed and flustered. "In my class?"

"On you actually," Greg proudly pronounces.

Susie giggles. "On how many times Greg could use the *F* word before you kicked him out."

With a voice as cold as the north wind and as sharp as broken glass, Mrs. Bird points toward the door as she commands, "Please go to the office, Greg." Not even this little rapscallion is going to make her be anything short of polite!

Laughing at his victory, Greg smirks, "I'm f—in' outta here. See you f—s later." Before he shuts the door behind him, though, he slams the old bird one last time, "Hey, *f*— even works as a noun!"

Greg laughing

☺ ☺ ☺ ☺ ☺

Dealing with the F Bomb

Mrs. Bird stands as soon as Mr. McGregor opens the door and walks into the room. She quickly smoothes her skit as she steps forward, hand stretched out in greeting. She forces a smile, painfully obvious in its lack of sincerity, and welcomes the man into her room. "Mr. McGregor, pleased to meet you."

Mr. McGregor grunts as he walks past Mrs. Bird, shoving both hands into the pockets of his pants whilst glaring at her extended—unclasped—hand, an obvious peace offering. He seats himself at the student table directly in front of her, and Mrs. Bird determines, *I bet that's a spot he never sat at when he was in school!* Ignoring her obvious look of disgust, Mr. McGregor begins the meeting. "We've talked so d— much over the f—in' phone, it's about time I get to see your face."

Great! Mrs. Bird internally laments. *I'm about to tell the man his son swears too much, and the first thing out of his mouth is gutter trash.* Even though the man is already seated, Mrs. Bird sticks to her rehearsed plan. "Yes, well, please sit down." His slight head shake and his hand gesture, indicating that he is already seated, throws the poor woman even more off guard. Trying to regain composure, Mrs. Bird walks toward the classroom door and looks out into the hallway. "Where is Greg?"

"He's coming," Mr. McGregor says as he leans back in his chair and props his feet up on the table. "He just stopped to take a p—."

My Lord, she postulates, *I am looking at Greg twenty years from now.* The thought makes her smile and puts her back on strong footing. "Please take your feet off the table," she requests politely. Complying with a roll of his eyes, Mr. McGregor slams his boots on the floor. The man is no prize to look at. His receding hair has grey roots and is far too long. He actually has it pulled back into a ponytail, which accentuates his bald spot. *If the man had any sense at all*, Mrs. Bird muses, *he'd pull a Bruce Willis and shave it all off.* Like his son, he is too skinny, which confirms her belief that the man is also on drugs—*Crack no doubt*, she decides. *Hmm…* She considers the possibility of crystal meth. Mr. McGregor briefly scowls and exposes yellow teeth. No sign of decay though. *Okay*, she admits, *maybe not crystal meth—yet*. His fingernails are dirty, and, to bottom it all off, he is wearing sandals like an over-aged hippie. Mrs. Bird smiles. His toes are sticking out of the holes in his socks! All in all, she is feeling quite superior to this man. "Well," Mrs. Bird says, seating herself behind her desk, "we'll get started as soon as Greg gets here."

"Why the h— does my kid have to be here in the first place?"

"Because we are talking about him."

Barging right over her answer, he asks, "So what's your problem with my kid? He's no trouble at home."

The man certainly has no finesse, she thinks wryly, *Greg must have inherited that from his mother*. "Well, your son, though a charming young man in his own right, is often belligerent in class. Perhaps the biggest problem I have outside of his skipping classes and arriving late would have to be his swearing."

"He says you swear." He glares at her. "If there's one thing I can't stand it's a f—in' hypocrite!"

Indignant, Mrs. Bird sits up straight and announces, "I do not swear! In fact, it has been over ten years since I last uttered inappropriate language. No sir," she emphatically adds, "unlike your son, I have learned to bite my tongue. I know when it is and is not appropriate to use foul language."

Mr. McGregor leans forward scowling at the woman. "Are you calling my son a liar?"

Mrs. Bird's hands are now tightly fisted on her hips, "If he says I swear, then, yes, sir, your son is lying!" With fire now shooting from her eyes, Mrs. Bird begins her anti-Greg rampage. "Your son, on the other hand, is constantly using taboo language in my classroom—"

Mr. McGregor boldly mimics the woman, "Taboo language! Are you cracked?"

Ignoring the man's rude behaviour, Mrs. Bird barges on, "He is constantly referring to male and female anatomy as well as repeatedly using the *F* word." Not even pausing to take a breath, Mrs. Bird rambles on, "Your son uses the *F* word every single day in my class regardless of the fact that I have asked him to please curtail his language. His response, quite frankly, has been '*F* that. This is the way I f—in' talk.' I swear to you, sir, every second word out of your boy's mouth is *F*."

Playing the smart a— (a trait Greg definitely inherited from him), Mr. McGregor points out with all sincerity, "At least he's only using the letter. It's not like he's saying the whole word."

"Mr. McGregor," she says, thinking *Either this man is an idiot or he is a reprobate like his son,* "he does say the whole word."

Greg listening in on the meeting

Greg is standing in the hall and, since the door was left open, has been listening to their entire conversation. Timing is everything, and the perfect entrance has just presented itself. Entering on cue, "F—, yeah, I say the whole word. Why would I p— around with euphemisms? My dad taught me to say exactly what I mean."

Snapping at his son, Mr. McGregor responds to him, "Shut up, Greg." Turning his scowl back on the teacher, he continues in his son's defense, "The boy's right, though. I did teach him to shoot straight from the hip."

"Well, I don't want what his hip has to offer in my classroom."

Greg responds, "You ain't ever gettin' what my hip has to offer." Turning to his father, he adds, "See what I mean, Dad? She's a f—in' pervert."

Shaking her finger accusingly at Greg, Mrs. Bird warns him, "I am going to forget you even said that."

Wheeling on his son, Mr. McGregor raises his voice. "I said shut the f— up! And stop using the f—in' *F* word in her classroom!"

Hearing Mr. McGregor refer to it as the *F* word after having just blurted it out twice himself makes him look ridiculous. Mrs. Bird shakes her head. Although she hates clichés, she can't help but think, *The apple really doesn't fall far from the tree.*

"Why? You say it! Mom used say it! Everyone I know in the world says it, except Mrs. Bird. And I'll bet you any money she says it all the time—just not in school."

Feeling she now owns this meeting, Mrs. Bird smiles and gestures for Greg to take a seat next to his father. "Greg, that is the very point I am trying to teach you." Looking pointedly at Mr. McGregor, Mrs. Bird hopes he picks this lesson up too. "There is a time and place for everything. When you are at a party you can usually swear without offending anyone, but in the classroom, as in most workplaces, swearing—especially using the *F* word—is inappropriate and will not be tolerated."

Greg counters with, "But I can't help it. It just slips out of my mouth. I have no control. It's part of today's language."

Mr. McGregor looks admiringly at his son. "The boy's got a point. It is harder to control your language today. The *F* word—"

Greg laughs at his father's use of the euphemism, causing Mr. McGregor to turn red, whether out of anger or embarrassment Mrs. Bird is unable to determine. He does not, however, stop supporting his son. Mrs. Bird condescends this to be one point in the man's favour.

Mr. McGregor continues, "As I was saying, the *F* word is everywhere." Greg looks as if he is going to speak again, but Mr. McGregor yells, "I said *shut the f— up!*"

Although annoyed with Mr. McGregor's rough manner, Mrs. Bird is pleased to see the young man so easily shot down. "Swearing is a conscious choice, Greg." She wonders briefly if this man actually beats his son. *Perhaps I should mention my suspicions to counseling.*

"No, it's not," Greg insists. "I don't think when I talk. I just talk."

"Well, Greg, I'm asking you to start thinking before you speak." Mrs. Bird glances Mr. McGregor's way with a look that asks, Surely this is not too much for a teacher to ask?

"That's impossible," Greg demands. Turning to face his father, he insists, "I can't do it. Dad. It'd be like quitting cold turkey." It is time to play his ace in the hole. Looking his dad in the eye Greg adds, "You know how hard that is."

Suddenly looking very old, Mr. McGregor stares down at his hands. After a long sigh, he surrenders, "My son's right. Okay. Here's the deal. Greg promises to try to stop swearing in class, but, if he slips up now and then, you'll cut him some slack."

There's that da— Mr. Willow's favorite expression again. That son of a ... he met with the man behind my back. Well, that's it, Mrs. Bird decides. *No more pussy footing around this issue. I've had all the abuse I plan to take!* "No deal."

"What?

Stunned are you, Mrs. Bird wants desperately to say, *that a teacher dares refuse your request?*

"It's like I told you, Dad," Greg announces. "She hates me. She wants to kick me out."

"I do not hate you, Greg. It is your swearing I don't like." Turning to face Mr. McGregor, presenting her most professional expression, Mrs. Bird says, "The swearing stops now. I have been dealing with this issue all semester. The next time your son uses the *F* word—or any other inappropriate language—in my classroom, I will have him removed for good."

Leaping up from his chair, Mr. McGregor demands, "You're not going to f—in' kick my kid out of school!"

Mrs. Bird remains impassionate. "Not school. Just my class."

"We'll see about that!" Grabbing his son by the shirt, he lifts him to his feet. In the process, Greg's chair tips over and skids across the aisle. "Come on, Greg." As they march out of the classroom and down the hall, Mr. McGregor loudly announces, "What a f—in' b—!" Greg's laughter rings in Mrs. Bird's ears.

The Final Ruling

Walking into class, Greg proudly announces, "I get to swear in your classroom and you can't kick me out." Mrs. Bird glares at the boy but says nothing.

Frank, refusing to remain silent, blurts out, "You've got to be kidding! Miss, that's not fair."

"Shut up, squid," Greg says with a smile. Nothing can deflate him now.

Mr. Willow may be making some stupid concession for this kid, but there is no way Mrs. Bird is going to let him ridicule another student in her class. "Apologize to Frank."

Greg ignores her. "Mr. Willow told my dad that you couldn't kick me out of your class if I swore every now and then."

"True. I won't withdraw you when you swear. However, I do have the right, under the School Act, to suspend a student one class at a time for inappropriate behaviour. And swearing is, as you well know, inappropriate behaviour. So, I will be sending you to the office every single time you utter a profanity. Let the *F* word slip out just once without thinking and you'll pack up your bags and go work in the office. Maybe after Mr. Willow gets sick of seeing you every day for the next few weeks, he'll change his mind about withdrawing you. And if not, well, that's okay, too, because you will be swearing somewhere else for a change."

Once again, Greg speaks without thinking, "F— you!"

Smiling sweetly, Mrs. Bird says, "Go to the office, Greg."

Mrs. Bird waving good-bye to Greg

☺ ☺ ☺ ☺ ☺

Cutting Him Slack

Bird is standing at the front of the class cleaning the day's work off the board when Willow enters. She smiles at him even though she knows he is not going to be the bearer of good news. "Willow, how ya doing?"

"I'm okay, Bird. You?" Willow, too, is smiling.

"Fine, my block four English class ran a lot more smoothly today with Greg down in the office. Getting tired of him already?"

"Yeah." Mr. Willow grimaces. "You waste no time getting to the point."

"I never was one for niceties. That used to be something you liked about me. Before you became admin, that is."

"Well, about Greg—"

Yup, here it comes, she muses. *God, you are every bit your name, a willow bending in the wind.* This thought causes a smile to battle for possession over her scowl. "Don't make me take him back. You have no idea what a pain in the posterior he is."

Willow grumbles. "Even before all this happened you'd been sending that boy to the office at least twice a week. Believe me, I know." Before Bird can get a word in edgewise Willow rambles on, "And I understand." After observing her expression, he begins to explain, "I know you don't believe me, but it's true. I haven't forgotten what it's like in the classroom. I taught for five years before becoming an administrator. But the fact is, Bird, there's more to this kid than you know."

"Let me guess. He's a crackhead."

"No, but he is heavy into drugs—pot, hash ... nothing too extreme—"

Before he can finish Mrs. Bird quips, "Yet."

"Did you know he's trying to quit?"

"Good. I hope he's successful." Glaring at Willow she adds, "I still don't want him back in my classroom."

"His father is trying to quit too—he got into crack."

Not even the least bit worried that she is showing her age, Mrs. Bird imitates Gomer Pile: "Surprise, surprise, surprise."

Willow tightens. "This is no laughing matter, Bird."

"I know its no laughing matter," Bird replies a bit too curtly, "but neither is having Greg in my class!"

"Look, Bird, it's like you're always saying, the apple doesn't fall too far from the tree."

"I do not speak in clichés. If I were to say anything about Greg, it would be that he's a little turd crapped out by an even bigger turd."

Willow grimaces at the base metaphor. "I'm going to let that slide. You're clearly at your wit's end."

"You figure!" Bird ejaculates.

"Look," Willow remains calm. "You need to know the score here."

"Oh, I know the score!"

"The real score."

Bird shakes her head in disgust. *Now what?* Peering icily at Willow, she says, "Fine. Enlighten me!"

"Last month, Mr. McGregor got the ultimatum from the plant. Go to Alberta Alcohol and Drug Commision and get cleaned up or lose his job." He pauses. "That was the same day he hit Greg with his car." Willow looks sternly at Mrs. Bird. He actually expects some sympathy as a result of this story. "Greg agreed to go with him. They have had a tight little ongoing drug dealership established. Dad shipped the marijuana and hash up from Edmonton, and Greg pulled in the teenage clientele."

"Good," Bird ejaculates, "then have the RCMP throw 'em both in jail."

"There's no hard evidence, only suspicion."

"Great. So my class has to suffer for their choice?"

"I believe Greg pulled out of the deal when his dad got into crack and crystal meth." Willow sighs. Not even this piece of intelligence solicits sympathy from her. "All I'm asking is that you cut Greg a little slack."

It is Mrs. Bird's turn to grimace.

Willow persists, "Both Greg and his dad have decided to give up drugs." He stares at her in recrimination. "Quitting isn't easy, Bird. You, of all people, ought to know that."

Bird closes her eyes. "Thanks for bringing that up, Willow."

"I'm sorry, but I need to give you something you can use to relate to this boy with."

"That was a long time ago."

"I know, and I only bring it up because … well …," he says, his tone softening. "Look, the reason you're so good with these kids is because you have something in common with them. Show that side to Greg."

Mrs. Bird doesn't fall for it. "You know, you really gnaw at me sometimes. This kid is out of control, and, instead of dealing with the problem by exacting a little discipline, you'd rather pamper him."

"There's no Mrs. McGregor. You know that, right?"

Exasperated, she answers, "No, I didn't. You don't tell me anything until after the explosion."

Willow is relentless. "She left him five years ago—she took their little girl with her."

Bird, too, is unyielding. "We all have hard luck stories. But we're not all scoundrels." Mrs. Bird tries to control the anger boiling up inside.

"She wanted to take Greg too, but he wouldn't go. Said he couldn't leave the old man alone. You always say he never takes responsibility. Well, he was only thirteen years old."

"You're killing me here."

"I'm trying to kill your argument."

"All right, all right, I cave."

Placing an arm around her shoulder in friendly conciliation, Willow says, "Don't see it as caving, Bird, see it as reaching out to grab the hand of a drowning child."

In her most cynical of voices, she counters, "Nice metaphor."

Willow is on a roll. "What makes this school a Catholic school?"

Rolling her eyes, she mutters, "Jiminey Cricket," under her breath before parroting the appropriate response, "The compassion we show our students."

"No," Willow emphasizes. "What makes us a Catholic school is *the compassion we show our students*." He stretches out the empathy through the extension of every vowel.

She gives in. She knows she might as well anyway. Once Willow has made up his mind to save a kid, there is no changing him. "Look, you're right. Okay. I know you're right. I'll talk to the kid. I'm just so da—, darn frustrated with him."

With a smile and a wink, Willow pats her on the back, "I know. You're a good egg."

Mrs. Bird glares at the man. "I hate clichés, especially when it's a comparison meant for me."

Nothing can daunt Willow now. He has saved yet another wayward child. With a huge smile and a hug, he utters, "Sorry."

Awkward in his embrace, Bird—never one for this touchy feely crap—grumbles, "Look, I said I'd speak to the kid and I will." Pushing Willow back, she rants, "But he has to meet me halfway. He has to at least try."

Stepping back and looking her square in the eye, he says, "Thanks, Bird. I knew you'd come through for him. You're a great teacher, you know. With you, kids always come first."

Gently removing his hands from her shoulders (wanting to be a lot less gentle), she says, "You don't need to stuff piffle down my throat, Willow. I've already agreed to give Greg a second—no—a thirty-third *thousandth* chance."

"How many chances has God given you? How many more chances will you ask for before you die?"

"You won already. Okay? Don't rub it in."

"Let me know how your meeting with Greg goes."

After Willow leaves the room, in a dancing sway that too closely resembles Gregory McGregor's victory dance, Mrs. Bird looks up at the crucifix on her wall. A rare moment in Mrs. Bird's life occurs as she begins to pray. "Is this what you want, Lord, because, I don't know. I swear all we ever do is enable these kids without teaching them any sense of responsibility at all." Shaking her head and grunting a few times to avoid cursing, Bird relents, "I know he's right. I hate it when he's right. All right, Lord. I'll give Greg another chance. Honest, I will, but you are going to have to help me because all I really want to do is strangle the living crap out of him."

Mrs. Bird talking to the cross above her door

☺ ☺ ☺ ☺

Meeting with Greg

In the hallway. Prior to class. Short, sweet, circumspect. An index finger points.

"One swear. That's it."

"Three."

"Two."

"Deal."

A handshake.

The cold winter wind blows through the cracks. It's over forty below out there. Fifty with the windchill factor.

E-mail Lament

From: PBird@hell.ab.ca
Subject: advice, or just venting
Date: December 10, 20— 11:16 AM MST
To: EFlett@hell.ab.ca

Forgive me for venting, but I just can't seem to help myself these days. Did you read Willow's e-mail yet? The one that goes: "People, too many students are wandering the halls these days. When approached they say they have been kicked out of class. Must I remind you of the importance of keeping kids in the classroom? Remember, it is our duty to keep these kids in the classroom, not toss them out to be wandering the halls."

Well, here is what I have to say to that! First off, Willow, most of these kids are throwing hogwash at you. Can't you smell malarkey when it hits you in the face? Maybe 10 percent of all the ones wandering the halls have been booted out. The rest, I assure you, are skipping! *Kids are so brazen with skipping out today that they don't even bother leaving the school. They don't even try to hide.*

Oh, Livy, don't get me wrong. Yes, I agree 100 percent that the best thing for these kids is to keep them in the classroom, but how? It gets harder and harder every year. Kids, society, and educational values are changing. So radical a shift has occurred that it seems we're hurtling into an abyss.

What is this shift? Is it the faster pace of society? Is it the technological advancements and our ever-growing dependency on computers, cell phones, and the Internet? Is it the greater emphasis on movies, TV, and video games? Or maybe it's everything being thrown at us so quickly that we can't digest it using reason or morality? And how do we address this shift in the classroom?

Not only this, but attitudes towards the way we raise our children today hinder us. Student rights are explicit, but little to no emphasis is placed on responsibility—or discipline, for that matter! Discipline today is only acceptable if the child approves. Why is this? Why have we allowed this to become the norm? If the child opposes the discipline, it can no longer be enforced. That is a reality—a reality I'm living with every day in this school. I can support this with specific examples. How do we maintain order in the classroom without a clear sense of discipline? How can we retain students in the classroom if they can skip without consequence?

We are in a conundrum, Livy. I see it all too clearly, like mud splattered against the mirror.

From:	EFlett@hell.ab.ca
Subject:	Re: advice, or just venting
Date:	December 10, 20— 3:00 PM MST
To:	**PBird@hell.ab.ca**

You said it in a nutshell!

From:	PBird@hell.ab.ca
Subject:	Re: Re: advice, or just venting
Date:	December 11, 20— 7:23 AM MST
To:	EFlett@hell.ab.ca

Perhaps, but I've still no answers. I feel like an elastic band pulled so tight I'm ready to rip in half.

From:	EFlett@hell.ab.ca
Subject	Re: Re: Re: advice, or just venting
Date:	December 11, 20— 7:25 AM MST
To:	PBird@hell.ab.ca

Oh, Prissy, it worries me when you talk like that.

From: PBird@hell.ab.ca
Subject: Re: Re: Re: Re: advice, or just venting
Date December 11, 20— 7:36 AM MST
To: EFlett@hell.ab.ca

Maybe so, but I feel like I'm falling down an endless well into the dark abyss.

From: EFlett@hell.ab.ca
Subject: Re: Re: Re: Re: Re: advice, or just venting
Date: December 11, 20— 11:45 AM MST
To: PBird@hell.ab.ca

You know, Prissy, I was thinking. You should send everyone your reply to Willow's e-mail. We all need to hear what you just said.

From: PBird@hell.ab.ca
Subject: Re: Re: Re: Re: Re: Re: advice, or just venting
Date: December 11, 20— 3:10 PM MST
To: EFlett@hell.ab.ca

Are you insane? I didn't even send it to him! You're the only one who got it. And don't send it to anyone else, please. I'm in enough crap with that man already. Even the Alberta Teacher's Association wouldn't back me on that!

From: EFlett@hell.ab.ca
Subject: Re: Re: Re: Re: Re: Re: advice, or just venting
Date: December 11, 20— 3:34 PM MST
To: PBird@hell.ab.ca

Don't be silly. Willow loves you.

From: PBird@hell.ab.ca
Subject: Re: Re: Re: Re: Re: Re: Re: advice, or just venting
Date: December 7, 20— 3:35 PM MST
To: EFlett@hell.ab.ca

If that's true, then why is Greg still in my classroom?

From: EFlett@hell.ab.ca
Subject: Re: Re: Re: Re: Re: Re: Re: Re: Re: advice, or just venting
Date: December 11, 20— 3:36 PM MST
To: PBird@hell.ab.ca

Is he still swearing up a storm?

From: PBird@hell.ab.ca
Subject: Re: Re: Re: Re: Re: Re: Re: Re: Re: Re: advice, or just venting
Date: December 11, 20— 3:37 PM MST
To: EFlett@hell.ab.ca

He keeps it down to two swears a block.

From: EFlett@hell.ab.ca
Subject: Re: Re: Re: Re: Re: Re: Re: Re: Re: Re: Re: advice, or just venting
Date: December 11, 20— 3:38 PM MST
To: PBird@hell.ab.ca

Two swears a block. How thoughtful of him. Looks like he can control his language after all.

From: PBird@hell.ab.ca
Subject: Re: Re: Re: Re: Re: Re: Re: Re: Re: Re: Re: Re: advice, or just venting
Date: December 11, 20— 3:49 PM MST
To: EFlett@hell.ab.ca

He always could.

☹ ☹ ☹ ☹ ☹

Dogs are Better than Children

Priscilla and William Bird cuddle together on their loveseat recliner. William is gently stroking Mrs. Bird's shoulder-length hair. "Your hair is so soft," he coos.

"It helps that I no longer dye it."

"You don't need too," he says smiling down at her. "You look beautiful natural."

"God, I'm so glad I married you." She smiles and reaches up to pat his face. "You don't even mind the fact that I gained weight do you?"

Knowing he's being set up, but still feeling comfortable being able to spout the truth, he agrees with her, "Of course not. You were the skinniest girl I ever dated when we first met. In fact," he says, about to score some major brownie points for this line, "I started dating you regardless of how thin you were. You know I prefer big-bodied women."

Priscilla slaps him on the chest, "You just want to get laid."

Laughing, William asks, "Is that so bad?"

"Of course not." Priscilla squirms a little and begins to giggle. "That's the other reason I married you. You're so amazing in the sack."

Priscilla's mood darkens. William knows where her mind is. They just talked about sex, and Priscilla always equates the act these days with getting pregnant. "Is it day fourteen?" he asks.

"Yup." Before William can say anything loving or supportive, Priscilla resorts to cynicism and wit. "You know, babe, I was thinking ..."

"That's always dangerous," William says with a smile, meeting her quip for quip.

Looking over to the rug where their little shih tzu is sleeping, Priscilla exclaims, "I've decided that dogs are better than children."

"Another bad day at school, eh?"

"Always, this semester."

"What's-his-name again?"

"Yup!"

"So, tell me, why are dogs better than children?" William decides playing this game is better than listening to another ten-hour lament on the antics of her latest miscreant.

"Well, for starters, when they are mad at you, the worst they can say is, 'woof.'"

William can't help but laugh. "That's very true." Priscilla's latest story from school has revealed that what's-his-name is a foul-mouthed fiend. Sensing that this conversation is actually relaxing his wife—a rarity these days—William encourages this little sport, "Why else?"

"Well ..." she thinks for a moment. "Dogs are always happy to see you. They always greet you at the door wagging their tails. Kids grow out of that real fast. You don't have to send your dog to school, which means you never have to deal with teachers. And," she says, illustrating her next point by rising up and sitting on his lap, "if you do take him to school, you have to go too. The classes are more for you than they are for the dog." She is now on a roll and begins citing all her ideas as a list. "You don't need a babysitter for a dog, you crate him when you go out. They never have sleepovers. You can spoil them absolutely. They will never throw a wild party and wreck your home—which brings me to the best part. You can stick them in a kennel whenever you go out of town. Can't do that with a kid. *And*," she finishes, extending the vowel to emphasize the significance of this next point, "dogs don't get drunk or stoned."

"Good point," William agrees. "Continue."

"If they have homework, *you* have to do it with them, and the only one you can really blame if they fail is yourself." She smiles and pats her husband on the chest over this next point: "University."

"What about it?" William asks.

"You don't have to pay for it. That's tens of thousands of dollars saved."

"But you always have to pick up their poop," William tosses in as a counter argument.

"So what?" Priscilla replies. "I'd rather spend a doggie lifetime picking up poop than putting up with—" She actually has to pause to count the numbers out on her fingers. "Rather than put up with seven teenage years."

"Good point," William agrees. The horror stories his wife brings home are enough to convince him that the last thing he needs in his life is a teenager.

"And then there's *sex!*"

"Sex?" William's interest is piqued (okay, a little more than his interest).

"Who cares if your dog goes out and gets laid? If he gets the neighbor's dog pregnant, well, that's their problem, not ours. *And,* if we don't want our dog propagating, we can always get him neutered. Try doing that to your kid."

"I doubt the law would allow it," William tosses in for effect.

"And nobody cares if your dog goes and humps another dog of the same sex. People just laugh and think its funny. But, when kids of the same sex start humping, man, the poop really hits the fan."

"True." William pauses for a moment, then asks, "Would it bother you if a child of yours was gay?"

"I don't think so. I've taught so many gay kids over the years, it just doesn't bother me anymore. Most of them have been my best students." She pauses for a moment. "I wonder if Frank's gay?"

"Who's Frank?" Having only heard about what's-his-name over the semester, William doesn't know about Frank.

Rather than answer, Pricilla leans back onto her husband's chest and says, "There's one more reason that dogs are better than children."

"What's that, dear?"

"No one will ever call me Grandma."

William closes his eyes and resumes gently stoking Priscilla's hair. He can feel his wife softly shaking against him. Any moment now she is going to ask him ...

"William?"

"Yes, dear?"

"Can we try again?"

William leans his head back and sighs. "Priscilla, we've already tried four times."

"Please."

"It's too hard on you. I just—I worry about you. Losing another one—"

"The last time—"

"Every time is the last time, hon." Looking down on her, wishing he could give her a better answer, he says, "Your body just can't take it." She refuses to look at him. William shakes his head. She is forcing him to utter the truth. "You're too old."

Sitting upright, Priscilla glares defiantly at him. "I heard a story about a—"

William places a finger to her lips. "About a fifty-year-old woman who gave birth to a healthy baby girl." Closing his eyes he sighs. "I know. You've told me that story. And I heard about the sixty-year-old woman too—" Stopping Priscilla from interjecting with a slight wave of his hand, he continues, "I know she flew to India. I know she gave birth to twins. And," he says with emphasis, "even if you were that stupid and we could afford something that outrageous ..." He opens his eyes and looks straight into his wife's eyes, "I would still say *no!*" Shaking his head adamantly, he tells her, "I will not have you die on me."

"Oh, you're right," Priscilla announces as she gets up off his lap. "You're always right." Waving her hand, she effectively stops a conciliatory remark. "I know you're right."

So much for getting laid, is William's first thought, for which he immediately self-recriminates. His hand covers his mouth and his head shakes as he watches her cross over to her little shih tzu and pick him up. The little dog growls his displeasure at being awoken and manhandled against his will, but settles in comfortably enough when she sits in the rocking chair and cradles him. Tears stream down her cheeks as she rocks back and forth. Appearing sympathetic, but really just enjoying the taste, the little shih tzu begins to lick the tears off her face.

Mrs. Bird cradling her dog like a baby

☹ ☹ ☹ ☹ ☹

Doctor's Appointment

It's cold outside so Mrs. Bird is bundled up. Her first layer of clothing consists of a flannel undershirt worn beneath a dark blue turtleneck. Over this she sports a thick wool sweater. It's brown and slightly tattered, but she no longer wears it for show, only warmth. A pink wool scarf is wrapped around her head and neck, and covering it all is a full-length fur coat. (This is the North; nobody throws paint on real fur up here.) Just as she turns to lock her classroom door, Damien shouts at her.

"Where do you think you're going?" Damien commands as he storms over.

Mrs. Bird turns to look at the young man. Incredulously she asks, "Excuse me?"

"Where the hell are you going?" Damien demands.

"Not that it's any of your business," Mrs. Bird replies curtly, "but I have a doctor's appointment." As if to emphasize the point, she begins putting on her mittens.

"You can't leave," Damien insists. "I'm supposed to write that test I missed."

Mrs. Bird looks the boy in the eye. "You mean that test you *skipped out of*?"

"Whatever," Damien growls. "Mr. Willow said I could write today after school."

"No," Mrs. Bird reminds him. "Mr. Willow said you were to make arrangements with me to write that test after school." She is starting to sweat in all her winter gear, and this little interview is beginning to exasperate her.

"Well, I'm here," Damien insists quite loudly, "and I want to write it now."

"Well, I can't stay," Mrs. Bird responds sharply. "I have a doctor's appointment."

"I took today off work so I could write this stupid test," Damien spits out. "This is the only day off I have this week."

"Well, that's unfortunate, Damien, because this is the one day this week I can't stay." And then, very slowly, she reminds the lad, "I have a doctor's appointment, and I have to leave *now*."

"Mr. Willow said I could write this test," the flustered youth spits out. "You have to let me write it."

"Mr. Willow said you were to arrange a time with me. You didn't do that."

"But I'm here now." Damien can't seem to comprehend Mrs. Bird's refusal to accommodate him.

"Tuesday, Wednesday, or Thursday after school," Mrs. Bird replies quickly. "Pick a day."

"I can't. I work. Today's the only day."

"That's too bad because I have to leave."

"B–but," Damien stutters, "it's Christmas break next week a—and diplomas as soon as we get back. Mr. Willow won't let me write it if my mark's below forty."

"You should have thought of that a lot sooner."

"I can pass this test. I actually studied for it."

Bending forward as if talking to a child, she repeats slowly, "I—have—a—doctor's—appointment. Good-bye, Damien."

After turning a classic firebrick red, Damien turns on his heels. "Mr. Willow's gonna hear about this!"

"I'm sure he will," Mrs. Bird snaps back as she heads down the hall.

Damien confronting Mrs. Bird bundled up for forty below

Of course, Damien storms down to Mr. Willow's office as soon as Mrs. Bird abandons him. Mr. Willow had told him he couldn't write the diploma unless he brought his average up to a passable level, and this test was supposed to do just that.

So Willow does what he does best. He approaches Mrs. Bird the next morning. Poking his nose into the staff room long enough to give her the fishhook finger, he waits for her in his office. Back in the staff room, Wood and Payne laugh—Willow and Bird are at it again.

Once Bird is inside his office, Willow motions to the chair next to his desk.

I hate this spot, Bird laments. *He does this on purpose—giving me a low chair and pumping his up with his testicles!* Having given herself something to smile about, Bird sits. "No round the coffee table for me today?" she asks glibly.

Mr. Willow glares. "Damien came to see me yesterday after school." His face is tight with anger.

"Really?" Mrs. Bird asks coyly. "And what did he have to say?" Mrs. Bird's reaction is smothered in sarcasm.

Even leaning forward with his hands clasped together and elbows on his knees Willow, can still look down on the woman. "You and I agreed that Damien was to write that test."

"We didn't agree," Bird reminds him. "You ordered and I complied."

Willow growls. "Do you call walking out on him yesterday complying?"

Bird's smile is sickly sweetly, "What exactly did he tell you?"

Willow leans back in his chair, taking a moment to consider Bird's posture. She is like a peacock preening its feathers. "He told me you wouldn't stay after school yesterday so he could write his test."

Bird turns haughty, "Is that all?"

"All right." Willow sighs in defeat. "Tell me your side of the story."

"Oh, I get to speak! How exciting." Noting the rise in Willow's brow, Bird tones things down. "Fine. He came to my room at half past three and demanded I let him write the test."

"Why didn't you let him?"

Bird sighs as she folds her arms across her chest. "Putting aside the rude manner in which I was approached, I was already on my way out. You see ..."

Willow makes the fatal error of interjecting, "You could have stayed. He needs that test to graduate."

"No," Bird spits out derisively, "he needs that test so our stats don't look like crap!"

"Enough!" Willow demands. "We agreed he could write that test. You should have stayed."

"I couldn't!" Bird, no longer cooperating, pauses briefly. Willow is going to have to work for this.

"Why not?"

"I had a doctor's appointment," Bird recites at a clipped pace. "A doctor's appointment I had made two months ago, long before Damien ever skipped out of that test ... long before you decided I had to stay after school so Damien could make up that test."

"Oh," Willow replies softly.

"Oh," Bird replies curtly. Feeling the need to hit hard, she barges on, whilst rapidly tapping her chest. "I would have had to pay for that doctor's appointment. There's no Alberta Health care for *skipping out* on your doctor! No, sir! They wouldn't've cared about *my valid absent!*" Her finger is now slamming against her chest. "They'd've simply charged me for not giving them twenty-four-hours' notice!"

"So," Willow asks contritely, "when can Damien come in to write his test?"

"Whenever it suits both you and him." Bird hardens. "I will put the test in your mailbox and you can administer it."

Willow smiles weakly. "Works for me." Bird is ardent. There will be no bending on her part anymore.

When Bird walks back into the staff room, she heads straight for the microwave, opens it, and sticks her head inside to the enormous glee of Wood and Payne.

Remembering the Good Ones

Mrs. Bird is infamous for not remembering names—student names, parent names, even the names of other staff members. Her students are used to this. They expect her not to know their names until a third of the way into the semester. Even then, at least one student is left forever unknown. This is the quiet one, the good one, the one who never interrupts the class, never asks or answers questions … the one whose grade remains constant (usually around 78 percent). Ironic, isn't it, that teachers get so bogged down by the loud and obnoxious students that they seldom have time to remember the good ones; the quiet, but central focus of our future? Such is the way it is for Mrs. Bird. This notorious bad habit of hers is highlighted by the fact that one of her co-workers is a past student. This is one she could never remember the name of in class and the one she still cannot remember the name of today. Little Miss Melissa Williamson.

Whenever the two educators bump into each other in the hall, the conversation is always the same.

"Hello, Priscilla." Melissa always calls her old teacher by her first name.

"Hey, kiddo, how's it going?" Mrs. Bird exchanges Melissa's first and/or last name with *kiddo* as she does not remember either.

"Great!" lovely little Miss. Williamson smiles. "I modified one of your lessons to fit into my social studies class."

"No!" Mrs. Bird beams. "How could you have possibly done that?"

"Remember in grade ten when you taught the Holocaust alongside the novel *The Chrysalids*?"

"Yes, of course." Mrs. Bird smiles whilst internally trying to register the fact that she taught this girl grade ten.

"Well," Melissa continues, "I had my social eleven class do a PowerPoint on the Holocaust."

"Isn't that just lovely," Mrs. Bird says, patting the young lady on the back. "You keep up the good work, kiddo." This, of course, is Mrs. Bird's way of ending the conversation before being exposed as a phony—the horrible teacher who can't even remember the name of one of her students—someone she now works with!

After every encounter with Bird, Williamson laments with other staff. Today she is with Payne. The two women watch as Bird scoots down the hallway in avoidance. "She doesn't know me. She doesn't remember me. She taught me English in grade ten and she doesn't even remember who I am." Turning to her friend for commiseration, she continues, "I work in the same building with her, as she still doesn't know who I am!"

Two women watching Mrs. Bird scooting down the hallway

"Well, don't take it so hard," Payne says. "She's horrible with names. It took her months to remember me."

"But she does remember you. Why?"

"I eat lunch with her in the staff room," Payne explains. "She sees me every day."

"Well, if that woman has taught me anything, it's to remember the names of all the kids I teach."

"Good luck with that," Payne adds sardonically. "By the time you get to her age, you'll have taught so many kids any hope of remembering them all will be gone." Stopping for a moment to calculate the numbers, she finishes, "Bird has probably taught close to six or seven thousand students by now!"

"At least she could remember the good ones," Williamson pouts.

"I agree," Payne interjects to stop Williamson from whining. "The jackals take up far too much space in our memories. Quite frankly the last person I want to remember down the road is Gregory McA—hole McGregor."

Williamson giggles. "I thought you hated that expression."

"I did, until he taped a 'kick me' sign on my back yesterday." Williamson bursts into laughter. "Don't laugh, its not funny—you wouldn't laugh if it happened to you!"

"True, you're right," Williamson adds. "But it's still funny." To keep Payne from arguing, she adds, "Besides, admit it, you'd laugh if it happened to me." Then she returns to the original topic. "So," she says, "back to McGregor. The odds are you'll remember him over the other kids, right?"

"Quite frankly," Payne states sharply, "I want to forget his existence before he even graduates."

"Okay, then," Williamson persists, "name me one of the good ones you taught—not the ninety plus kids, but one of the quiet ones—" She stops Payne before she can answer. "—from the first semester of your first year."

Payne screws her mouth, sucks in her breath, looks upwards, folds her hands, and taps her thumbs together. She even begins tapping her toes until she responds with, "That's harder than trying to list ten Canadian TV shows." Both women laugh. They had played that game at the staff Christmas party: in sixty seconds or less, list ten popular *currently running* Canadian TV shows (and *Hockey Night in Canada* doesn't count). No one could do it! Okay, everyone was drunk—but still …

"You can't, can you?" Williamson quips triumphantly.

"You got me there," Payne admits. "We must remember the good ones."

"We must *make an effort*," Williamson adds, "to remember the good ones. Or," she points out sternly, "as the old bird just illustrated, it will never happen."

Frank's Day in H.E.L.L.

It's Wednesday after school. Hump day is over. The week is almost done, and Frank Gibbons is finally going home. The halls are empty, but this is not unusual at four forty (especially in the last week before Christmas). Most kids like to get out of the building as fast as they can, except for the jocks. They always have practice, but that's at the other end of the building so Frank never runs into them. The drama kids stick around, too, when they have a show on, but that won't be until next semester. They're a nice enough group of kids, and Frank would hang out with them if they weren't always trying to convince him he's gay. The fact that everyone thinks he's gay really freaks Frank out. It scares him, and he doesn't know what to think. In fact, he tries not to think about it at all. If the kids at school would let him forget it, he would—but they won't. As far as the student body is concerned, Frank *looks* gay so Frank *is* gay.

Even this close to Christmas, Frank's routine remains the same. Monday and Wednesday he stays after school for extra help in math, and on Tuesdays and Thursdays he stays for science. This isn't exactly common knowledge amongst the whole of the student body, but anyone interested in knowing the daily whereabouts of Frank Gibbons would have very little investigating to do, especially if one wanted to locate him in a deserted hallway. And this is exactly what Damien Headstone does—muttering to himself every time he sees Frank, "It's time to beat the faggot out of the fag."

Not too long ago, Greg told Damien that the best way to deal with a faggot was to give him a good pasting. They were sitting in Tim Horton's eating snack wraps and drinking Coke when Greg offhandedly mentioned his dad's gay-bashing rampage at the bar. "Yeah, he said the little faggot made him wanna puke!"

"Did he kick the shit out of him?" Damien asks eagerly.

"Said he broke his nose and kicked 'im in the shin."

"Nice." This is Damien's stock reply to any story describing violence. "Shoulda kicked 'im in the nuts. Faggots having sex is gross," he says in approbation of Greg's father's recent brawl.

"No kidding," Greg concurs. "There's sh— up there."

Both boys shudder and respond in unison, "Gross."

"Hey," Greg says winking at Damien, "I saw Francine smiling at you in the hallway today."

"F— you!" Greg always refers to Frank as Francine around Damien. It helps keep up the reminiscence of Damien asking the boy out. Damien turns his usual shade of firebrick red. "One of these days, I'm gonna show that little faggot just where I stand."

"Does he make you 'stand to'?" The firebrick darkens. Greg was the only student in his English twenty-dash-one class to figure out what Shakespeare was alluding to in the porter's speech. He uses it every time he suggests Damien is hard for Frank.

"I'll f—in' plug you if you ever say that again!" Shoving a fist in Greg's face, Damien insists, "I'm no faggot and I'm gonna kill that little fudge packer next time I see 'im." Shifting his eyes from side to side, he continues, "I've been keeping an eye on him, and I know exactly where and when to—"

Greg waves Damien silent. "The less I know about this the better, man. I don't like Francine, but beating her up is criminal. She can't hardly defend herself."

"Quit talking about him like he's a her. *He's* a guy, and *he's* a fag!"

Never was a moment better for a change of topic as Damien's face is now a purple plasma ball.

Unfortunately, no change of topic happens today. It is now four forty, and Frank is at his locker preparing to go home. Damien's choice of time and place is perfect. By four forty, most of the staff are gone, and Frank's locker is next to the stairwell—there are no security cameras in there. Damien waits inside the stairwell since Frank would be alerted to trouble if Damien approached him. Damien, who never acts alone, has solicited the aid of Doug and Jamie—two mercenaries in Greg's army of friends. Jamie casually strolls up to Frank and asks him how he's doing. Doug leans against the locker on the other side of Frank and smiles.

"Uh, fine I guess." Frank stares intently at his lock as he tries to work the combination but only succeeds in fumbling it in nervous fingers. He is a little confused. Jamie hangs out with Greg and Damien. He has never once spoken to Frank.

Suddenly, Jamie has his arm around Frank's shoulder. "Hey, pal," he says just a little too friendly, "let's hang out."

"Huh?" These guys never want to hang out. Alarms start sounding in Frank's brain, but, before he can react, Jamie and Doug usher him toward the stairwell. Doug opens the door, and Jamie pushes Frank through to where Damien is waiting. Grabbing hold of Frank, Damien slams him face first against the wall and starts bashing him on the back of the head. Doug punches his side, while Jamie stands back and watches. Jamie, laughing heartily at the display, suggests to Damien that Frank is probably enjoying this. "My dad says fags like that S and M sh—."

"You getting off on this, fag?" Damien spits out. He starts thrusting his pelvis into Frank's buttock. "Is this the sort of sh— that gets you off?"

Doug reaches his hand into Frank's groin and grabs at his penis. "The little f—er's starting to get hard, Damien. I think he likes you."

Damien slams his pelvis even harder into Frank's back end and hollers, "Is this the sort of sh— you like? Is it?"

Jamie, unable to believe that Frank could actually have a hard-on, shoves Doug's hand aside and gropes Frank's groin. "Holy sh—!" he yells out, half in ecstasy, half in horror, "the little faggot *is* hardening for you."

Damien starts pounding his fist against the back of Frank's head. The fist pounding is so brutal, the other boys actually have to pull him off before he does serious damage. Footfalls echo down the hall alerting the three boys to danger. Like jackrabbits, they race down the stairs and out of the school. Frank stands pressed against the wall as if still pinned. Stunned, he hangs there a moment longer before his body slowly slides towards the floor.

Frank slumped on the stairwell floor, crying

☹ ☹ ☹ ☹ ☹

Closure?

Whose are those footfalls? Why don't they advance toward Frank? They stop suddenly. They turn around. They walk back down the hall. They return to the classroom. Those footsteps belong to someone who has forgotten to carry a class set of essays home to mark.

No one ever knows. Frank will never tell.

Teacher Bashing

Christmas break always provides the educator with a brief respite, especially from the politics of work. Unfortunately, one is always encountering attitudes towards educators out in the community. So, even though Priscilla is, for the next two weeks, just Priscilla, "Mrs. Bird" comes out to haunt her at her husband's staff Christmas party.

Every Christmas, William's boss throws a huge festive holiday bash for his staff. He holds this event in his rumpus room, which he has decked out as a party room.

Neil O'Brian of O'Brian Construction owns a home worth over one million dollars. It was the first home in H.E.L.L.'s community to reach that pinnacle. Although not of mansion proportions, as one might expect at such a cost, it is grand indeed. A half-moon driveway allows guests to be dropped off near the front door. The front yard is delicately designed with shrubbery, stone, grass, and flowers—during spring and summer only, of course. Currently, it is a series of white mounds, and driving through the half-moon driveway is like driving through a tunnel without a roof. The O'Brian's home is four stories with two stories above ground, one on ground level, and the fourth story below. This basement area is subdivided into two levels. The lower level is the basement where the furnace, water heater, water softener, washer/dryer, freezer, and other assorted essentials of life are kept which must be kept out of view of the visiting public. Only four feet above, and connected by a small staircase, is the upper basement level—the rumpus room. Here O'Brian has a variety of games set up, including a Ping-Pong table, billiard table, and a poker table. The room also comes equipped with a bar, big-screen TV, and stereo system. Oh yeah, he even has foosball! The best part is that he can easily fit over one hundred people comfortably in this space.

On the eve of the party, William and Priscilla arrive early. William is always one to arrive on time. This way they get to enjoy the fun the room has to offer without competition. They manage to play two games of foosball, a game of billiards, and even a round of Ping-Pong before the other guests arrive.

Once the room is comfortably crowded, the men and women, by nature, separate into groups. Most of the men congregate around the bar, billiard table, and foosball, whilst the majority of women sit on couches and chairs, even around the poker table, which they turn into a tea spot—well, okay, a drinking spot.

It is here, around this little table, that Priscilla is subjected to a night of teacher bashing. Report cards and parent/teacher interviews came late this year (the second week in November rather than the third week in October) and parents are still stinging from the blow of their children's marks and teachers' comments. One of the worst offenders at this "bash" session is Mrs. O'Brien, who works as an educational assistant in the public system. She is angered by the fact that her daughter's social studies grade is only 80 percent.

"She deserves a 90, I tell you," Mrs. O'Brien grumbles. "My daughter works hard studying every night. She hands every assignment in on time and knows more than her teacher does!" She pauses for a moment, eyes each women severely as if each were the man in question. "I work with him, you know. He's a lazy son of a b—ch." She shakes her head before adding, "I'd mention his name, but it would be unprofessional you know."

"Oh, I know," replies the wife of O'Brien's right-hand man. "I swear teachers are just the worst." This lady, entering into her sixtieth year, has no current story to tell but must always regale the women with her experiences. "Well, since we're on the topic of teachers, let me tell you about Mr. Roschman." She smiles at Mrs. O'Brien. "I can say his name as I don't work with him, thank God." Then to the crowd of ladies, she expounds, "Quite frankly, I hope the man is dead." All but Priscilla join in on the laugh.

"What did he do?" inquires one of the many listeners.

"Well," she says with righteous indignation, "when Timothy was in grade twelve, his grades took a tumble. At parent/teacher interviews, I expressed my concern. He only had a 58 average in his science class." She pauses to let the gravity of her son's circumstances set in. "So, I mentioned—" At this point, she leans forward, places her left hand on her left leg, her right elbow on her right leg, points her index finger, shakes it, and looks out at the women over her glasses before continuing, "—with tears in my eyes, mind you, that he wouldn't get into university with grades like that." There is a mummer of commiseration from the women. "Well," she continues, leaning back and tucking her arms under her massive breasts, "he actually sneered at me." She sneers in grotesque mimicry of the man. "And he said, 'They wouldn't even look at him.'" Numerous tsks and gasps applaud her story. This, however, is not the end. A huge smile crosses her face. "So, I spent the whole night studying with that boy preparing him for his next science exam, and he walked away with a 98 percent." Choruses of "good for you" and "good for him" and "You certainly showed him" shower the woman.

"I know what you mean," a much younger mother pipes up. "My Alex was doing so well in grade one and two. He was such a little scholar. Well, then he entered grade three, and his teacher was just a b—ch. I tell you, she hated my son. Well, his mark dropped from high 90s to low 40s. And, now, here he is in grade six, barely passing." Surrounded by confused looks, she explains, "Oh, I wouldn't let them hold him back. It's not *his* fault!" She shakes her head. "I don't know what that woman did to him, but she ruined him for life."

Priscilla smiles and takes this moment to point something out. "That would have been three years ago when he had that teacher, am I right?"

"Yes, three years," she replies bitterly, "and he hasn't bounced back yet."

"Wasn't that the year you got divorced?" Mrs. Bird inquires politely.

The young woman gets flustered and blusters out, "Alex handled the divorce very well. We—he—talked it through with both his father and me. We even let him choose who to live with." Finally, in a burst of indignation, she almost shouts, "My divorce has nothing to do with the way that teacher treated my son."

No, Priscilla thinks, *but it likely had something to do with the way he behaved in her class.* Getting up she mutters, "'Aroint thee witch,' the rump-fed ronyon cries."

"I'm sorry?" Mrs. O'Brien inquires.

"Oh, it was nothing," Priscilla chimes sweetly, then lies, "Just a line from *Shakespeare.* I'm teaching The Scottish Play, and sometimes it's hard to get the day's lesson out of my head."

"Oh, you're a teacher," Mrs. O'Brien says. At least she is blushing.

"Yes. And," she says, pointing toward one of the couches, "as I see another teacher sitting alone over there, I think I'll join her." Almost laughing like one of the weird sisters, she adds, "maybe we'll partake in a little parent bashing." Priscilla turns away from all the back peddling and crosses the room to join the other educator.

A smug Priscilla walks away from flustered ladies

☺ ☺ ☺ ☺ ☺

The Assignment

The first day back after Christmas break, Mrs. Bird assigns an essay. Choral groans of "You can't!" and "It's the first day back!" are slung at her. Mrs. Bird remains undaunted.

"There are only three weeks left of classes, Miss." Greg, as always, argues for the class.

"Don't even try to get out of it," Mrs. Bird warns in her sternest voice. "You'll be writing finals soon, and you need the practice. Besides," she emphasizes, "the topic is easy."

"According to you," Damien laments. The test he wrote before Christmas brought him up to a 42. He can't afford to take a zero now.

Reading his thoughts, Mrs. Bird smiles. "That's right, Damien, you are going to have to write it too." Her smile widens. "If you still want to write your diploma, that is." Turning her back to the class, she writes the assignment on the board reciting the words aloud as she writes: "Select a poem, extrapolate its theme, and support your assertion." Turning with a grin, she chirps, "See? Easy!"

"For you," Susie gripes. "You're an English teacher."

Even Frank looks despondent. Mrs. Bird looks at the youth questioningly. He simply lowers his head onto his desk. "Frank," she asks softly, "is everything all right?"

With the teacher's attention elsewhere, Greg turns to Susie and declares, "I'm going to write this d— essay and really p— the old bird off!"

Getting no response out of Frank, Mrs. Bird turns back to the class to further her instructions. "All right, class, I want you to take out *Heath Introduction to Literature* and select your favourite poem." When only Mary responds with the appropriate actions, Mrs. Bird claps her hands together. "Chop, chop! Let's get going." Two or three more reluctant students pull out their textbooks.

215

In an unprecedented move, Greg raises his hand. Although stunned, Mrs. Bird cautiously asks, "Yes?"

"When's it due?" Greg asking a question is one thing (he always has something nefarious to say), but Greg expressing interest in an assignment is—well—unheard of.

"Tomorrow." In an attempt to inhibit the communal moan, she adds, "And I'm giving you this block to work on it."

Greg's hand rises again. Mrs. Bird nods. "What if we don't like any of the poems in this book?"

Trying to wheedle his way out of it, no doubt, she reasons. "Pick the one you like the best out of all of them."

"I mean," Greg is being excessively polite, "what if our favourite poem happens to be a song?"

"Ah," Mrs. Bird exclaims, "disc poetry." Conceding but with exception, she decides, "Yes, you can use disc poetry—but nothing too obscene."

Greg smiles.

Oh, Mrs. Bird. Had you but said "nothing obscene." But, no, you had to stick in that little qualifier "too." Teachers today need to be *very* explicit lest semantics be their undoing!

Front board with writing assignment

☺ ☺ ☺ ☺ ☺

Laying Down the Law

The rumpus room in the Cardinal home is L shaped. Prior to the installation of a three-piece bathroom (for Susie's use only), it had been rectangular. The bathroom is lodged in the far left corner of the rectangle. In the area between the stairwell and the bathroom is a series of coat hooks. On the floor is a boot mat. Even though Susie has to remove all outer footwear upstairs, she insists on carrying them downstairs to her own space, keeping her life enclosed—disconnected and as far away from her parents as possible. She has one long bedroom with a walk-in closet, the outer wall of which lines up with the stairs. Kitty-corner from the bathroom is an entertainment center with a supersonic stereo system plus a TV with videocassette and DVD players. A bookshelf lines the back wall. It contains few literary accoutrements, but does display countless toy rabbits. Susie often twitches her nose like a little rabbit, a habit that resulted in friends and relations giving her the nickname "Bunny" when she was quite young. As a result, she always gets some form of stuffed or porcelain rabbit for her birthday, Christmas, and Easter. Susie's desk is housed against the short wall. Although Susie sits at her workstation often, she seldom ever uses it for homework. While there, she is Twittering, Facebooking, blogging, instant messaging, e-mailing, or searching the World Wide Web. She accomplishes actual schoolwork only when her dad stands behind her watching every word she types. She grumbles every time he does this. "Dad," she screeches out, "this is so annoying." Her hands form eagle's claws (so much for being a fuzzy little bunny). "I can't do anything with you standing there."

Both stoic and stolid, Mr. Cardinal's response is always the same, "You never do any work *except* when I'm standing here."

"You're invading my private space."

"You're private space just happens to be inside *my house*."

218

An angry sigh issues out of Susie's lips. "You never let me have any fun." Indeed, as long as her father stands there, she can't do anything she wants. No party chat. No boy chat. No online sex with Greg. The worst of it is, Mr. Cardinal has been known to stand there for over an hour just to make sure Susie gets her homework done.

Father looking over daughter's shoulder while she works

This tenacious behavior on the part of Susie's father turns out to be a useful parental tool because Susie works like a little demon at school so she can show her dad all her completed homework before going downstairs to have a little fun. And tonight Susie plans on having a lot of fun.

Greg is coming over. Her dad actually approves of this visit. Greg had called just before supper to ask for permission to use Susie's desktop and printer:

"Hello, Mr. Cardinal."

Mr. Cardinal recognizes Greg's voice immediately and puts up his guard. "Susie's not home," he lies.

Before he can hang up Greg cries out, "No, wait, Mr. Cardinal." Asking contritely, "I was hoping I could speak with you."

"Me?" the man asks suspiciously. "What do you want to talk to me for?"

"Well, sir," Greg is really playing up the polite, "I was hoping you would allow me to come over this evening to use Susie's computer."

"You want to use my daughter's computer?" Mr. Cardinal remains gruff. "What's wrong with your own?"

"My dad pawned it, sir."

Mr. Cardinal pauses, then repeats slowly, "Your father pawned it?"

"Yes, sir." Greg's voice cracks. "He was a little short of cash last month."

"Humph." Mr. Cardinal grimaces. Beginning to soften, he asks, "What do you need Susie's computer for?"

"I have an essay due for English class and—"

"English class?" Mr. Cardinal is starting to get annoyed again. "Susie never mentioned anything about any essay being due."

Greg improvises, "Susie handed hers in on time. Mine is late, but Mrs. Bird says I can hand it in tomorrow. She'll only accept it tomorrow, sir. And my handwriting is so bad she insisted I type it."

"Humph." Mr. Cardinal concedes, "All right then. You can come over. But you are to remain at that computer—no hanky-panky with my daughter, you hear?"

"Yes, sir, and no, sir, and thank you, sir."

☺ ☺ ☺ ☺ ☺

The doorbell chimes, and Susie leaps to her feet. Greg is finally here, and she can't wait to let him in. She races up the stairs and opens the door at the top only to discover that her father has already let Greg in. Susie smiles. Greg is wearing a backpack. He never wears a backpack. He's really playing the part. Having listened in on their phone conversation, Susie knows all about the excuse Greg used to convince her father to let him come over. Slipping past her dad, Susie grabs Greg by the hand and starts dragging him towards the stairs.

"Hold it right there!" Mr. Cardinal orders. "Greg is here tonight for one thing and one thing only, to use your computer."

"Yeah, I know." Susie smiles sweetly, hoping her smile will work its wiles on her father. It never does, though.

Taking her by her other hand he pulls her away from Greg. "You are to remain up here while Greg works on his paper."

"What?" Susie is indignant. She has been waiting hours for Greg to come over, and there is no way she is going to be kept from his side. She knows this essay-writing thing is just a hoax to get him to her home. And she loves the idea of the danger involved in having sex with her parents home knowing she is downstairs alone with her boyfriend. This is too exciting a prospect to give up on. "That's my space! You and Mom said I could have it. My living room! My bathroom! My bedroom! *Mine!*" At this point, she slaps her chest in emphasis. "I can go down there anytime I want! I live down there! So I don't need your permission. "

"Of course, Bunny," Mr. Cardinal says good-naturedly. "Go down if you want." He reaches out and stops Greg on the top step. "But, if you do, Greg goes home."

"Please, sir," Greg asks, "I really would like to write this essay."

Mr. Cardinal stares at his daughter. "Either you stay up here with your mother and me or Greg turns around and goes back home."

"No, sir, please. I can't pass if I don't get this mark."

Susie gives him a wink. He is really playing this up. "Yeah," Susie pipes up. "You promised he could use my computer." Grabbing Greg's hand again she says, "Come on, Greg, let's go."

Mr. Cardinal becomes a wall before the basement door. "Only Greg goes down there. You stay up here. Otherwise he goes home."

Susie sighs. "You might as well go home, Greg. Dad's not going to let you downstairs."

Greg pales. Turning to his girlfriend, he pleads, "Susie, I really do want to write this essay. I found the perfect song and everything. I can get a good mark. I know I can!"

Mr. Cardinal notices the boy's expression and opens the door to the basement. "Greg can go downstairs if he wants to, but you have to stay up here."

As Greg starts to descend, Susie sputters out her shock, "Greg, what are you doing?"

"I'm going downstairs."

"Without me?"

He shrugs his shoulders, "Your dad says you can't."

"But, why?" Susie is truly befuddled. It never dawns on her that he actually came over to do homework.

"I kinda wanna write this essay."

"Fine." Susie is too confused to be angry.

Mr. Cardinal smiles as he closes the basement door behind Greg.

☺ ☺ ☺ ☺ ☺

It is nearly nine o'clock when Greg finally comes upstairs. Mr. Cardinal is sitting at the kitchen table reading the newspaper. When Greg emerges, Mr. Cardinal flips down a corner of the paper to look at the boy. "So," he asks, "you finally done?"

"I think so," Greg replies. He is holding his masterpiece in his hands.

Mr. Cardinal glances at the paper. "Let me have a look-see."

"Ah." Greg blushes. "You wanna read it?"

"You spent two hours in my basement working on it," Mr. Cardinal reasons. "Hand it over, son."

Greg passes the man his work and waits for the subsequent explosion. First an eyebrow cocks. Then he lowers the paper momentarily to scrutinize the young man. He stifles a few grunts (and laughs) as he finishes the paper.

Greg can see the struggle to hide a smile so he asks, "Did you like it?"

Mr. Cardinal clears his throat, lays the paper on the table, stares down at it for a moment, and then comments, "Well, you'll be lucky if they don't kick you out for it."

"I—ah," Greg stammers trying to remain serious, "did the assignment just the way she asked."

"Oh, I can tell," Mr. Cardinal replies. "However," he continues as he takes a moment to inhale through teeth and release a very long breath, "even you have to admit that you are walking a thin line here."

"But, it's the best thing I've ever written," Greg says emphatically.

"No doubt," Mr. Cardinal adds. Reaching into his breast pocket he pulls out a pen and begins re-reading and marking up the paper.

"Sir," Greg blusters, "that's—that's my good copy."

Mr. Cardinal looks Greg in the eye. "If you're going to hand this in," he picks up the paper and waves it for emphasis, "then you need someone to proofread it for you. That way," he adds judiciously, "at least she can't fail you for your writing skills." After a few moments of editing, Mr. Cardinal hands the essay back. "Now go back downstairs and make the corrections."

Greg is stunned. No adult has ever helped him with homework before. He stammers, "Ah, thanks, sir."

Mr. Cardinal waves Greg off with his hand. Before Greg can go back downstairs, Mr. Cardinal asks, "How you getting home after this?"

Greg shrugs his shoulder. "Same way I came. Walk."

"Not at this hour of night. I'll drive you."

Two acts of kindness in one night. Greg fails to respond. He just stands there staring dumbly at the man.

"Well …" Mr. Cardinal harrumphs. "Get back to work."

Greg starring dumbly at Mr. Cardinal

☺ ☺ ☺ ☺ ☺

Getting Sh—tered!

It's Friday after school, the start of Christmas break. And it's Yuletide at the McGregors! When Greg comes home, he discovers the family festivities are well under way. The kitchen is decorated with mountains and valleys of dishes all along the countertops. Cigarette ash lingers like snow in the air. There is even a bulky decoration sitting atop an empty beer box (Pilsner). It's a double bobble—Santa Claus f—ing Rudolf. At one light touch, both heads go wild causing grown men to giggle like little girls. None of this bothers Greg. What disconcerts him is the sight of his old man's favourite posture—a whiskey and smoke in one hand, a beer and a joint in the other. Two buddies from work sit around the table while Eddie, the drug dealer from Edmonton, sits sentry next to his best friend, Danny "Boy" McGregor.

Danny "Boy" lifts his drink in salute. "Merry f—in' Christmas, son."

"I thought we were on the wagon?" Anger and resentment mingle.

"Moderation, son." The old man is smiling. He's happy. No more jitters. "Everything in moderation. We just have to keep the partying to the parties."

"But we quit," Greg utters dismayed. "You said we *quit!*"

"Get off your old man's case, kid," one rough-around-the-edges drunk man mutters.

"Yeah," another—the hippie with the long hair—replies. "That's the sort of sh— you'd expect him to say to you."

"Oh for f—'s sake, kid," Eddie exclaims, "you're no f—in' angel. Sit down and have a toke." With that, he leans forward and offers the boy his joint.

Greg waves it away. Danny "Boy" smirks, justifying his behaviour by encouraging his son to participate. "Go ahead. No harm in having a little fun. We just gotta keep it away from work and school, that's all."

"Can you do that?" Greg asks skeptically.

"Hell, yeah," his father slyly replies. "I'll only use at home and on the weekends." Then, with a wink, he assures Greg, "Work'll never know."

"Well," Greg sits down at the table and motions for Eddie to hand him the joint. After a few long, luxurious pulls, he finishes his thought, "If you're not gonna f—in' try, why the hell should I?"

"Hey, Greggie," Eddie intones.

"Don't f—in' call me that. I'm not two years old anymore."

"Greg," Eddie says, apology inherent in his tone, "pick up the phone and invite a few of your friends over. Tell 'em we're gonna get sh—tered. Your dad and I got quite a stash to sell." He says this as he points to two kilos of marijuana and more crack and crystal meth than even Greg can measure.

Phone calls are made. Friends come over. The word spreads fast over Twitter and Facebook, and, before midnight, the McGregor house is full of beer-swilling, dope-toking, crack-smoking, meth-sucking partiers. Greg sits with the drinkers and the tokers. He knows enough about what goes into crack and meth, having helped his dad cook up the sh—, to ever want to take it. "Give me an organic high," he says to his buddies. It's healthier and safer. If you want that chemical shit, you need to talk to my old man."

Greg is sitting with Jared and Scott; both are in Mrs. Bird's English thirty-dash-one class—the high academic kids. The three of them are getting stoned. As the night wears on, Greg finds himself inside the most unusual conversation. At around four AM, his dad pops in Jimmy Buffet and keeps hitting replay on his favourite tune, "The A—hole Song." Greg loves the irony in the fact that this song is his dad's favourite. His father, as far as Greg is concerned, is one of the worst a—hole drivers out there. But the old man never sees himself in the words of the song; he sees only the people who cut him off. Jared and Scott laugh every time Greg's father replays the song. As they listen over and over, they spout out phrases like "that's subjectivity," "there's intersubjectivity," "Oh, wow, a priori," "choice and action," "the coward and the hero" ending with "change, is it possible?"

Greg just stares at them. "What the f— are you two talking about?"

They respond simultaneously, "Existentialism."

"What the f— is that?" Greg is truly mystified—or just really stoned.

Jared takes on as studious a pose as is possible in his drunken and stoned state. Scott bursts out laughing at his friend's absurd posture. Jared, too, gets an attack of the giggles.

"Stop f—in' around. What is it?"

Jared resumes his Socrates pose. "It's a philosophy of life."

"Of living," Scott interjects.

"Of living," Jared concedes. "Jean-Paul Sartre—"

"Noted twentieth-century philosopher," Scott adds whilst mimicking Mrs. Bird in lecture mode.

"States," Jared continues, "that man is what he wills himself to be."

"What the f— are you two talking about?" Greg asks, shaking his head. He is a little disconcerted by the mumbo jumbo they are presenting to him.

Seeing a baffled Gregory McGregor creates a series of body-shaking giggles in the young men. Greg, being stoned too, can't help but laugh along. And for the next hour, Jared and Scott ramble on about the elements of existentialist thought and whether or not there is a God.

"It's sh— you're learning in class, right?" Greg asked, dismayed, whilst attempting to be dismissive. At first he thinks these two are just plain weird the way they discuss this philosophy. However, as the dim grey of morning festers through the front window, Greg actually starts to consider what these "wacked out kids" are saying. Although refusing to admit it, deep inside his core, Greg is jealous. Jared and Scott are actually excited about what they are learning. They actually see an aspect of their education playing a very real role in their lives. *Why can't I feel this way?* he wonders. Shaking his head at this thought, he mutters, "What the f—?" Not pausing to contemplate, he turns to Jared asking (while not trying to look interested), "Do you think I could borrow that book of yours?"

"Sure," Jared replies. "I have it in my backpack."

Scott stares at his friend disbelievingly, then giggles. "You brought your homework?"

Jared, in his own defense, says, "I went shopping after school."

"F—," Greg mutters. "If you bought anything, I doubt its still in there."

"Fortunately I couldn't find anything." After a swig on his beer, he says, "I hate buying Christmas gifts. The malls are always packed."

"Buy early, that's what my mom always says," Scott adds judiciously.

"F— that, guys," says Greg, becoming annoyed at the direction this conversation is taking. "I'm talking about the book."

"What book?" a bleary-eyed, stoned Scott asks.

"That Sartre stuff you were talking about."

"Oh yeah." He turns to Jared, "F—, you got that? Here?"

"It's in my backpack."

Scott giggles, "You f—in' brought you homework to a party."

"F— off. I went shopping after school!"

"Okay. Okay. Just give me the f—in' book." Both Jared and Scott giggle. Slowly, Jared rises and staggers down the stairs to a pile of coats and boots and backpacks near the front door. The stairs make the journey a precarious one, but he arrives unscathed and, after a few moments of picking up items and tossing them out of the way, he finds his backpack and retrieves the book. "I found it," he says, holding it up in display for no one in particular.

"Stay down there," Scott yells out. "We gotta go." Turning to Greg partially for support up, he says, "Thanks for the party, man. Great way to bang in the holidays."

Greg escorts the sodden youth to the top of the stairs and watches as he descends. Scott looks like a seaman going down into the bowels of a ship in the midst of a tempest—except the act is in slow motion.

Jared is still standing there with the book held in mid air. "Toss me the book, man," Greg reminds him.

Jared smiles as the electric truth of this philosophy is played out through his action.

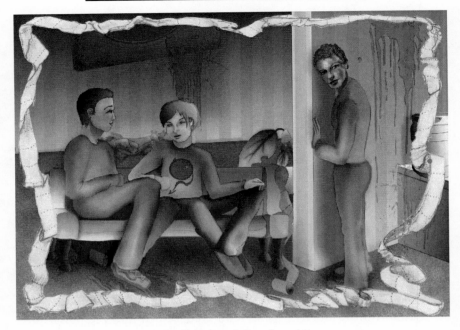

Greg talking with Jared and Scott

Over the Christmas break, Greg reads the book and considers its ramifications. *This Sartre guy is really wacked,* Greg figures. *But, if he's saying what I think he's saying, then I am responsible for who I am. He says I can change. He says, if I think about it and I'm really honest, I will have to admit that all I really want to do is good. He says that everything I do reflects humanity. He makes me feel important and not just some drugged-out stupid kid.* Greg never tells Mrs. Bird he is studying this. He just keeps asking questions of Jared and Scott, who seem more than willing to discuss the concept with him. He is baffled at the notion they are actually excited about writing a paper on this. *Could I do that?* he wonders.

And then kismet, karma, synchronicity—call it what you want, but it happens for Greg on Monday, January 6—the first day back at school. Mrs. Bird gives them a stupid assignment. Right there in her class, inspiration hits. *She just said we could use song lyrics. Jared and Scott said "The A—hole Song" fit Mrs. Bird's favourite philosophy perfectly.* Greg smirks knowing he has his perfect opportunity. He'll show her what he is really capable of and in the most irritating manner possible.

Jimmy Buffett's Existentialist Quandary by Gregory McA—hole McGregor

Jimmy Buffett's song "The A—hole Song" is one of the great existentialist quandaries of the twentieth century. In "The A—hole Song," Buffett questions what exactly has produced the a—hole persona of the driver who "nearly cut [him] off the road" (Buffett line 2). He wants to know whether this man was "born an a—hole" (Buffett line 6) or if he "worked at it [his] whole life" (Buffett line 7). In this one line, Jimmy Buffet is asking whether God created the a—hole, or if the man, through choice and action, turned himself into one.

If God really is the reason this man is a bad driver, then we have one heck of a sick God up there. If we are, in fact, all a part of God's design, why would the God of love include such a man in his design? There is no possible justification for creating an a—hole. The Christian Existentialist would argue that God created man in his own image but granted man free will, thus allowing him to choose to be an a—hole. In other words, man is free to design his own future … create his own essence. Although God created man, he leaves man free to create himself. Thus God did not create the a—hole, the a—hole created himself.

The idea that man creates himself is the very root of Jean-Paul Sartre's theory of existentialism. In his essay *Existentialism and Human Emotions*, Sartre claims "existence precedes essence" (Sartre 1984, 17). According to Sartre, the man has indeed "worked at it [his] whole life." If "man is nothing else but what he makes of himself," (Sartre 1984, 17) then the a—hole is indeed an a—hole by his own choosing. But this is positive. If the a—hole can design his a—hole persona, he can also redesign himself. There is always the possibility of change. Or is there?

Unfortunately, Jimmy Buffet's song leans towards the concept of quietism; the idea that action is useless since everything is hopeless (Sartre

1984, 20). This is clearly shown in the line when he says, "I've got a feelin'/ you'll be an a—hole the rest of your life" (Buffett lines 16, 17). Although Buffett does not actually condemn this man to a lifetime existence as an a—hole, he does suggest that he was born that way.

Sartre slams this perspective when he discusses the coward and the hero in his essay *Existentialism and Human Emotions*. In his analysis, the hero chooses to act heroically while the coward chooses cowardly acts. So, Sartre would say this man is an a—hole "because he had made himself a[n a—hole] by his acts" (Sartre 1984, 34). Perhaps Jimmy Buffett is hoping the a—hole was born this way, as it really sucks to think someone might actually choose to be an a—hole. But this is not hopeless. Like the coward, who is free to change who he is and become a hero, so too is the a—hole free to change his personality. What is unfortunate, though, is that the hero may, at some point in his life, choose to act like a coward. So too may a good man choose to act like an a—hole.

So, where is the hope? According to Sartre, it is through conscious action. In other words, it means one should live as a conscious man—one who is aware of his actions and considers the negative consequences. More so, even if he can't see all the consequences, he is ready to accept responsibility. Perhaps, if the man who cut Jimmy Buffett off had waved just to show he was sorry, Jimmy Buffet might not have seen him as an a—hole.

Although Jimmy Buffett's "The A—hole Song" is a comical rant against bad drivers, it is also the quintessential existentialist debate of the twentieth century.

Bibliography

Buffett, Jimmy, "The A—hole Song." retrieved from: http://www.lyricsfreak.com/j/jimmy+buffett/the+A—hole+song_20214732.html.

Sartre, Jean-Paul. *Existentialism and Human Emotions.* New York: Citidel Press, 1984.

The Perfect Grade

What Greg never anticipates, though, is Mrs. Bird's reaction to his paper. Rather than freaking out and kicking him out of class like she usually does, she reads Greg's essay out loud to the class. In her respect for such a well-researched, humorous essay, she includes all the swearwords and expressions. She lets the class know that Greg earned the only perfect grade she has ever given a student on an essay, and tells the boy that she hopes he will continue to work hard and produce more work of this caliber in future. Greg is stunned. His only intention was to p— the old woman off. He had no idea what he was doing was that good. *I really can do it*, he muses smiling. For the first time in five years Greg, basks in the glory of academic achievement.

Mrs. Bird reading Greg's essay to the class

☺ ☺ ☺ ☺ ☺

Extra Foods

January is always the coldest month of the year. There is seldom a break in the cold streak of minus thirty or forty below, even with global warming. Today is no different. Sundogs, those beautiful rainbows caused by light refracting off crystals of ice in the air, circle what is said to be a ball of fire currently at too great an angle to make any difference on this part of the earth. With all the moisture crystallized into ice, each breath feels like a million little pins stabbing into the lungs. When William and Priscilla arrive at the grocery store, they spend the first twenty minutes driving around in circles waiting for a spot close to the door to open up. Then, as William collects a cart from the outdoor stand, Priscilla races into the store. The cold has so permeated the shopping cart that William keeps his gloves on for the first thirty minutes inside the store.

William and Priscilla spend every Saturday afternoon buying groceries at Extra Foods—a giant green warehouse filled with inexpensive food. Shopping for Priscilla is a relaxation ritual. She putters about grabbing various items from the shelf while William trails along pushing their cart. Every so often, she will turn to her husband and inquire, "What about this, honey?"

"Any MSG in it?" William always asks.

Priscilla sighs and reads the label for ingredients before shrugging and shoving the now-unwanted item back on the shelf. "Why can't they make anything without MSG anymore?" is her usual lament.

Priscilla loves grocery shopping because she always runs into people she knows. Being a teacher, she knows more of the town populous than the average person, so a shopping day never passes without numerous hellos and short conversations. A ten-minute shopping trip always turns into an hour and a half as she visits with the neighbours.

This Saturday is no different—except for the old student she runs into. Priscilla taught Bradley Henshaw a number of years back in grade eleven.

It has been a few years since she last bumped into him. In those days, he had been slightly overweight and employed out at the oil mines making fifty dollars an hour driving the big trucks. She remembered how proud she had been of him for landing such a good-paying job. He had had big plans, Bradley Henshaw had. He had even told her was looking into buying a house. Priscilla had advised him to wait a few years, build up a savings account first, but he was gung ho, especially since the banks were offering mortgages with no down payments. Priscilla didn't approve, but it wasn't for her to say. Bradley wasn't her son, and his life was not hers to choose. "Well, you do what you think best," was all that she could say.

Today Bradley Henshaw is a different man. When he calls out her name, Priscilla turns to stare into the face of a stranger. "Yes?" She inquires a bit taken aback by the ghastly image addressing her. Before her stands a gaunt man with greasy hair and very dirty clothes that are clearly not weather appropriate. His nose is red; the drippings have turned into icicles. His lobster-red hands are clenched into fists that shake violently. His smile widens as he waves.

"Do I know you?" she inquires, desperately hoping he is not a ghost from her past come back to haunt her.

"Come on, Miss, it's me," he stammers through chattering teeth. "It's you're favourite writer?" With shoulders tight, he taps against his chest with a clenched fist in a repetitive staccato. "At least that's what you always said."

Mrs. Bird blinks in surprise. "Bradley? Bradley Henshaw?"

"In the flesh," he proclaims proudly.

His words are nearly inarticulate, whether from the cold or a drug-induced state Priscilla is unable to make out. Hearing the unlikely expression she responds, "Nowhere near as much flesh as I remember."

"Yeah," he quips, "I used to be fat."

"Well, I wouldn't have said fat," Mrs. Bird corrects him, "but certainly not this thin. Why you look like the next slight breeze might blow you away. Just look at you."

"Yeah," he giggles shyly. "I lost a little weight." Bradley looks down to the ground between his feet.

"A little!" Mrs. Bird cries out. "You should put some of it back on."

"Nah," he replies more to his feet that to Priscilla. "I like being skinny."

"Well," as long as you're healthy." Priscilla winces. *What a dumb thing to say. He obviously isn't.*

William, who is standing next to his wife leaning on the cart, which is now filled with bags of groceries, motions with his head to the car. Priscilla, pretending all is well, smiles at her husband. "William, this is Bradley Henshaw." As the two men shake hands, Priscilla adds, "I taught him in grade eleven, right?"

"Yeah," Bradley says with a glance at the grocery cart.

"So," Priscilla asks, "what are you up to these days?"

"Nothing much," Bradley whispers as he stamps his feet in the mud, slush, and the snow.

"Sill working out at the plants?" Priscilla asks more hopeful than anything.

"Nah, quit." His answers are short and to the point. This is not a conversation he wants.

"Well—" Priscilla begins trying to find a way to gracefully end what is clearly painful for both parties, but Bradley blurts out what he needs. "I'm pushing people's carts to their cars today."

"Really?" Priscilla asks, brightening slightly. "Do you work at Extra Food now?"

"Ah, nah." He shakes his head slightly. "I—I push people's carts to their cars and unload their groceries for them and return the cart for the loonie." His eyes shift back and forth in his head. "A friend of mine says he'll give me a—a—a tattoo if I can come up with twenty bucks."

"Really," Priscilla says. "Well, that's nice of him, I guess." Pondering a moment, Priscilla studies Bradley's appearance. His hair is matted. *He needs a toque,* she thinks. *His head shouldn't be so exposed.* And, even though he is hunched over, his shoulders still hug his ears. *Oh, your face!* She sighs. *Your face is so gaunt. How could this have happened to such a nice boy?* Bradley's eyes are like those of a puppy that's been badly abused. Priscilla wants desperately to help him. "You don't really need that tattoo, do you?" she asks, feeling a burst of maternal love for the pitiful creature.

Before the young man can answer, William calls out, "Priscilla."

"Yes, dear?" Priscilla turns her back on her student.

"It's time to go."

"Of course." When she turns to say good-bye, Priscilla discovers that Bradley has already moved on to another couple asking if he can push their cart.

William softens his tone when he sees tears glistening in his wife's eyes. "There is nothing you can do for him, dear."

"I could give him money." She reaches into her purse and pulls out ten dollars.

William grabs her hand and closes it around the bill. "He will only use it to buy drugs."

"What about food?" Priscilla replies desperately. "We could give him some food."

William shakes his head sadly. "He doesn't want food. He wants drugs." After a short pause, William releases the grip on his wife's hand. "I'm sorry, babe," he says gently.

"I could have at least given him my scarf," she says while caressing the soft knit material.

Shaking his head, he reaffirms, "You can't help him."

Priscilla sighs as the tears start to flow. "Oh, William, take me home."

Mrs. Bird talking to Bradley Henshaw outside Extra Foods

☹ ☹ ☹ ☹ ☹

The Broken Shell of Youth

Mrs. Bird, although an appreciator of great literature, is not prone to the act of writing. Even still, after her peculiar encounter with Bradley Henshaw, she finds herself oddly compelled to put pen to paper. William takes it in stride, allowing her to do what she needs to release the emotional turmoil brewing inside. She spends the rest of the afternoon and most of the evening writing and revising a poem. Although she questions the literary value of her own work (as do most amateur writers), she determines to share this with her students.

"On Saturday," she begins, "I ran into one of my old students."

"That must happen a lot," Susie suggests.

"Yes," Mrs. Bird replies, "it does." Then, with a sigh, she adds, "But most times it's a pleasant experience."

"What happened?" Greg asks. "Did you run into a loser yesterday?"

Mrs. Bird, choosing to ignore this outburst, carries on with her litany. "I sat down and wrote this poem yesterday."

Noting the swell of her teacher's eyes, Mary adds sympathetically. "It must have been a rough experience."

"Yes, it was." Mrs. Bird has to pause in order to avoid crying.

"What's the poem called?" Damien asks, in a rare outburst of sympathy.

"the broken shell of youth."

The class quiets down, and Mrs. Bird begins, "I guess I don't need to repeat the title. Ah ... okay, here goes:

it makes me sad
to see him standing there
ears frozen
head shaking
hands hiding inside pockets

searching for warmth
begging for loonies
pushing people's carts at extra foods
for a twenty-dollar tattoo

i make him uncomfortable
standing there
pretending all is well
fighting back the urge
to give him money
knowing where it would go instead

he was a shy kid
a lonely kid
when he was at my school

his shell is broken now

shattered

beneath the foot of drugs"

A long pause ensues, and Mrs. Bird begins apologetically. "It's not the best poem, I know, but—"

Suddenly a chorus of voices burst out. "Miss, that's awesome!" "Wow, Miss, did you really write that?" Mary says poignantly, "I thought it was beautiful."

The tears Priscilla has been struggling so hard to control stream forth, and the class is awed into silence. Before them stands a teacher willing to share her deep-felt emotions for someone who was once one of them.

"I'm sorry," she stutters through sobs. Removing her glasses, she lets them dangle at her chest. She wipes one hand over her eyes and searches blindly on her desk with the other hand for the tissue box. As she appears unable to find it, Susie gets up, grabs a tissue, and places it in her hand. After a couple of nose blows, Mrs. Bird is able to continue. "When I think of that boy, and then I think of you—" through blurry eyes she looks at Greg, "kids ..." Her head shakes slightly as she looks at him, the tears veiling his ghostly countenance.

Greg slams his chair back away from the table and runs out of the classroom.

A Cry for Help

When Greg arrives at Mr. Lloyd's office, the counselor's door is shut. Inside, Mr. Lloyd is conferencing with a parent. After pacing up and down the small waiting room for a few minutes, Greg wheels around and begins pounding on Mr. Lloyd's door.

Annoyed, Mr. Lloyd emerges. Greg can see the parent scowling in the background. Quickly closing the door, Mr. Lloyd motions for Greg to sit down on the chair that resides outside his office door.

Ignoring the gesture, Greg blurts out, "I need to talk."

"I'm in a meeting," says Mr. Lloyd, gesturing with his head towards his office whilst cocking his eyebrows, "with a parent." Pointing again at the chair, he adds, "Sit and wait quietly please."

Before he can reopen his door, though, Greg grabs his hand as it rests on the door handle, "*No!*" he shouts. "I need help!" With the expulsion of these words, all the air is blown out of Greg. He crumbles to the floor. "I—I can't keep doing this ..." he sobs. "I—I—need help."

Mr. Lloyd, helping the boy up off the floor, sets him gently on the chair. His voice is calming, reassuring, "I'll help." Greg slides off the chair. He is shaking as the man kneels down next to him and enfolds the boy in his arms. Mr. Lloyd finds himself cradling the young man like a child. "I'll help, Greg, I promise."

Mr. Lloyd cradling Greg in his arms

A knock from inside his office reminds the counselor of the parent waiting for him. Suddenly, the presence of the man is an annoyance. Greg's issue is paramount. In the five years Mr. Lloyd has known the boy, Greg has never once asked for help. This is a crucial moment. Greg's need must be addressed or the boy may be lost forever. There is no way Mr. Lloyd is going to allow that to happen. He utters a quick and silent prayer: *Lord, grant me the strength I need to help this boy.* Then he reassures Greg, "I just need to get rid of this parent and then we'll go into my office." Making sure Greg understands he is not being abandoned, Mr. Lloyd adds, "It will only take a moment, okay?"

Greg nods and allows Mr. Lloyd to help him sit back into the chair.

Removing the parent is not an easy task. He has taken time off work for this appointment. Greg can hear the intensity in the raised voice battering Mr. Lloyd with excessive abuse. "I don't know why he's putting up with it," Greg mutters to himself. "After all the sh— I've put him through, I'd be telling me to f— off." When the disgruntled parent finally opens the door to Mr. Lloyd's office, he takes a moment to scowl at Greg and mutter a few curses under his breath. As he exits, he slams the door behind him.

Mr. Lloyd opens the door quietly. "Come in, Greg," he says as if he hasn't just been yelled at.

"How can you let it roll off you?" Greg wonders aloud.

Mr. Lloyd waves it off. "Forget about him, Greg. You're what's important now." Mr. Lloyd opens wide his door and steps off to the side, giving Greg room to feel safe. As soon as Greg is seated, Mr. Lloyd begins—with silence, giving Greg the time he needs to gain composure. Waiting patiently, he hands Greg a box of tissue. Greg goes through half the box before he hands it back. Finally he begins, "Mrs. Bird—"

When Greg fails to continue, Mr. Lloyd prods him slightly, "What about Mrs. Bird?" Mr. Lloyd knew this had something to do with Greg's English teacher. This is block four which means her class. *What that woman needs is a little lesson in patience and understanding*, he muses.

"She read a poem," Greg replies.

Blinking his eyes and giving his head a slight shake, he inquires, "She read a what?"

"A poem," he repeats.

"Well, Greg," Mr. Lloyd says slowly, trying desperately to keep sarcasm out of his voice, "she *is* an English teacher." Taking a moment to cough so he doesn't laugh, he adds, "It's not unusual for her to read poetry."

"No," Greg insists. "She read her own poem."

"Oh." Mr. Lloyd is still confused. "What's wrong with that?"

"She cried."

Mr. Lloyd searches his mind for a connection. "Why did that bother you? What was the poem about?"

Greg avoids the first question by answering the one about content. "It was about some kid she'd taught."

Sensing Greg's discomfort, but knowing the key to that distress—his sudden epiphany—lay somewhere inside this poem, Mr. Lloyd persists. "Tell me more."

"She said she saw some kid begging for drug money."

"Really?" Mr. Lloyd's interest was piqued. "Did she say who it was?"

"She didn't have to. I knew."

"How did you know?" Mr. Lloyd dearly wants to know. He has been trying to get Greg out of the drug trade for years. Today might just be the beginning of a new life for this kid.

"She said he was pushing people's shopping carts for loonies."

"How did that fact let you know who it was?" It is obvious to the counselor that Greg wants to reveal himself, but he is uncomfortable doing so. Mr. Lloyd tries to help him along with leading questions.

"He bought crack from my dad and paid with twenty loonies."

Mr. Lloyd's jaw dropped. He had known for years that Greg dealt alongside his dad, but he never had any proof until today. And now, because of some poem Mrs. Bird has written, Greg is admitting to it. "Your dad sold a student crack?" Mr. Lloyd's voice is ominous. He holds no mercy for anyone who deals drugs to his students.

"No," Greg states as a matter of fact. "The kid dropped out a few years ago."

"Oh." Mr. Lloyd pauses briefly then asks. "Do you think that makes it right?"

Greg raises his voice, "If I did, would I be here?" The anger bursts out so suddenly Greg flushes. "I—. Sorry, I'm just—"

"It's all right, Greg, I understand."

Greg shakes his head, "I don't deserve—"

"It's okay, Greg," Mr. Lloyd says soothingly. "Let's go back to what happened."

"Well, this guy, see, Bradley Henshaw—" Greg adds the name expecting Mr. Lloyd to know him. Mr. Lloyd shakes his head. There is no recognition. This Henshaw must have dropped out before he started working at Father Hugh. "Well, anyway," Greg continues, "my dad said he'd sell him a hit cheap. 'Henshaw's a good customer,' he says. 'For guys like him we gotta give a few away just to keep 'em comin' back.'" There is a long pause as Greg stares into space, then, squeezing his eyes tight, he slowly drops his chin to his chest. Bursting into tears he cries, "I can't live like this anymore." Mr. Lloyd hands him back the box of tissue. After Greg tears through the other half of the box, he looks up, pleading, "What can I do to change?"

This is exactly what Mr. Lloyd has been waiting for. "You need to leave your father." Greg nods. "And move back in with your mother." Countering Greg's objection before he is able to utter it, Mr. Lloyd adds, "I know she hurt you." Greg looks down. "But she still loves you."

"How do you know?" Greg blurts out, his anger evident in the splotches of red staining his cheeks.

"She has kept abreast of your circumstances through me."

"You been tellin' her about me?" Greg asks furiously.

"She is still your mother, Greg, and has every legal right to know how you are doing at school. Even if I didn't want to tell her anything, I would still been obliged by law to keep her informed." Taking a moment to let Greg ponder this, he waits to add again, "She still loves you."

"I don't know if I still love *her*." Greg sighs.

"Her mistake," Mr. Lloyd points out, "was having an affair. Balance that with your father's errors."

Greg doesn't need to be reminded of those. Mr. Lloyd waits patiently allowing Greg to mull those over in his head. Greg draws in a deep breath and sighs. He looks up, eyes red and swollen. "Will she have me?"

"I know she will."

"I don't know if I can live with her."

Mr. Lloyd crosses his fingers under his desktop as he asks hopefully, "Are you willing try?"

"What choice do I have?" Greg asks.

"There are always choices, Greg." With far less enthusiasm, Mr. Lloyd informs Greg, "Social Services can set you up in an apartment. You're too old for a foster home now. You'd have to work part time to supplement." Tapping his desk and shaking his head, he continues, "It's a far tougher route. At your mom's, at least you'd have support." Taking a moment to eye the lad seriously, he asks, "Have you quit?" He raises a hand to stop Greg, "I mean really quit."

Greg lowers his head. "No."

"You are going to need support, Greg."

"Will she really want me?" Greg begins to stutter. "I—I haven't spoken to her—since—for five years."

"I'll phone her right now and ask." He reaches for the phone, but, before he picks it up, he asks for Greg's permission, "Is that okay, Greg? May I call her?"

Greg's answer comes in the form of a nod.

Mr. Lloyd cannot help smiling as he dials the boy's mother. Silently, and to himself, he says, *This is it. Greg is on the road to redemption. Greg is on the road to recovery.* Just before Greg's mother picks up, Mr. Lloyd takes a brief moment to thank God for delivering him this blessing.

245

At the End of the Day

It's the second week of January. Everyone is tired. Everyone is antsy. Everyone is ornery. It's been minus forty below for close to a month now. Cabin fever is at its peak, especially for the teachers. All the students want to do is sit and play. No one goes out for lunch, which makes supervision hell, and the days feel like moisture trapped inside an icicle. With only twenty minutes left to go before the bell, students are up and about wandering around the classroom in between tables. Only a few remain in their seats, silently working on the homework assigned. Mrs. Bird flits from her computer desk at the back of the room to the front table and back again as she tries to get work done and students re-seated and focused.

Snippets of conversations swell in every direction—voices bouncing off voices, making little to no sense. "Damien, sit down! Greg, get back to work!" is interspersed with "You did what?" followed by "at three AM?" Hushed details of student exploits are drowned by the sound of Mrs. Bird screeching out her exasperation: "Enough party talk! I gave you this class to catch up on your work before finals. They're next week you know! And is this how you thank me?" Students sing out chorally, "Thank you, Miss," sincerely ... sugary sweet.

"Susie, show me what you've done so far."

A button nose squints, and pouty lips emit a desperate plea, "I just don't get it, Miss. What's an alley?"

Trying not to smirk or roll her eyes, Mrs. Bird searches for a polite response. "An alley is a small road, usually dark at night as it has no lighting. It is either a road behind and between two houses or a small road between two buildings. Since this story is set in London, England, we can assume it's a roadway between two buildings."

The girl's dimples swell, and Mrs. Bird truly feels that she has taught someone—that a brief moment of education has just occurred.

"Thank you, Miss."

For the first time that day, Mrs. Bird smiles down at one of her students, "You are welcome, Susie."

Greg, too, is taken in by Susie's demure attitude and dimpled smile. "You are so cute!" he says as he leans in to kiss her on the cheek.

"None of that in my classroom, you two."

"Sorry, Miss," the two cohorts chime, as if an apology will always exonerate the crime.

Her mind scattered by all of the surrounding noise, Mrs. Bird forgets to check Susie's work and moves on to the next bottleneck of activity. "Frank, what's with you today? You're usually so hard working."

"What? Don't tell me Frank's in trouble!" Greg turns to look at Damien who is laughing in response. They high five.

"Be quiet, Greg!" Mrs. Bird turns on him, annoyed, before resuming her talk with Frank. "What is it Frank, tell me? You've started sleeping in class. That's not like you. And your marks have slipped since Christmas."

Damien's laugh is so thunderous and earsplitting, the whole class turns to look at him.

"What?" Damien asks defensively. "I'm just laughing."

"Must you be so loud about it?" Mrs. Bird demands.

"Sorry, Miss." Damien smirks as he shrugs. "I never did learn how to laugh quiet."

Turning her back in a futile attempt to make the boy disappear, Mrs. Bird mutters, "Get back to work, Damien."

Returning to her model student, Mrs. Bird taps Frank on the shoulder to get him to lift his head, "Come on, Frank, what is it?"

"I'm tired, Miss. That's all. I'm just tired. Besides, you know I'll get it done."

"I know, Frank, I'm just worried, that's all. You're marks have dropped and—"

Frank explodes. "All I want is to be left alone. Can you do that?" Looking sullenly at his teacher he mutters, "Just leave me alone." He returns to hiding his head underneath his arms.

The whole class is stunned by Frank's odd behaviour, except for Damien, who seems to laugh at everything Frank does these days.

Mrs. Bird expresses her concern through an apology. "I'm sorry, Frank." She pats him on the shoulder before turning to leave the young man alone.

Greg sputters. "Sure, Little Girl Gibbons can be a jerk and you apologize, but as soon as *I* step out of line—"

Trying desperately to stifle her rage and frustration, Mrs. Bird turns on Greg. Speaking through clenched teeth, she says, "You stay out of this! This is none of your business." Mrs. Bird, more worried about Frank than Greg, chooses to ignore Greg's barely audible, "Whatever."

Only a half turn away from Frank, Mrs. Bird's attention is directed to another stretch of heavy student traffic. Damien has decided to get up and go for a walk around the classroom. "Damien, sit down."

Damien ignores her.

"Damien, will you please sit down?" Too much noise, too little work, too much attitude thrown at her over the course of the day finally takes its toll. In a state of serious rage, Mrs. Bird roars, "Damien! I said *sit!*"

Indignation sets in. Beset with emotion, Damien acknowledges his teacher's presence at last. "I'm not a dog!"

"I know that, but I've asked you to sit twice now—both times politely—and you have ignored me."

"I didn't hear you."

With teeth clenching and unclenching, Mrs. Bird spits out, "What? Are you deaf? I'm standing right beside you."

"I was talking to Greg."

"Clearly. And I was trying to stop you."

"Why don't you just leave me alone?" Damien asks. "I'm not causing any trouble."

"You are not working." Mrs. Bird is so angry now she can't even contract her words.

"Why do you care?"

"I am your teacher." Her fists are now clenched and punching away at the air. "I do not want you to fail."

"It shouldn't matter to you whether I pass or not," Damien reasons as he leans against Greg's table.

"Just—sit—down—*now.*"

Greg looks up at her, indignant. "I am sitting."

Had Mrs. Bird *been* a bird, her wings would be flapping wildly against the bars of her cage. Turning on Greg, she hollers, "Was I looking at you? *No!* I was looking at Damien. Did I say, 'Greg, sit'? *No!* I said, 'Damien, sit'!"

"All you said was 'sit,'" Greg reasons, "and you're standing next to me."

"That's because Damien is standing next to you! What I should be saying is, 'Greg, sit'—*Arghhh!*"

"I am sitting!"

"Greg, stop talking and start working!"

"Ouch!" Greg winces as Susie pinches him, stopping him from uttering the "f" word. "I mean, gee, Miss, you don't have to yell."

"Then get to work, and I won't have to yell at you!"

A forgotten voice brings Mrs. Bird back to the original culprit.

"Yeah, right!"

Damien's posture, with his arms crossed as he leans against Greg's table, coupled with a smirk across his lips infuriates Mrs. Bird. "Damien," she growls through gritted teeth, "I told you to sit!"

"He's not a dog, Miss."

"Greg, be quiet!" A fist slams against the table, and students jar in their chairs.

"Everyone in this room, sit down and stop talking right now. Damien, sit down! Tony, sit down! And no one—*I mean, no one*—talks."

An ominous hush falls on the room. Mrs. Bird stands there, bent over with her fist pressing against Greg's table as she stares him down, daring him to utter something.

"Quit staring at me, Miss, it's freaking me out." He winces again.

In a whisper of frost, Mrs. Bird says, "I said no one talks. One more word out of you and you're out."

He winces before saying, "Fine."

"Good-bye!"

"Whatever." After one final wince, Greg packs up his bag and walks out.

"Miss," Susie says tentatively, "Greg never swore once this class."

"What does that have to do with anything?"

"Before class started, he told me he wasn't going to swear even if it killed him. He asked me to help him. I was to pinch him every time it looked like he was going to swear. I pinched him eight times all block. The last time was just before he left."

Mrs. Bird remains leaving over the table, supporting her weight on leaden arms. A slight shudder and shake occur before she takes in a strong breath of air, which brings her upright. Without pause, Mrs. Bird walks out of the classroom. "Greg."

Already at the other end of the hallway, the boy stops and, without turning, answers, "What?"

"I'm sorry."

Everything slams to a halt as silence screams throughout the building. A classroom is filled with stunned expressions, and the hallway expands and collapses, bringing two people closer together. Greg turns to face his teacher.

"I'm sorry. I was wrong. Look, I have no excuses, and this justifies nothing, but I've had one heck of a day. My head has been pounding since third block, and this class ..." Her eyes close for a moment, her hands twitch as if trying to grasp at a concept. "And you guys—you guys are just crazy today, and I took all my frustration and anger out on you."

Somehow, Greg has moved from one end of the hall back to where Mrs. Bird is standing. "Yeah, I guess I'm sorry too."

"Look, how about I try not taking everything out on you, and you try to get a little work done in what's left of this class?"

"Deal."

Two hands clasp, and, for the first time that semester, student and teacher feel as if they have actually come to some sort of truce.

Greg and Mrs. Bird shaking hands

☺ ☺ ☺ ☺ ☺

Planning for Paintball

Exam week is a joyful time. There are no more classes, only the odd student coming in every now and then for extra help prior to finals. And, although there is a substantial amount of marking, for the first time in the semester teachers actually have time to do it. Mrs. Bird is relaxed. She feels no pain in her shoulders or neck today. Her radio is tuned to CKUA, Alberta's (and perhaps even the world's) only decent station. Currently enjoying the jazzy tunes of Lionel Rault's *Nine to Noon*, Mrs. Bird taps out the rhythm with her pencil as she peers over a student essay patiently waiting to be marked. There is a timorous tap on the door. Mrs. Bird looks up to see Frank waving to her.

"Hi, Miss. Miss me?"

"Always, Frank." Pleased, she waves him in. The fact that Frank is smiling reassures Mrs. Bird. She has been exceedingly worried about the boy. When his average dropped ten percent, she made her first (*and only*) phone call home. Mr. Gibbons, failing to hear Mrs. Bird's concerns about Frank's welfare, concentrated only on the fact that Frank's grades were no longer up to par. "How," he bellowed through the receiver, "can a ninety-plus-average student's grade suddenly slip into the eighties." Unfortunately for Mrs. Bird, she was the fourth parent to call and inform Mr. Gibbons of this. The last thing Mr. Gibbons wanted to hear at that point were more stories about his son's morose, unsocial behavior—not that Frank has ever been on friendly terms with his peers, but he even stopped bugging his teachers. Mr. Gibbons swore that his boy's marks were going to improve. He ignored completely Mrs. Bird's insistence that Frank's grades were not the real concern.

"What could be more important than marks?" Mr. Gibbons roared.

"Frank's mental health."

"Are you calling my son a looney?" The incensed father raged. "You know, half you teachers think he's gay, the other half think he's crazy.

Well, my boy is both straight and sane. He'd do a lot better at school if you people would just leave him alone."

"No, sir," Mrs. Bird tried desperately to backtrack. "I just want you to—" And she heard a click—actually a slam. Fifteen minutes later, Mr. Willow was in her classroom informing her she is not to contact Mr. Gibbons again. "Can we at least have Lloyd talk to the man—or Frank?" she asked disparagingly.

"Of course," Willow replied. After a short pause to reassure the educator, he added, "Frank's one of our better students. You don't have to worry about him. He'll bounce back."

Today appears to be the day to prove Willow true. Frank is finally showing signs of his old self again, and Mrs. Bird is feeling a profound sense of relief. Anticipating a science fiction debate, Mrs. Bird asks with a smile, "So, what is it today, Frank? A comparison of the two *Battlestar Gallacticas*? *Star Wars IV, V*, and *VI* versus *I, II*, and *III*? Or do you want to debate the plausibility of a fifteen-year-old girl kicking the crap out of fifty muscle-bound men?"

Too excited to even entertain his favorite topics of conversation, Franks blurts out, "Uncle Teddy says I can have the paintball field for a Sunday afternoon in February." Then he adds with a gush, "as long as it's not colder than minus twenty!"

"You're uncle owns a paintball field?" Mrs. Bird asks, feigning interest to encourage the boy's re-found enthusiasm. "And he operates it in winter?"

"Yeah," Franks blurts out. "Winter paintball is the best. It's harder to camouflage. Way more challenging than summer paintball."

"How so?" Although not really interested, Mrs. Bird wants to encourage Frank's good mood.

"If it's just snowed, you leave tracks and your enemy can find you easier. Unless there's a storm—then the wind'll cover 'em for you." Gushing with enthusiasm, he finishes up, "Winterball's cool, Miss. You'll love it."

Missing the "you'll" in Frank's words, and hearing only "you'd" instead, Mrs. Bird continues, "I see. And where is your uncle's field?"

"In the forest just north of town. He calls it The Oil Barrel."

"I've heard of the place. Mr. Wood talks about it all the time."

"Yeah, I figured he might want to play too."

Mrs. Bird catches her breath and swallows. "Too? Umm, what do you mean 'too'?

"I was hoping I could get a student/teacher game set up."

Mrs. Bird's mouth hangs open for a time before finally uttering, "Oh. And you want Mr. Wood to play. Good choice. He loves the game." Discreetly turning back toward her pile of marking, Mrs. Bird attempts to hide behind her work.

Frank either ignores or fails to notice this subtle hint. "Yeah, and I was thinking you'd like to play."

"Ah," she says, desperately pondering ways of getting out of this. She inquires, "What does Mr. Willow have to say about this?"

"Oh, he's cool with it."

Mrs. Bird can't help but snort. Looking up at the young man skeptically, she asks, "Really?"

Frank, hemming and hawing slightly, says, "Well, he sorta said— actually, kinda suggested—well, as long as the game's not connected with the school, he doesn't care what we do."

"Well." Mrs. Bird frowns. Trust Willow to find a way of avoiding sanctioning the act whilst not refusing any ardent student request. "Let me think on it."

"You'll love it, Miss." Searching for the perfect argument, he says, "Just think, you'll get to shoot at your students!" Frank sees the wry smile appear before it quickly disappears. "You've got to admit, Miss, you'll love it."

Frank's smile is intoxicating, and Mrs. Bird basks in the young man's bliss. It pleases her no end to see him happy again. "Well, all right. My husband may kill me, but I'm in. This is real nice of your uncle to give us a free day like this."

"Well ..." Frank grimaces. "It's not entirely free, just the field rental. We still have to rent the guns and paintballs—" Then he interjects into his own sentence as if to halt any chance for Mrs. Bird to renege, "It's so much cheaper! Only fifty bucks a person!"

Mrs. Bird sighs. *Why does everything have to cost so much these days?*

Seeing skepticism in her eyes, Frank asks, "Are you still in?"

"Of course, fifty bucks isn't so much," she lies. "I can handle that."

"Good." After a brief sigh of relief, he adds, "And, I sort of need your help."

"With what?"

"Well, advice."

"Okay. Ask away."

"Help me get students and teachers to join in."

"Oh, no," Mrs. Bird replies emphatically. "I can't do that! If anyone got hurt playing paintball, Willow'd have my as— … ahh, posterior region in a sling!"

Smiling, Frank tosses in, "You can swear, Miss, I don't care."

"Seriously, Frank. I can't go around asking students to play paintball—"

Before she can even finish, Susie pops her head into the classroom. "Did someone say paintball?" Darting back out into the hallway she squeals, "Greg, someone said paintball!"

From a distance, Greg's chagrin can be heard. "Ah, man."

Susie leaps into the classroom. "Who's playing paintball?"

Mrs. Bird, seeing a way to avoid helping Frank, turns to encourage Susie's zeal. "Frank is organizing a student/teacher paintball match."

Susie's eyes widen. The fact that Frank is the "gay nerd" doesn't seem to affect her. In fact, Frank has actually hit on an idea that might just improve his status amongst the student population, and provide an opportunity for students to aim a gun at a teacher's head and actually be able to shoot— albeit paint, but, still, just the idea is intoxicating! Actually, providing teachers with an opportunity to aim a gun at student's heads and actually be able to shoot—albeit paint—is also intoxicating—in a healthy/sick sort of way. (It may sound bad, but it really is good.)

"Cool!" Susie blurts out before her boyfriend can make his way into the classroom to talk her out of this.

"Great!" Mrs. Bird reacts immediately. Here is someone to take the burden of organizing a student team off her shoulders. "Maybe you can help Frank here organize a student team."

"I—I'll organize the teacher team," Frank stammers, suggesting Susie would be free to work without him.

Before Susie can yelp out an affirmative, Greg enters the room. "What have you just agreed to?" Greg demands authoritatively.

Mrs. Bird laughs. Greg might just end up in her sights after all. "Frank here has access to a paintball field—free of charge, not including gun and paint ball rental, for a Sunday afternoon, and he is planning on hosting a student/teacher paintball match."

At this Susie, starts to bounce up and down excitedly. "Paintball Greg! I get to organize the student team, and we get to shoot at teachers!"

"Forget it!" Greg says. "I'm not spending half a day freezing my balls off just to hang out with Little Girl Gibbons and a bunch of teachers."

"Of course," Mrs. Bird quips, "Greg is clearly intimidated, fearing, no doubt, that he'll get shot in the back end by *me!*"

Greg's focus, however, is not on old Bird's cynicism. Susie's persistent jumping up and down in pleading fashion, jingle jangling her boobs in front of him (continuously—perhaps purposely—aiming her nipples at his eyes) is holding him at attention. "Please, Greg. Please." Determined to have her way, Susie moves in close enough for her gargantuan breasts to rub against Greg. "Please, Greg, I want to play paintball. Please, please, please, please, please!"

Susie bouncing up and down for a mesmerized Greg

Every please is accented by the rise and fall and rub of Susie's pert nipples causing Greg to agree without realizing it.

As Susie dances around the room singing variations of the word *yipee*, Mrs. Bird lets out a laugh. "Serves you right, young man, for letting your groin make your choices for you."

"Fine!" Greg, trying to make the best of a bad situation, sets his condition: "Only if Damien agrees to play too."

Frank turns white and screams, "*No!*" at the top of his lungs and then runs out of the classroom.

Before the door has a chance to slam shut behind the young man, Mrs. Bird is chasing Frank down the hall. Susie and Greg follow at her heels. Frank, seeing Mrs. Bird chasing him, seeks refuge inside the boys' washroom. Little does he know, but Frank has just chosen a toilet-paper-matted and moldy stall as his confessional.

By the time Greg and Susie arrive, Mrs. Bird is pacing up and down the hall just outside the washroom door frantically chewing her right thumbnail. "Greg!" Mrs. Bird seizes the young man by the collar and orders, "You stand watch." As she moves towards the door, four hands aggressively hold her back.

"Miss!" Susie exclaims.

"You can't go in there," Greg insists.

Summoning her most authoritative voice, Mrs. Bird insists, "I can, and I will." Looking towards the door, she explains, "That boy needs someone to talk to."

"Sometimes," Susie counters, "a guy needs a guy to talk to."

Both Mrs. Bird and Greg look at her incredulously.

"Maybe he needs a girl to talk to," Greg adds smugly.

Before Mrs. Bird can yell out "Greg!" Susie balls her fist and slugs him in the chest. "You get in there and you talk to him." When Susie takes charge of a situation, this little woman is *in charge!*

"Ahhh …" Mrs. Bird instantly attempts to counter this suggestion. "Greg might not be the best person for Frank—"

Susie does not let her finish. "You heard me, Greg. I said get in there!" All Greg can do is shrug his shoulders and do as he is told.

Just as Greg is about to enter the boys' bathroom, Mrs. Bird grabs his shoulder. "Before you do this, I want you to remember one thing. What a man chooses to do reflects who he is. You, who studied Sartre on your own, should know this better than anyone. If you intend on going in there, then decide right now to do what's right. If you walk through that door, you are choosing to help, not make things worse. You got it?"

Greg pauses, thinks for a moment, then nods. Mrs. Bird releases her grip.

Mrs. Bird sighs, hoping beyond hope that Greg really is the decent man inside she believes him to be.

The Confessional

Inside the washroom, Greg finds Frank has locked himself inside the stall. *Yuck*, Greg can't help but think. *He must really be f—ed if he's sitting in there.* Waiting in silence, listening to the other boy sobbing, Greg ponders what exactly it is Susie is hoping he will say. *It's a vicious world*, Greg muses, *and Little Girl Gibbons is only going to get whipped by it.* Finally, Greg decides to let come what comes. "All right, Frank," he shouts, "how long you plannin' on cryin' in there?"

The alarming sound of Greg's voice causes Frank to squeal, "Leave me alone."

"For f—'s sakes, give it up. You're not a baby."

"You don't know anything."

"Then tell me!" Greg is a little too emphatic in his demand, and the fact that he slams the stall door with his fist doesn't help matters.

"No!"

Pacing up and down past the urinals, wrinkling his nose periodically at the stench, Greg tries his best to calm down. Playing Mr. Sensitive is not exactly his forte. Walking back to the stall, he decides to try apologizing. *It always works with Willow. Who knows*, he figures, *it might just work on Little Girl Gibbons.* "Look, Frank. I'm sorry."

"Go away!"

Greg spins on the spot to avoid hitting the stall door again. *What is it going to take to get this little sh— to talk to me?* Staring hard at the stall, he mutters to himself, *Susie better put out after this.*

"You know," he says straight to the stall door, "this makes no sense. Here I am set to play this stupid game of yours and we don't hear a peep out of you. Not one f—in' word, and, the minute I mention Damien, you freak out."

"Shut up!" Inside the stall, Frank lifts up the toilet seat and prepares to vomit. When nothing comes out, he sits back down on the floor leaning against the dirty porcelain base.

"F—, Gibby, you make no sense. I treat you way worse than Damien ever did. He's never done nothin' like I've—"

Franks leaps up and slams open the stall door. His eyes are wet and wild, and his nose is red and runny. Knots of hair protrude atop his head like miniature ponytails, as he has been grabbing and tangling his hair whilst crying. "You never tried to rape me!" After blurting this out, Frank screams and slams the stall door in Greg's face.

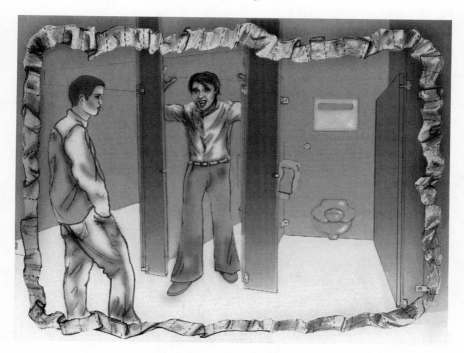

Frank screaming in Greg's face

Greg is too stunned to move. Silence rings with the memory of the slamming stall door. Whole worlds collide and break apart scattering dust into infinity.

"What the f—?"

"Just go away … please," Frank begs.

Greg slowly leans forward, planting both fists firmly against the metal door. Although his head drops between his arms, there is tension throughout every muscle of his body. "Not until you tell me exactly what happened." Greg's face turns red and all he can think about is Uncle Ambrose.

"I can't," Frank pleads. He is back to heaving and sobbing. Then he venomously demands, "Why do you care?"

"My uncle—" Greg's mouth slams shut. Silence breaks a chink in the wall between them. Putting the focus back on Frank, Greg demands, "What—exactly—did—he—do."

It is interesting. These five words placed together in this exact order construct a question, but there is no query in Greg' voice. He is giving Frank an order. An order punctuated by the shot of every word. Greg needs to know, and Frank needs to tell him. The words *my uncle* resonate between them. There in the stench of the boy's bathroom, sitting next to a toilet surrounded by matted and moldy tissue, Frank begins confessing to the most unlikely of confessors—"Father" Gregory McA—hole McGregor. When Frank finally finishes, Greg explodes. He is enraged. Memories flood Greg's mind of an eight-year-old boy forced to fondle his uncle Ambrose. Damien will pay for what Uncle Ambrose did back then.

"That Mother f—in' son of a b—ch!" Frank listens as Greg slams his way out of the bathroom swearing, "I'm going to kill the f—in' bastard!"

As Greg rushes out of the bathroom and past them, Mrs. Bird ushers Susie his way. "Go after him, Susie. See what's wrong. Try to calm him down."

Once the two teenagers have vanished, Mrs. Bird enters the boys' washroom. Frank, no longer hiding in the stall, is standing at the sink splashing his face with cold water.

"Frank?" Mrs. Bird inquires timorously. Her concern for Frank, coupled with the impropriety of standing in the boy's bathroom, turns this otherwise-strong woman into a meek little canary.

Starting at the sound of her voice, Frank yelps, "Miss? What are you doing in here? It's the boys' can."

Glancing around at the sights and smells of the boys' washroom, Mrs. Bird wrinkles her nose in disgust. Wet toilet paper litters everywhere, and the urinals are stained yellow. One urinal even has excrement in it. Shaking her head, she looks back to Frank. Addressing the young man, she begins with an apology, "I'm sorry, Frank, but I was worried about you."

"What if I was, you know—" He looks at the urinals uncomfortably and he shakes his head slightly in their direction to finish his sentence.

"Well, yeah," she too looks at the urinals uncomfortably. "Thank goodness you weren't."

"I'm okay," Frank says weakly, his eyes flicking towards the door as Mrs. Bird begins to advance and extends an arm to hold him. Feigning an assertive stance, he says, "Really, Miss. Everything is okay." His red swollen eyes and runny nose prove otherwise.

☹ ☹ ☹ ☹ ☹

The next day, when Damien Headstone walks into school, he has a fat lip, bruised cheek, and one nasty shiner. From this day forth, no one dares tease Frank when Greg is around.

Damien with copious bruises

☺ ☺ ☺ ☺ ☺

Boot Camp

Between Willow, Wood, Frank, and William, Mrs. Bird is put through three weeks of intensive training in preparation for the big day. "Killing" Greg—shooting him with paint—has become her sole consuming thought. Every day after school, she runs with (or rather lags far behind) Willow, who shouts encouragements at her. "Atta girl, Bird, you're doing great." To which she always replies, "I can't believe you like running in twenty below weather!"

"You should have started up with me in the fall," is his stock reply. "You'd've acclimatized much better. Besides," he quips back, "you're running out here with me."

Yes. Bird grimaces—then grins, *But I'm on a mission!*

Her husband helps her build upper body strength by having her hit his punching bag in the basement. (William takes kickboxing classes to help diminish the stress he feels as a result of his wife's stress.) Frank and Wood have the odious task of teaching her how to hold a gun, aim, and shoot. Frank also teaches her the layout of the field. Now this proves to be expensive (and frickin' cold), but Mrs. Bird is convinced it will be all worth it if she can at least get one hit on Greg. So, every Saturday afternoon, she spends running the field with Frank, learning its every hiding spot and where one is most likely to hit the opponent.

"I like to head out for the farthest end of the enemy field as fast as possible, Miss," Frank explains. "That way I can get at them from behind … unsuspecting like."

On Sunday after church, she is at the paintball field again, this time on her own trying desperately to hit barrels at a distance and paint cans hanging from trees. *If I can't even hit a still object,* she moans, *how can I ever hope to bean Gregory McGregor?*

After two weeks of aching muscles, William insists his wife take a much-needed rest from this little obsession of hers. "No," he insists, "you cannot train tonight."

"But I have to," Priscilla whines, "those kids will brutalize me in the first attack."

"Oh, give me a break. You are not worried about *those kids*. You're just scared what's-his-name is going to shoot you more times than you shoot him."

Priscilla starts to behave like a spoiled child, balling her fists and shaking them up and down in a very constrained manner. Her eyes are squinted shut, and she is practically pleading as she says, "I don't care how many times he shoots me just as long as I can hit him once in the a—!"

All William can do at this stage is simply laugh—at his wife, that is—and remind her not to swear.

"Fine. Whatever. *Buttocks!*"

Mrs. Bird jogging with Willow

☺ ☺ ☺ ☺ ☺

Winter Woodsball

In H.E.L.L.'s community, when one plays paintball, one plays Woodsball. And, for the ardently insane, there is Winter Woodsball: Me Canadian. Me play Winter Woodsball. One must live at a certain level of insanity to partake in winter sports at minus twenty below; however, the level must be a bit higher if one is going to play Woodsball—the ultimate approach to paintball, as the game makes players truly feel they are inside a war zone. The coveralls provided by the Oil Barrel Woodsball Club in spring, summer, and fall are green-and-brown army camouflage. But the coveralls provided during the long winter months are white. In this way, ordinary citizens can pretend to be Arnold Schwarzenegger—the men at least, while women image themselves to be Starbuck!

In mid February (after another frickin' freezin' spell), all the participants wisely wear skidoo suits under their white camouflage coveralls. They also wear white sorrels (honking boots with thick felt liners). After all the participants have rented their gear and signed the appropriate forms, the referee shouts out, "All right, everybody. Come line up over here." He has to cite the rules and regulations before the games can begin. "You're lucky today," he begins, "it's only minus twenty-four." Everyone chuckles. Only in Canada can you get away with saying, and with all sincerity, "it's *only* minus twenty-four." Okay, there's Russia—and the poles—but nobody technically lives there! "I had thought," the referee continues, "to cancel, but Frank asked so nicely I just couldn't say no." The small crowd cheers. "If they show up, I told him, I'll let you hold your game. And—" he points admiringly to the crowd, "you're here!"

Glaring at the motley crew before him, he begins with the necessary information, "Okay, the rules are simple. You must wear your headgear at all times. Never take it off. This mask is designed to keep you from getting hit in the face or losing an eye. If you ever take it off while out on the field," he says, shaking the head gear in his right hand for emphasis,

"I will disqualify you from the game *and* from ever playing on my field again." Looking sternly at the crowd, he asks, "Understood?"

Everyone—already in military fantasy mode—stands at attention and shouts, "Understood, sir."

"Good." Having people respond to him in military fashion gives the referee the air of a general. He starts to pace back and forth in front of the group as if at inspection. Holding his paintball marker in the air, he shouts, "This is your weapon. You are to keep the safety lock on until you are firmly established in your team's fort." Lifting the marker to show where the lock is, he continues, "Here," he says whilst pointing to a small button under the trigger, "is where the lock is located. Push it and it shows red. This means the lock is now off and you are able to begin shooting. Push the button back, hide the red, and the gun is locked. That means you can no longer shoot." The referee is not looking at Frank or Mr. Wood. His focus is on the newbies—Mrs. Bird, Greg, Susie, and the others. "I want you to practice locking and unlocking your gun." All the newbies do as they are told and a series of clicks is heard as the plastic guns are unlocked and locked. Mr. Wood snickers. Greg points to his eyes with two fingers and then points at Mr. Wood with one. Mr. Wood laughs outright at Greg's antics. The referee ignores their silent mode of conversation. "These markers are semi-automatic. This means you don't have to pump the marker between each shot. The triggers are electric." Casting a glance over confused faces, he explains in layman's terms, "it means you can shoot fast. This," he points to the big funnel atop the marker, "is the hopper."

"What's a hopper?" Susie asks. The remaining newbies exhale a sigh of relief. Someone else asked the stupid question.

"It's the loader." Seeing nothing but dense expressions on the newbies, he elaborates, "You fill it with paintballs." Shaking his head and grinning at his nephew, he adds, whilst tapping his right breast pocket, "You might want to take extra ammunition out there. Just in case you run out." Noting the look of confusion on the Newbies faces he explains, "Frank's rifle is a sniper riffle with cigar case cartridges. The sniper makes every shot count so he doesn't use a hopper." The referee's smile quickly vanishes, though. "Now," he says, pausing to impress the gravity of his next statement. "Once established in your fort, you are to wait until I give the signal, like this." He retrieves a starter pistol from his holster and, pointing it skyward, lets off a shot. Mrs. Bird jumps and stares in the direction of the sound, and Greg snickers. Mrs. Bird turns to Greg and gives him the two-finger-one-finger salute. Everyone laughs. Even the referee has to take a moment to catch his breath before starting up again. "When you shoot at people, make sure they are at least five yards away from you. A shot at close range is very painful and is considered to be bad sportsmanship." Looking sternly at this untrained platoon, he warns, "If an unsuspecting enemy walks into your sights, you are encouraged to ask for a voluntary kill or surrender. This will save the victim from suffering serious damage, which, as I said, can occur with hits at close range. Let us respect our friends out on the field." Already, Mrs. Bird is calculating how close she can get to Greg without getting caught. Catching herself entering into the malicious zone, she shakes her head and dismisses the idea. Greg, on the other hand, is chuckling at the thought of blasting the old bird so that feathers fly in every direction. The referee, noticing their silent intentions adds, "Although it is not officially against the rules, if I catch anyone purposefully hitting the enemy at close range, you will be expelled from the game and banned from further use of my field. We play a clean game at The Oil Barrel." Once again studying the platoon—Mrs. Bird and Greg especially—he demands, "Is that *understood*?"

"Understood, Sir!"

"Alrighty then. Let's divide into teams."

The students all race to the left while the teachers push through them to the right.

"Hmmm," the referee mutters as he studies this division. "There seem to be more students than teachers here. I like an even game at The Oil Barrel, so we have to move a couple of students over to the teachers' side." Waves of dissent rise up from both teams. The referee, having none of this, insists, "Two students must join the teachers' team or the game is forfeit."

Greg leans in to Frank and complains, "Your uncle is a real stickler."

"He knows what he's doing," Frank replies. The boy may not be successful at defending himself in a physical confrontation, but, when it comes to his uncle, he would die for the man. "I'll join the teachers," Frank offers.

Mrs. Bird, forming a fist and pulling it into her side, shouts, "Yes!"

Greg responds instantly. He grabs Frank by the collar and pulls him back. "There is no way we are giving over our best player." Frank grins. The cool kids actually need him. Turning to address the opposition, Greg insists, "You already got Mr. Wood. We're keeping Frank. You can have Susie."

Turning an indignant glare on her boyfriend, Susie demands inquiringly, "What?"

"Look, babe," Greg reasons with her, "this is war."

"No way," Wood interjects before the two can start fighting. "We already got Mrs. Bird."

Mrs. Bird flies into an even bigger hissy fit than Susie, "*What?*" Mrs. Bird's jaw drops. "I've been training for three weeks!"

Wood, who had a big part in her training, replies, "We'll take Terry." Then, conceding to the politically correct notion that they have to take at least one girl from the students' team, he adds, "and Jill."

Greg holds Frank back

"Good," replies the referee. He nods and starts the game. "We will begin with a little game we like to call elimination. The first team to take out all of its opponents wins. Lock your markers." A rustle from the newbies occurs as they look to make sure their weapons are locked. "And make your way to your forts! Students, take the fort on the far side of the creek. Teachers, you get the fort on the right." Just as the two teams are about to disperse, the referee calls them back. "Wait!" Looking up at the cloudy sky he adds, "It might start snowing—"

"Good," Frank shouts. "That'll cover our tracks."

"Yes," the referee agrees, flashing a proud smile at his nephew. "But," he warns the crew, "it will also cover the edge of the creek bed." That sucker's icy. You might slip—or, even worse yet, break though. I'm sure it's completely solid because it's not very deep. But you never know. If you crash through to water, it'll be mighty cold. So stick to the bridges." Eyeing the group carefully to ensure they all understand the danger, he gives them the go ahead. "Alrighty then!" He motions in the direction of the forts. "When you hear the signal, the battle begins."

Blood Will Have Blood

Tripping over roots hidden by soft snow while icy wind lashes in her face is not Mrs. Bird's idea of a good time, but the adrenaline rush caused by the threat of yet another paintball in the buttocks keeps her moving. So, too, does the high she feels every time she imagines shooting Greg. *I'm gonna get that little miscreant if it kills me*, she mutters to herself. And kill her it might, except that a fluke opportunity suddenly presents itself.

In this last game, called capture the flag, Mrs. Bird finally takes Frank's advice about getting to the other side of the field as fast as possible and sneaking up on the enemy from behind. There he is—Gregory McMiscreant McGregor. *Oh, to hell with William's decorum*, she figures. *McA—hole!* Safely hidden behind a pile of empty oil barrels used to create a small bunker, Mrs. Bird, creeping in as close as is acceptable within the standards of good sportsmanship, aims straight at the young man's posterior region and fires.

Mrs. Bird shooting Greg in the buttocks

Greg utters, "Son of a *b—ch!*" This is the first hit he has taken all game. The young man has a natural talent for stealth. His first target, as always, was to be Mrs. Bird, and he was scanning the field in search of her when he got shot. Angrily, he stands. He looks first at his buttocks to ensure the paintball actually broke and splattered him with the telltale green. Seeing it has, he swears to himself again, then lifts his gun as instructed, and shouts, "Hit!"

Mrs. Bird is ecstatic. Leaping out from behind her barrels, she begins swirling snow around with dancing feet. "I got him! I got him!" Her yell alerts all the other students to her presence, and Greg watches with glee as Mrs. Bird gets shot from every direction. Mrs. Bird is not daunted by this attack. She accepts every pelt with honour even though the hits do make her scrunch down and grunt. Even this odd looking dance does not lessen her happiness.

On their way off the field, neither Greg nor Mrs. Bird wants to waste any bullets, so they decide to empty their magazines on one other. They combine laughing, running, and yelling as a part of their exit. The referee, not sure how to handle such a blatant abandonment of his rules, stands stunned at this exhibition. Clearly paintball is really just a game and not a true military endeavor for this man. Finally he comes to his senses just as the two miscreants run out of ammo. "All right, you two, get off my field."

Back in the small cabin where "killed" soldiers go to wait out the rest of the game, Mrs. Bird and Greg actually share a laugh.

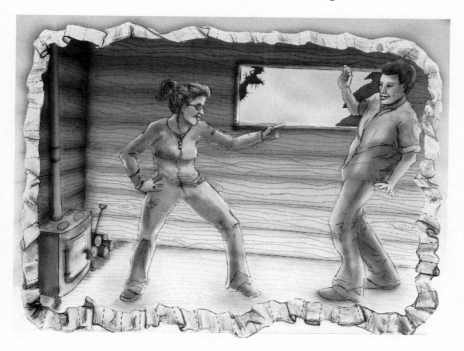

Mrs. Bird and Greg laughing

☺ ☺ ☺ ☺ ☺

Whatever Happened to ...?

A teacher is like a sieve through which thousands of soul will pass; try as one might, no teacher will ever know the impact he or she has had on most of them—positive or negative—if any. As the years pass, students come and go, and many are forgotten. At some point in time, memories begin to blur, and individuals become conglomerates of student types. Frank, for example, is the one who always hangs around the teachers during break and lunch and after school. No one ever really wonders what happened to him because he is always there. Every semester some teachers run and hide when they see him coming, while others understand his need and endure even the stupidest of conversations to keep the poor kid from being alone. Mary is another one whose future remains uncertain, but one can venture a guess. She moves on, to another city perhaps, and, like her mother, gets a job in the service industry. Yes, she gets married—no Hollywood folly about only the beautiful people hooking up. Neither is this Hollywood fantasy about losing hundreds of pounds of weight to reveal a hidden, immaculate beauty. Fat Mary marries and has kids of her own who, like their mother, and her mother before them, endure ridicule and abuse at the hands of their peers. Guess all one might, no one really knows.

Even though teachers remain in ignorance of the future lives of the majority of students they have taught, sometimes they hear stories.

"Hey, Bird!" Payne is dancing into the staff room with the best news she has heard in weeks. "Guess what Lloyd just told me?"

Considering Payne's exuberant posture, Bird assumes she is talking about Damien Headstone. "Headstone's trial?"

"No." Payne sits next to Bird on the couch. "Did you hear the verdict?"

"Yup." Bird smiles. She has been waiting patiently since the boy graduated, ever since he turned eighteen, for something like this to happen. "Wood told me all about it this morning."

"What did I tell you?" Wood, having just entered the staff room, responds to the mention of his name.

"All about Headstone's date rape trial."

"Yeah." Wood, too, is smiling. Headstone did not make many friends among the staff during his stay at high school. "Three years in adult prison." Wood's smile diminishes into a grimace. "Three years isn't long enough for that bastard if you ask me."

"Lord save him," Payne replies.

"May the Good Lord do nothing of the kind," Wood counters angrily.

Bird leans over and whispers into Payne's ear, and points discreetly to Wood. "His niece was the victim."

"Oh," Payne mouths. Then to Wood, she says, "I'm sorry."

Wood, ignoring her completely, continues, "That boy is a rapist. He deserves what he's gonna get. And I hope he gets it right up the—"

Before Wood can finish laying his curse, Payne interjects, "But he's so young, and adult prison is so ruthless."

"Not ruthless enough if you ask me," Wood shoots back.

"Wasn't Damien the one who pointed a knife at you?" Bird reminds Payne.

"Yes, but—"

"But, nothing," Wood interjects. "And didn't his mother say it was just a joke?"

"Yes," Payne replies meekly.

"Yeah," Bird adds, "if I recall correctly, that was in your first year. Damien pointed the knife at you and asked Greg if he should cut you up."

Payne grimaces. "I never forgave Willow for not withdrawing him."

"Yeah, that was wrong," Bird agrees.

Wood's anger flares up. "You should've gone to the cops. He might've gone to jail then and Becky never would've dated him!" Shaking his head vigorously, he recites a little too emphatically, "Never leave criminal acts to administration."

"Well, that's all water under the bridge now," Payne says. "And, believe me," she adds to reassure them, "if anything like that ever happens again, I will definitely bring in the police." Returning to her original topic, she continues, "But that's not what I came in here to tell you guys." What Lloyd told her has her bouncing up and down in her seat.

"All right then," Bird laughs. An excited Payne is always a humourous Payne. "Out with it."

"Remember Gregory McGregor?"

"Who could forget him?" Bird laughs.

"I could," Wood replies. "I decided years ago that it is not worth my time remembering the a—holes. I save a place in my memories only for the good ones."

"True," Bird agrees. Payne chuckles remembering Melissa Williamson's rant. Bird, missing out on Payne's humour, continues, "But I got to like McGregor in the end."

"You?" Wood can't believe what he's hearing.

"Yeah," she replies, "he was okay in the end. Hey," she queries, "wasn't he supposed to marry Susie Cardinal?"

Wood replies, "They were engaged for about a week."

Payne laughs, "Until old man Cardinal found out about it."

"Who would've thought Susie'd be ruled by him," Wood wonders.

"That simply means Susie knew she and Greg weren't meant to be together," Bird replies. Payne looks at her incredulously. "Really, think about it. If she had wanted to marry Greg, come hell or high water she would have married him."

"If you ask me," Wood concurs, "old man Cardinal gave her the way out she was looking for." Noting Payne's look of confusion, he adds, "McA—hole proposed to her at the grad party when they were both drunk. She never would have said yes had she been sober."

"I saw her last week at Safeway," Bird pipes up. "She's working out at the oil mines driving the big truck now."

"She looks good, too," Wood adds, "now that her hair is back to its natural colour."

"Yeah," Bird agrees, "I noticed that. You know she almost looks Métis." Wood and Payne stare at her. "What?" Bird asks. "That wasn't racist, was it?"

Wood and Payne burst out laughing.

Bird sits forward, both hands shooting into open palms. "What?"

"She *is* Métis," Wood barely manages to spit out.

"No!" a befuddled Bird replies.

"Yeah," Payne adds, "her father is half Chippewa. Didn't you know that?"

"No," Bird answers, "I only ever dealt with the mother."

"And she's a quarter Dene," Wood adds laughing. "Geez, Bird, get in the game."

"It's a little late for that," Bird muses. "She's long gone from our lives now."

"So," Wood asks Payne, "what's your news about McA—hole?"

"He's not such an a—hole anymore." Payne giggles. "You'll never guess what he's up to now!"

"Spill it then," Bird insists. "What did Lloyd tell you?" Payne always takes too long getting her stories out.

"Gregory McGregor has been accepted into the education program at the University of Alberta."

Bird starts to laugh as she elbows Wood in the side. "That's your old campus, isn't it?"

Wood is incensed. "I can't believe they accepted him."

"He did upgrade," Bird reminds him, "and finished with a decent average." Turning to Payne with excitement, she asks, "So what's his major? English?"

"No, according to Llyod he's going to be a counselor."

The room shakes with laughter.

Mrs. Bird imagining Greg sitting behind a counselor's desk

A little deflated but still proud, Bird congratulates the boy, "Good for you, Greg. Good for *you!*"

Epilogue

Mrs. Bird is sitting at the staff room table. It is a rare lunch hour, because she is alone. She reads through a news article she found in her mailbox. She has a secret friend who likes to put amusing news articles there. This article does more than amuse Mrs. Bird; it appears to be upsetting her. As she reads, she ejaculates the occasional "What?" followed by "No way!" "I can't believe this!" "Ridiculous!" Her body gesticulates along with each expression. Hands fly up in the air, her head shakes, palms slam against the table—she even rocks back in her chair to put her hands on her head so great is her disbelief. Livy enters the staff room and stops to watch Mrs. Bird's exaggerated pantomime.

Livy is a beautiful woman. She was once a fashion model and retains much of her youthful beauty. Her thyroid started acting up when she hit forty, though, and now her five-foot-four frame has to support over two hundred pounds of flesh. She always dresses in the latest style and bedecks every finger with an expensive ring. Her earrings, bracelet, broach, and necklace are always a matching set. She sits across from Bird, "Well, Prissy," she asks wryly, "What's so funny?"

"Funny?" Bird looks up and smiles. "Livy, welcome to the staff room."

"Well, I do work here you know," Livy replies, pretending to be incensed.

"Yes," Bird agrees. "But we never see you in the staff room."

Livy is Mrs. Bird's best friend on staff, but they almost never see each other. E-mail has become their preferred means of communication as Livy works downstairs in the art room and Priscilla works upstairs in the language arts department. Even though Mrs. Bird comes downstairs every lunch hour to visit with other staff, Livy prefers to eat in the art room since kids like to work on their art projects during lunch and after school. Livy provides extra help every lunch hour and every day after school. Bird thinks she's crazy, but they've decided to stop arguing and agree to disagree on this point.

"I have no kids today," Livy says with a smile, the smile that won her the cover of *Glamour* magazine when she was twenty-one. "What are you reading?"

"Someone left this article in my mailbox, and it's got me burning."

"Oh," Livy says with a little squirm.

"Not that kind of burning," Bird replies with a scorn. "It's all about the demands university students are making of their professors these days."

"Oh." Livy laughs. "I read that. It was in last week's *Edmonton Journal*."

"It really irks me that kids are trying to get away with this stuff."

"I know," Livy agrees. "To expect a B just for showing up. It's outrageous." Grabbing the paper from Bird, she scans the article for facts. "It also says university students expect their professors to be available at the student's convenience whether it is convenient for the professor or not."

"And that's not all," Bird says, snatching the paper back then pointing at it for emphasis, "it also says they think they should get marks just for trying."

Livy and Bird discussing the article

"Absurd," Livy says, mimicking Bird. "I knew you'd like the article."

Mrs. Bird looks up, smiling. "*You* gave it to me. Thank you so much!" She sighs. "This article really makes me think about the kind of students we are putting out there into the world. To think that university students today should expect such highfalutin treatment." Livy nods her head in agreement allowing Bird her moment to rant. "I mean, we graduate these kids! We are the ones preparing them for university, and this is the nonsense we've produced."

Playing the devil's advocate, Livy says, "Now, Priscilla, you know we aren't supposed to prepare them for university, just teach the curriculum."

Priscilla rolls her eyes and sighs. Her eyes cross as she exhales.

After a short chuckle Livy asks, "Are you blaming high school teachers for this trend in student attitude?"

"No." Bird pauses to consider the question. "Well, maybe yes—but no, society as a whole, I think." She taps the table with her knuckles. "Parents, the pampered child, the self-entitled mentality of the average kid today. Rights, rights, rights—without any responsibility. We're all to blame, really. We did it to them and we did it to ourselves, I guess."

"How?" Livy asks.

"Look at our education system—'leave no kid behind,' 'no one fails,' 'completion rate, completion rate'—with no emphasis on quality content. It's ridiculous."

"Aren't these all noble ideas?" Livy is still playing the devil's advocate.

"No. They may sound good, but, in truth, students no longer have to work for their education, so, when they get to university, they rebel against professors who expect them work."

"Well," Livy asks, "what's your solution?"

Mrs. Bird shakes her head. "I don't have a solution anymore that you do. All I know is that, ultimately, education has one purpose: to facilitate the conscious mind. The conscious mind is aware that it is responsible for every action, and that every action reflects and affects humanity. It is our job to produce conscious, responsible members of society. When I read articles like this one," she continues, poking her finger at the paper for emphasis, "it is evident that this is no longer happening."

"I doubt it's happened since the days of Socrates and Plato."

"Oh, Livy." Mrs. Bird sighs. "You're so right." Closing her eyes and shaking her head, she adds, "We *must* look back."

Socrates and Plato

☺ ☺ ☺ ☺ ☺